CHEAT DAY

A Novel

Liv Stratman

SCRIBNER

New York   London   Toronto   Sydney   New Delhi

Scribner
An Imprint of Simon & Schuster, Inc.
1230 Avenue of the Americas
New York, NY 10020

This book is a work of fiction. Any references to historical events, real people, or real places are used fictitiously. Other names, characters, places, and events are products of the author's imagination, and any resemblance to actual events or places or persons, living or dead, is entirely coincidental.

Copyright © 2021 by Liv Stratman

First Scribner hardcover edition May 2021

SCRIBNER and design are registered trademarks of The Gale Group, Inc., used under license by Simon & Schuster, Inc., the publisher of this work.

For information about special discounts for bulk purchases, please contact Simon & Schuster Special Sales at 1-866-506-1949 or business@simonandschuster.com.

The Simon & Schuster Speakers Bureau can bring authors to your live event. For more information or to book an event, contact the Simon & Schuster Speakers Bureau at 1-866-248-3049 or visit our website at www.simonspeakers.com.

Interior design by Wendy Blum

Manufactured in the United States of America

1   3   5   7   9   10   8   6   4   2

Library of Congress Cataloging-in-Publication Data is available.

ISBN 978-1-9821-4054-0
ISBN 978-1-9821-4056-4 (ebook)

For Kate Stratman, Alicia Kohlhepp,
and Anna Hight

Probably one of the most private things in the world is an egg until it is broken.

—M.F.K. Fisher, *How to Cook a Wolf*

CHEAT DAY

PART ONE // Valentine's Day

CHAPTER ONE

We started the Radiant Regimen on Valentine's Day. I'd decided to cook a nice dinner: leg of lamb and a salad with roasted acorn squash and walnuts in some lemony dressing.

"Why don't you make that couscous my mom gave you?" David asked. He was keeping me company, trying to catch up on his endless work emails. We spoke to each other from across the kitchen island, the messy surface where we looked at our devices and scattered our junk mail and lost our keys and ate our meals. "All you have to do is boil it."

"I know how to make couscous," I told him. "But wheat is off-limits with the new program."

Our apartment was filled with the meal's woody aroma: clove and paprika and the roasting flesh of a small, tender animal's hindquarters. Oven heat fogged David's glasses when he looked up from his laptop screen. Woogie—our large, temperamental cat—perched on a stepstool between the small kitchen and the dining room, which we never used. Woogie observed us, always, as though watching a TV series he didn't much like anymore but felt the need to see through to the finale. He was a very fluffy creature, with long, soft orange fur and walrus whiskers.

His appearance was far less serious than his personality, a fact I always felt a little sad about on his behalf. We sometimes joked that he was cursed, an old Norse wizard trapped in a cat's body. His ridiculous tail swooshed behind him with disinterest, pendulum-like, while he looked at me, his eyes almost closed, as though David and I were boring him to sleep.

Taking the big knife from the block, I leaned over the cutting board next to the stove and put my full strength into chopping a tough, misshapen squash.

"Remind me the rules for this di—" David stopped himself. "This program again? I forget."

I wiped my hands with a dish towel before passing him the hardcover copy of *Way to Glow!: Your Guide to Complete Wellness Through the Radiant Regimen.*

David pursed his lips as though he might complain, exaggerating the book's heft as he set it down next to his laptop.

"Please don't lose my page," I said as he began to examine the introduction of the book, titled "So, What *Can* You Eat on the Radiant Regimen?"

"This is intense," he said, frowning. "Really strict."

"Look at the benefits first," I said. "Not just the rules. Look at Diana Spargel's *story.*"

"This gal?" David said, turning the book over and tapping the photo of Diana Spargel, inventor and lead spokesperson of the Radiant Regimen and author of *Way to Glow!,* along with two bestselling companion books—*Glow on the Go!* and *Glow Up: Aging Gracefully with Healing Foods*—on the back of the jacket.

"You lost my page," I told him. "And don't say 'gal.'"

"Your recipe is on page two-fifty-five," David said, still looking at the back of the book. "I don't know why I said 'gal.' I've never said that word before in my life."

"She must look gal-ish to you," I said, turning to him, a taunting smile on my face. I couldn't help myself. David prided himself on being somewhat less sexist than other men, and I never missed a chance to challenge him, to point out how this was, in its own twisted, nerdy way, a kind of condescending machismo.

"She looks like a nice lady—a nice woman. Person. A woman-person." He drew a circle with his finger around Spargel's face. "She looks . . . smart."

"She certainly does *not* look smart," I said. "*Maybe* she looks nice. Whatever 'nice' means. Don't overcompensate for calling her a gal on account of your own embarrassment."

Diana Spargel, who indeed appeared to be glowing in her glossy author photo, with a golden-brown suntan and loose waves of beachy blond hair, was described in her short bio as a "naturopathic healer and nutrition expert." David read this sentence aloud, shrugged. I could tell he wanted to tease me a little, say the Radiant Regimen seemed pseudo-scientific and entirely too extreme, but he didn't. He'd already agreed to do it.

"Where'd you hear about this one?" he asked.

"The Radiant Group is a whole online wellness empire—this is a famous program, David. Everyone knows about it."

"Who's everyone?"

"Okay, everyone on Instagram."

"Ah, yes, social media," David said. "Epicenter of reliable information."

"You're a hypocrite," I said, but without real malice. "You have tennis elbow from looking at your phone." David nodded, acquiescing.

He became frequently and easily distracted by the useless trappings of the Internet's bad advice, as well as its vapidity: a GIF of a politician rolling her eyes theatrically; the meme of a baby wearing a tuxedo and sunglasses; a video featuring a two-pound barnacled rat drinking a smoothie someone left on a subway bench, straight from the straw. David had the terrible habit of holding his phone's screen up to my face, forcing me to look. It was harassment, to be accosted by someone else's algorithmically determined clickbait. I had my own content to wade through! Plus, he was a workaholic, the most distractible and Internet-dependent kind of person there was.

David was a computational building information modeler, an esoteric kind of architectural engineer. I wasn't very interested in computers, and we'd reached a point wherein I no longer fully understood his profession. When we'd met in college, he was studying architecture, and then he'd gone to graduate school for architecture, and then he'd gone to work for an architecture firm. But he wasn't an architect. On this point, he could be kind of pushy. It was a whole thing. Before I could bring up any of this, though, as a point in my favor in our endless debate over whose Internet habits were more insufferable, my phone began to vibrate. I was keeping it propped up on the bottom shelf of my wall-mounted spice rack. I looked at the screen.

"It's Melissa," I told David, turning off the stove heat.

Melissa: my older sister, my former boss. With our cousin Angelo, she co-owned Sweet Cheeks, the bakery on Fourth Avenue where I'd been the general manager for nearly the entire six years the place had been in business. I'd gotten mad and quit a couple of months earlier, around the holidays.

"Melissa! What does *she* want?" David asked, but he'd turned back to his laptop before he was even done speaking, offering me a kind of mental privacy to take the call.

"We'll find out," I said, swiping my thumb across the photo of her face that appeared when she called. "Yeah," I said, instead of "hello." "What is it?"

"You answered!" Melissa shrieked, triumphant. Her voice fizzled in my ear. In the background, I heard the familiar clamor of the bakery's operations: metal pans banging, water running, a timer going off. Someone shouted something in Spanish as a second timer started to buzz. The exhaust fan whirred.

"What are you still doing there?" I asked her. "It's, like, dinnertime."

"Well, if you must know, I'm extremely busy," Melissa said, her tone exasperated, as though *I* had called *her* rather than the other way around. "Valentine's Day is a pretty big deal over here, you may recall. I still have a handful of special orders to frost, and there's been a line out the door all day."

"Is this why you called? To tell me how busy you are? I'm busy, too, you know."

"I did not know that, Kit," she said. "I had no idea you were busy. Because it isn't true."

"As a matter of fact, I am celebrating Valentine's Day with my husband," I said, drawing out both syllables of the word "husband," as though Melissa had no particular connection to David and might not know to whom I was referring.

David looked up from his laptop, his dark brows furrowed. In a flat, loud voice, he said, "Hi, Melissa."

"He says hi," I told her, though of course she'd heard him.

"Yeah, sure, okay. Hi, David," she said. "So what are you doing? You going out? Can you drop by the bakery for ten minutes first? Me and Angelo need to talk to you."

"Angelo and *I*," I said. "Just tell me why you're calling. I am not coming by the bakery. I'm making dinner. I need to hang up before my whole kitchen burns down." I looked around, imagining that Melissa could see into my house through the bakery storefront five blocks away—the squash I'd been chopping, the open bottle of olive oil I'd massaged into the lamb's sticky skin, the Ziploc bag coated with the dust of a homemade spice mix I'd sprinkled over it, the baker's string, the parchment paper, the big, horrific baster with which I should've been basting the lamb at that precise moment. "I'm roasting a leg of lamb. And making a salad."

"Oh, okay," Melissa said, her tone dipping into a familiar register: her own particular combination of pity and dismay. "You're doing one of your diets."

"As it so happens, David and I started the Radiant Regimen today," I snapped. "It's not a diet. It's a wellness program."

"'Program' is just a culty word for 'diet.'"

"You know what *your* problem is, Melissa?" I said. "You don't understand nuance. You suffer from binary thinking. I'm flushing the toxins from my system to cleanse my liver and the—"

"Okay. Relax, psycho," Melissa cut in. "Make your lamb. Do your *program*. Have a wonderful, romantic time with your husband." Now *she* drew the word out. My phone was heating up in my hand. "But can you come in tomorrow? It's important."

I tugged at the sagging belt of my bathrobe, which hung open above sweatpants and an oversize Mets T-shirt. I had dressed in outside clothes earlier, when I'd gone to the produce market and the Turkish butcher. Immediately upon returning from these errands, though, I'd changed back into my indoor clothes. (Incidentally, my indoor clothes also functioned as pajamas.)

David, wearing gym shorts and a black T-shirt he'd been given for free at some industry conference, with the words THE SYMPOSIUM FOR TALL TOWERS AND NEW CITY DEVELOPMENT / SINGAPORE 2015 emblazoned across the chest in a severe font, had returned fully to his emails. I could tell he wasn't paying any attention to my call, though surely he was aware of the annoyance coming off me, the way a person might be aware of water dripping from the tap or a window not closed all the way, some harmless imperfection he knew he should probably check on. His laptop's noxious glow turned him whitish blue, radioactive. I tried not to feel my own pale body in its soft robe, or the strands of hair escaping the staticky ponytail, hanging loose and messy at the back of my neck. I was sweaty from the oven, red in the face.

"What do you want?" I asked my sister.

Suddenly, everything felt gross and stale. I had been excited about the Radiant Regimen, and proud of my auspicious start, cooking what I thought of as one of the advanced special-occasion meats, a dish requiring patience and discipline, characteristics I'd need in order to complete the program successfully. The Radiant Regimen was seventy-five full days. No breaks, no cheating, not even for a wedding or anniversary. It was the most ambitious dietary plan I'd ever undertaken. But now Melissa had called and ruined it; she'd had to say barely anything to make me feel desperate and foolish and unemployed, a hopeless sucker who couldn't stop falling for the wellness industry's specious claims and vain promises.

"Come to the bakery," she said. "How about noon tomorrow?"

"Maybe," I said. "I mean, I have a lot going on tomorrow. But I'll try."

"Great. See you then."

She hung up before I could protest further. No goodbye, no thank-you.

I muted the phone's ringer and put it back on the spice rack with the screen facing the wall. A symbolic gesture. Melissa wasn't going to call again, and nobody else would, either.

I turned on the oven light and crouched down to get a look at my lamb. It appeared how it should. Thick meat glistening around a thin but sturdy bone, the whitish-pink flesh now dark, the coating of spices and herbs crusted over it like a thin bark. We'd have one or maybe even two meals of leftovers.

"So?" David said. "What did your sister want?"

"She wouldn't tell me. She just kept asking me to come talk. I'm going to go see her and Angelo tomorrow."

David grunted. "She only calls when she wants something."

"I think I will go back to work," I told him. "If she asks. It's not as though I have other offers pouring in, or anything else going on."

"Of course that's why she called. But you know, you haven't even tried to get a new job," David said. He sounded a little bored.

I considered starting an argument, but he was right.

I'd quit the bakery in December, in the middle of a bad day, suffering from what my grandmother used to refer to as my *intensificazione,* slicing the air with her fingers, raising her arm to the ceiling in increments. My grandmother had been dead for seven years and here I was, intensity unreduced, escalating ever higher on the ladder of high-strungedness: *up, up, up.*

The day I'd quit had been busy, the decaf drip coffee machine leaking putrid brown water, and I was tired, agitated, hated my life. So when Melissa whistled in my face and told me to focus, to cheer up, I tossed my apron onto the kitchen floor at her feet, tears stinging my eyes. My voice and hands shook when I said, "This whole place is bullshit," and stomped out the back door. Melissa watched me go with her arms folded, her face calm. This was the third time I'd resigned by storming out.

Given this history, I knew it was ridiculous and unfair, but still I wished David took more interest in my professional life. It had been nearly two months, and I hadn't so much as walked by the bakery. The other times I'd "quit," I was back at work within a week. In those instances, Melissa had called after I'd had a couple days to cool down and feel appropriately embarrassed. She was good at guilting and flattering me in one move, bringing up an impending health inspection or a large catering job, saying how much better the staff liked me than they did her or Angelo, reminding me that I had nothing else to do. I wondered if David wished I didn't work for Melissa. He never would have said so. But I suspected he'd prefer I had ambition to match his own workaholism, a job in the city, my good education put to good use. He must've thought I was wasting my time. In fairness, I suspected myself of wasting my time, but it wasn't something I really knew how to change. I'd always been this person. Besides my college years far uptown and a couple years after graduation when David and I lived in the East Village, I'd spent my whole life in Bay Ridge. In this very dwelling, in fact.

Now I looked around the kitchen and tried to regain whatever papery confidence Melissa had blown sideways with her big, loud disapproval.

"I *am* going to look for another job," I told David, even though I wasn't, and we both knew it. "But with all the changes I'm already making—" I gestured at *Way to Glow!* and my cooking "—I should have a routine. Without the stress of starting something new."

David nodded agreeably. He was used to me talking about an impulsive decision as though it were an idea I'd been considering well and for a long time. I went back to the squash, turning the gas on the stove and dribbling some more olive oil onto my heaviest cast-iron pan.

When the food was finally ready, I had the idea that we should eat in the dining room, but I hadn't asked David to clear the table of scarves and gloves and backpacks, or to wipe it down because surely the cat had napped on it, flopping over to lick his feet and stomach and anus in a crude, absent manner, many times, since we'd last had a proper meal. So I scooped the food onto our chipped kitchen dishes, and David and I ate side by side at the counter, over the junk mail. David closed his laptop, but it was still in front of us, plugged into the outlet on the wall next to my head, sucking up electricity, giving off heat, an unsubtle reminder of David's essential professional busyness. It didn't matter that it was Valentine's Day. It wouldn't have mattered if it had been the Fourth of July or Labor Day. Nor did it matter that this particular Valentine's Day was a Sunday. Sunday for David was simply a long windup to the workweek, Monday's pressure so heavy it seeped backward, took over the rest of the weekend, as if we were living in our own recent past.

But the meal was excellent, the meat juicy and the vegetables crisp. I willed myself to be optimistic. Over the past week, I'd read *Way to Glow!* straight through, taking notes and marking the best recipes with Post-its. I'd signed up for several yoga classes and researched something called "infrared saunas," which Diana Spargel recommended for sweating out "stubborn" toxins. The Radiant Regimen's particular methodology may have been new, but my seeking it out was an old

9

routine, one more addition to the repertoire of diets—*programs!*—I'd been doing since college.

I think of this dinner now, though, as *before*. I had no way of knowing my life was about to change, that this would be the last time David and I sat together and failed to notice each other or that our two lives were fused into one certain, sturdy shape. I'd meet Matt Larsson the next day, and the fact of my marriage—which had been a part of me, as natural as my endless search for the perfect diet, my belief that satisfaction and self-acceptance were things I could purchase, study, and employ (I just had to find the *right* things!)—would reveal its provisional nature.

THIS WAS 2016. I was thirty-four, and David and I had been married seven years. We didn't have kids. We lived in the upstairs apartment of the house on Eightieth Street, a ten-minute walk from Melissa's bakery, a forty-minute train ride to David's office in midtown. We worked different hours, and I thought he worked too much, but our life together was peaceful, even sweet. David was preoccupied, but so was I, always trying and failing to find the right way to eat. When I really press myself, I still can't think of anything to hold against David as a reason for why things happened the way they did. I just start thinking about all the reasons it doesn't make sense: David was smart, good-looking, and easygoing; he had a job he loved. His relationship with his family was steady and returned me to a steadiness I'd lost. He was funny, and we made each other laugh almost every day. I was fully attached to him.

But how can that really be true? Doesn't an affair start somewhere far behind the action itself? Isn't betrayal the product of a slow, underground roiling of barely discernible unhappinesses—disagreements over money, the gradual loss of physical attraction, regret over wasted time and lost friends, a sense of one's own life becoming too narrow, a sense of having chosen the wrong person—that gets larger and stronger over months and years before, finally, an affair churns to the surface? I'd always thought this must be the case; cheating was a *symptom* of some deeper decay. But that was before I had a contradictory experience of my own. Because Matt Larsson was specific, a person with a history and rationale all his own. What I know now is there is no recipe for a clean marriage, and you can't plan for everything. I don't believe any person alive is ever fully satiated, though I suppose I can speak only for myself.

CHAPTER TWO

I was late for my meeting with Melissa and Angelo the next day. David was already gone by the time I woke up, and remnants of his morning lingered: an empty mug in the sink, cold coffee on the stove. Woogie circled my path, rubbing against my shins.

I fed the cat and made a new pot of coffee. Then I got to thinking about the day's food. Dairy was off-limits on the Radiant Regimen, so I'd have to take my coffee with unsweetened almond milk. It mixed poorly, slimy chunks of residue floating in the cup, and did little more than make the coffee taste watered down. I resolved to learn to take it black. That was what Diana Spargel recommended, anyway. She herself rarely drank coffee, preferring to start her own days with antioxidant-rich green tea. I'd tried to develop a tolerance for green tea a couple years earlier, when I was doing a "bioactive compounds" diet developed by an influencer who had been, earlier in his life, a Tibetan Buddhist monk. But green tea tasted like stale cigarettes, and I had to pee every ten minutes. And I'd missed coffee. I made espresso at the bakery all day. I'd been drinking coffee since I was fourteen. It was one thing I'd decided to hold on to, and ever since I swore off any wellness program from which coffee was forbidden.

I scanned the cupboards and parsed through *Way to Glow!*'s breakfast recipes. The kitchen was bursting with the groceries I'd purchased in preparation. I decided to make something from a section called "Rapid Radiance: Superfood Smoothie Bowls." It wasn't really all that fast, though. I had to dice and sauté half a sweet potato in coconut oil. Then I set the pan aside to cool and used the blender to puree some strawberries and frozen banana, which I spatula'ed into a cereal bowl and topped with the sweet potato, plus a handful of fresh blueberries, and some slivered almonds.

The smoothie was fine, even pleasant, but as I stood over the kitchen sink spooning it into my mouth, I couldn't help but think the worst part of the Radiant Regimen—besides its ban on alcohol—was going to be the exclusion of almost anything resembling a traditional breakfast. No grains, so no oatmeal or pancakes or toast. No dairy, no yogurt. No eggs. Most of Diana Spargel's recipes for breakfast were substitutions for the real thing: "porridge" made from chopped apples and soaked chia seeds, or an eggless "frittata" that was just mushrooms stir-fried with flax powder.

AFTER BREAKFAST, I DRESSED slowly, fumbling around my sock drawer for a particular pair, pausing occasionally to look at social media on my phone, standing in the middle of the bedroom in jeans and a bra, barefoot with the socks balled awkwardly in the same hand I used to scroll down the screen, as though it were some sort of emergency. Once I got outside, I realized I'd forgotten my hat. Winter was in the midst of its merciless conclusion, and my exposed ears stung, so I went back up and spent too long looking through the apartment for the right hat—my beige beanie—which I finally found hanging on one of the hooks in the vestibule. As I dug through my bag for house keys, my neighbor Adeeb came out of his apartment. Our house was a big duplex; Adeeb and his family lived in the three-bedroom on the first floor, and David and I had the upstairs unit, which included our big attic bedroom.

Adeeb nodded, saying a quiet hello, but he was down the walkway and through the gate before I'd finished turning the lock. The neighbors never locked their door; someone was always home.

I'd grown up in this house, and now it belonged to me and Melissa— both our names were on the deed. When our grandmother died, she left us the house and all its contents outright; the mortgage had been paid off long ago. We'd agreed to split the taxes, though I lived in my half, and Melissa rented her unit. She lived in a two-bedroom on Marine Avenue, on the sixth floor of a renovated building. She had laundry right off her kitchen.

Adeeb was Melissa's tenant. He had a big immigrant family; I was never sure how many people lived downstairs. Relatives might be there for months at a time, coming on short-stay visas from Pakistan. Sometimes when the family hung out on the stoop in summer, I'd peer through the open door of their apartment as I passed, trying to get a sense of how they set things up, who occupied which of the high-ceilinged rooms. I'd grown up in the downstairs apartment, but I hadn't been inside for years. Once, on the last night of Ramadan, I brought Adeeb a cake from Sweet Cheeks. His wife invited me and David to join them for dessert. I said I couldn't because I had a headache and needed to lie down. David frowned at me. He knew the truth—I was on a diet and didn't want to sit there drinking seltzer while everyone else had cake. David went downstairs and ate dessert with them. For an hour, I could hear them laughing and clapping while I tried to read a novel that wasn't holding my attention.

In truth, I missed my grandmother too much to revisit the apartment. I still expected sometimes that she would open the door as I was coming up the walk, look at me crossly, ask why I was always late, and tell me to have a baby. My grandmother had been my and Melissa's primary guardian for as long as I could remember—our mother had died when I was only a few months old. We barely knew our father, who'd been in the army and now lived with his wife and two children out in the California desert. Our grandmother was everything. She'd been tall and broad with orangey-red dyed hair. Her voice was low and pebbly; she spoke a strange hybrid of accented English and her native Barese, a language so distinct from other Italian dialects that people in stores and restaurants often confused her for Russian. Her death, a double stroke when I was twenty-four, had broken my heart.

FINALLY, I HEADED DOWN the block, passing the other duplexes, the semi-detached brick buildings and vinyl-sided homes, stopping at the crosswalk in front of Standing Tall Chiropractic, where my grandmother used to go on Tuesday afternoons to have her back cracked by a guy named Dr. Rusty. I crossed Third Avenue: thoroughfare of lunch counters and bagel shops, Italian red-sauce joints both fine and cheap, Greek pastry cafés, cigar lounges, unmarked soccer clubs, Irish hole-in-the-wall bars, nail salons, pizza windows. Along with these enduring institutions, there'd been a recent upcropping of new businesses, most of them a quaint but somewhat contrived mimicry of central Brooklyn's late-stage gentrification. In addition to Sweet Cheeks, Fourth Avenue had an Urban Outfitters, plus an independent clothing boutique selling oversize blouses along with other billowy garments made from linen or thrice-layered diaphanous gauze. There was a twenty-five-dollar cheeseburger place where the Sizzler used to be. Between the Victory Cabs cabstand and a Dunkin' Donuts, there was an ironic tiki bar with a live ukulele band. It was called the

Coconut Flake, and the hostess gave you a lei made from real carnations on your birthday.

Traffic was slow outside the bakery, only a few people were out, and I realized the sky was holding a snowstorm. The clouds were a low, lustrous gray. The Verrazzano Bridge hung at the edge of my periphery, where it always was, a pale green gate posted into the water. Wet snow started falling as I pulled the door open. The bakery's dense smell—chocolate and warm butter and risen yeast—enveloped me. Immediately, my mouth began to water. I felt the danger of being there, the way I always did when I was trying to eat well, to follow a diet, a nutritional program, whatever. All my life, I had been afflicted with a powerful, terrible sweet tooth.

SWEET CHEEKS WAS ONE of those bakeshops known as much for its creative dessert hybrids—the red velvet cookie, the banana split cupcake—as for its fine-tuned brand of millennial kitsch, the design so aggressively cute it felt almost mean. A neon sign hung in the window, the words CAKE IS THE ANSWER! aglow in bright pink cursive. Behind the glass counter, a girl named Athena—a tiny twenty-year-old with a lot of freckles, a tight red bandana tying back pigtails—was packing a big box with confetti cupcakes, which she took, one by one, from the rolling tray just out of view.

"Hello—" she started to greet me as though I were a customer coming in, but her gaze lifted before she could say, "I'll be right with you." Instead she let out a big, excited laugh and slapped the counter's flip-lift, racing through to throw her skinny arms around me.

"They found you!" she said, as though I were a little dog or a diamond ring. I let Athena embrace me on her tiptoes, looking over her small shoulder across the dining room's black and white penny tile. At a table in the farthest corner, Melissa and Angelo sat in silence, looking at their phones. Neither had appeared to notice my arrival.

"Well, I wasn't lost," I said to Athena. "I was just at home."

"But are you back?" she asked. "Please say yes."

"We'll see," I said in a low voice, nudging my head toward my sister and cousin.

Athena smiled, her Invisalign gleaming atop her white teeth, and returned to packing orders behind the counter. She picked up the final cupcake in the dozen box she was working through, gingerly placing it in the last corner of available space. The cupcakes lined up beautifully, three rows of four, and my stomach ached at the sight.

I made my way to Melissa and Angelo. "Busy today," I said, gesturing to the nearly empty room. Melissa raised one finger: Hold on. Angelo used his free hand to absentmindedly twirl a black baseball cap. It read SWEET CHEEKS, EST. 2010 in baby-blue block letters across the front. His expensive jeans and pink button-down shirt were pressed and spotless. Melissa was as disheveled as Angelo was neat, in waitress clogs and a full chef's apron smeared with crude-looking chocolate stains. Her long dark hair was pulled into a loose bun at the base of her neck.

I considered dipping back behind the espresso bar and making myself an Americano. Plain coffee was the only item on the Sweet Cheeks menu that I could have. But I didn't want to give Melissa and Angelo more leeway to keep ignoring me. I pulled a chair from a nearby table and sat down. After a long moment wherein neither of them acknowledged me or averted their gaze from their phones, I became annoyed. "What are you guys even looking at?" I snapped.

"Grindr," said Angelo.

"Tinder," said Melissa, and she swiped her thumb across the phone's screen.

"Okay, well. I'm guessing you didn't ask me here to help you find a date."

Melissa raised her head and fixed me with a steady but congenial stare. "No," she said, leaning forward. "We need to know when you're coming back to work." Her mouth had shaped itself into a concentrated straight line, as professional an expression as she could muster.

"I'm not coming back," I said. "I quit."

Angelo let out a small laugh—a high, dry sound. "You said that the first two times," he said, and set his phone facedown on the marble tabletop, folding his hands across his knee with a little kick.

"Right," Melissa added. "I let you have a long break this time, because honestly, you were out of sorts all December. Crabby and mean—how you get—and not telling anyone what was wrong."

"You were a nightmare!" Angelo chimed in. Melissa shot him a warning look.

"I'm sorry you felt that way," I said, aware that I sounded like a fourth-grader but unable to stop myself. "I guess it's better I'm gone, since I'm so difficult."

Melissa's mouth quivered with annoyance, but she blinked her temper away. "Come on, Kit," she said. "What are you doing with yourself? Aren't you bored? If I were home all day with nothing to do, I'd be so depressed."

I was depressed. For the last two months, I'd dragged myself through every day. I scooped Woogie's litter box, made the bed, paid the bills, and then, all reasonably productive tasks completed before noon, I spent the rest of the hours drifting deeper and deeper into the Internet's bottomless pool of imbecility, click-click-clicking through headlines. SEVEN SURPRISING SIGNS YOU AREN'T GETTING ENOUGH VITAMIN C. YOU WON'T BELIEVE WHAT THIS FORMER *BACHELOR* CONTESTANT LOOKS LIKE NOW. THIS MOM'S RESPONSE TO HER SON'S YOUTUBE POST WILL MELT YOUR HEART. Lately, there'd been an extra dose of derangement to drink in, as a clown car of candidates— a few of them obvious psychopaths—fumbled through the beginnings of the Republican primary. Mostly, though, I looked at wellness influencers' blogs and social media pages, the clean clutter of curated photos: blenders making green soups, complicated yoga poses, bikinis on tropical beaches. On a productive day, I peeled myself from my laptop and went to Duane Reade and maybe the grocery store. On an especially productive day, I watched talk shows at the Laundromat instead of my living room sofa.

I said, "I have plenty to do. I'm running my household."

"Housewives have children," Angelo said.

I tried again. "I'm getting a job at my yoga studio. Working the check-in desk."

"That's how you want to use your college degree?" Melissa asked, because she couldn't let go of the fact that I'd elected to spend four additional years in school and had little to show for it.

"It's not like I use my degree here," I said.

"That is just not true. You're our communications director!" she cried.

"I'm your floor manager," I said. "You don't need a college education to order paper goods and call the dishwasher repairman and get yelled at because the cake says 'Happy Birthday Shoshanna' in light pink frosting when the customer asked specifically for lavender."

Angelo, himself in possession of a business degree from Baruch, knew what to say. "We value the insight you bring to the business," he told me. He sat up straighter. "You have your moods, but you are the smartest person we know."

"Whip-smart," Melissa agreed, but her tone was less cajoling. She sounded listless, resigned.

I squinted, moving my gaze between the two of them. It was too much, these compliments. "What's going on?" I asked.

Melissa sighed, ready to confess. "We are making some, uh, renovations," she said. "In the kitchen."

"Small ones," Angelo interjected. "I'd love to have the whole thing totally redone, but you know, the money—" He cleared his throat, looking sideways at Melissa. "We don't have it at the moment. But we can't wait anymore on the shelves, and rather than go get some new ugly placeholders from Costco or wherever, we are having them custom-built. We hired a carpenter I found on a website."

"Craigslist?" I asked.

"No, boo, not Craigslist," he said, irritated for some reason. "A different website. A nicer one."

"Okay," I said sourly. "Sorry."

"His stuff is high-end," Melissa said. "This carpenter, he designs shelves and tables and all kinds of things. We had to describe what we wanted, and then we posted it, and contractors and whoever—they bid on it, saying what they'd do, and how much it would cost. He wasn't the cheapest, that's for sure. But he wasn't the most expensive, either, and the shelves he's going to build are perfect. It's hip. He's a designer, too— Oh! I bet David will love him. He did all the tables for a bar at this new hotel in the city."

She picked up her phone, typed furiously as she spoke, then held the device out to me. I watched a website load slowly on her screen. The Wi-Fi was always spotty in the bakery, which had that thick-bricked cavernous quality of so many New York dining establishments. Finally, I saw what Melissa meant. On a sleek, simply formatted webpage, I read: MARSSON STUDIO // Custom Interiors from Master Craftsman Matt Larsson.

"Oh, I see," I said, turning the phone horizontally to get a bigger view. "This is *fancy*."

Melissa nodded, satisfied by my approval. "We could have used your help, you know," she said. "Writing the request was hard."

I clicked through to the website's gallery. The furniture was understated but beautiful and had a kind of industrial Danish-midcentury look. There was a raw oak dining table with smooth glass inlaid over its purposely unsanded imperfections, and—from Melissa's aforementioned hotel bar—slim stools and high tables with raw steel legs, a few leather booths to match. The shelves were really impressive, a blend of wood panels fixed into sturdy metal frames and screwed into the wall through smooth circular jousts. I saw immediately how well this Matt Larsson's aesthetic would meld with Melissa's tastes and the rest of the bakery, where the dining room had the look of Malibu Barbie's nineteenth-century train station café. It was inexplicable but true that the marble-topped tables and heavy black bistro chairs looked nice, and right, alongside the pink neon and the tinted cake covers.

"Well, I think this looks great," I said, handing Melissa her phone. "But I'm not sure what it has to do with me."

Angelo opened his mouth, but Melissa beat him to it. "We can't afford to close the kitchen, not even for a day."

"Larsson will be coming in around closing and working late," Angelo added. "The commission will take a week this way, maybe a little more." He closed his eyes for a moment and his eyelids quivered. I realized he was exhausted.

"Why would I need to be here?" I asked. "Give him a key. Or have one of the dishwashers stay."

Angelo shook his head. "A supervisor has to be here. If something happens, the insurance won't cover damages or workers' comp: nothing. And you're the only one of us with an OSHA card."

When we'd opened the bakery, I'd insisted that someone take the thirty hours of occupational safety training offered by the Department of Labor. It got Angelo better insurance rates, so he agreed, but neither he nor Melissa was willing to do the course. Having the card had turned out to be a curse. Now my presence was the one required any time we undertook possibly unsafe or insalubrious repairs and projects.

I groaned. "Truly, no good deed goes unpunished with you two."

"Look," said Melissa, "there's just too much going on right now. You've gotta come back. And no more leaving every time you're in a mood. Otherwise, we have to promote Violet."

"Who's Violet?" I asked.

"We hired a new person—Violet Kim—right after Christmas," Melissa said. "That's what happens when you 'quit.'" She made bunny-ear quotes. "We have to hire new people. Tiffany went back to school this semester and had to go down to two days. Athena is babysitting her sister's kids on Fridays. It's been a lot of extra work—*your* work. We have too much to do."

"I can't be writing the shift schedule for these girls," Angelo said. "Making the schedule sucks."

"And, not for nothing," added Melissa, straightening her broad shoulders, "Violet's good. Experienced. She used to be a supervisor at Magnolia, and then she was at this third-wave coffee place in SoHo. She'd be a good manager."

"But she's a sourpuss," Angelo said, grimacing. "Not as bad as you, but still."

Melissa neither agreed nor argued. She behaved as though she hadn't heard Angelo at all. "We don't really have time to train Violet," she said. "And why would we? We have a manager. We have you."

Angelo rose from the table and went into a small supply closet behind the espresso bar. We used it partly for storage and partly as a kind of outpost for getting office work done. There was a chest of drawers built into the wall and a telephone connected to a private line. Behind this were stacks of paper coffee cups and hundred-packs of flattened lock-corner cake boxes in shrink-wrap. He rummaged around and came back quickly, dropping an overstuffed manila folder on the table in front of me with an agitated slap.

"Here," he said. "This is yours." In silver marker, written in Angelo's perfect, prissy cursive, were the words KIT ALTMANN, QUITTER: ABANDONED RESPONSIBILITIES.

Without looking, I knew what the folder contained: schedule mock-ups, time-off request sheets, supply order forms, temperature logs, job applications—all the tedious ephemera of my tedious existence, foisted back upon me. There was no more conversation, no more begging, no more flattery. While I had fully expected this meeting to result in my reinstatement, I hadn't, for some reason, planned on working that very afternoon. Though I had nothing else to do, this was a little disorienting, like realizing you're dreaming but not being able to wake up. Everything was the same. Angelo's phone rang and he answered it, wandering off toward the front of the room, where he liked to pace at the windows and berate whoever was unfortunate enough to be calling him.

"Why are you dressed so nice?" Melissa demanded as I took the folder and followed her into the kitchen to say hello to the back-of-house.

"This is how I always dress," I said, looking down at my black wool pants and cashmere sweater, two of my favorite items of clothing, the kind of thing I'd wear to go out to dinner or one of David's work parties.

Melissa rolled her eyes. "Okay," she said.

We went through the swinging double doors, where we were smacked with the kitchen's familiar heat. For the first half of the day, Melissa and her assistant baker, Guillermo, used both of the hulking commercial ovens nonstop. I let myself enjoy the buttery smell for a moment, knowing full well how fleeting the comfort was. From Guillermo's station, I got a whiff of the fresh bananas he was slicing and layering into clamshells of banana pudding. I could taste the cake pieces on my tongue, pillowy when mixed into the even softer pudding fluff. I'd have loved to eat some. Melissa, who said diets were for self-loathers and suckers, and who'd never recovered from her disappointment when I'd become a clean eater, was always telling me to eat more of the pastries. ("Why would I starve myself to be skinny," she'd asked me a million times, "when I could get hit by a bus tomorrow? This is *America;* I'm not dying on an empty stomach.") I'd have to constantly beat back the temptation to sneak behind the cooling racks to shovel broken cookies or a spoonful of buttercream frosting into my mouth. Everyone did it.

But I wouldn't, I resolved. Every diet I'd ever done had ended at the bakery, after hours, when the lights were low and there was nobody to see and I'd been on my feet all day, was famished, couldn't keep my willpower propped up another second. But it was going to be different this time. I was going to complete the Radiant Regimen. I'd make it to the end.

CHAPTER THREE

The kitchen bustled with its usual activity. Guillermo pulled heavy trays of sugar cookies from the ovens, shouting over the whir of the exhaust fans. At the long steel table in the back of the room stood Maria, the specialty decorator. She had cropped white-blond hair beneath a hairnet, perfect Soviet posture, and enormous noise-canceling headphones, which were surely pumping house music into her ears. She held a piping bag and was sculpting ornate flowers along the surface of a three-tiered cake. Maria had studied art restoration as a student in Kiev before she came to New York. She was incredibly talented and the most reserved person I knew. I didn't say hello; she couldn't stand to be interrupted while working.

As soon as Guillermo had the trays laid on cooling racks, he pulled off his giant oven mitt and hugged me, but with what felt like casual disinterest. No one had ever considered my absence as anything more than a hiatus. Melissa spoke with him, her Spanish quick and relaxed, as natural as her English. There was some discussion of baking times and oven temperatures. Melissa said *treinta y cinco minutos*, which I knew offhand to be the baking time for most sponge cakes, and Guillermo looked skeptical and argued for a two-bake process based on the addition of some novel ingredient or maybe the height of the pastry. They were always debating how to do things.

I went to the handwashing sink and took a clean white apron from the bin below, tying it tight over my sweater. Besides being overly dressy, my clothes were much too warm. The front-of-house staff wore cuffed blue or black jeans and checkered or plaid shirts of any color. We tied our hair back with bandanas into buns or braids, put on bibless aprons, and wore high-top sneakers. The look was supposed to have the whimsical practicality of Rosie the Riveter, but it was also comfortable. It had been my idea. Sometimes, when getting ready for my shift at home, I pretended I was dressing for a part in a movie in which I played the manager of a Brooklyn bakeshop. For some reason, this fantasy was much more pleasant than actually being the manager of a Brooklyn bakeshop. Now, without the surface comforts of the uniform, reality was uninteresting, even somewhat disgusting. Already, I could feel sweat soaking the edges of my bra, which would be drenched by the end of my shift, maybe stain my sweater.

Melissa finished with Guillermo and came over. "You should wear a chef's coat over that," she said, surveying me once more. "You'll ruin that cashmere."

"I'm already roasting," I told her.

Melissa's workstation was littered with the detritus of her five a.m. baking shift: anthills of powdered sugar, torn cupcake wrappers, a metal bowl of fudge with a skin drying over it. I observed her, her frowzy clothing and lined, tired face, a crusty streak of something—frosting or wet sugar or cake batter—smeared on the side of her jeans. Her soiled apron was untied at the hips, hanging loose like a sail around her neck, and the high bun that held her dark hair had collapsed behind a terrycloth headband. Melissa was sturdy; it was obvious how strong she was. She was in much better shape than I was, despite being heavier. She found a clipboard beneath a flurry of other papers and began to read something on it with what seemed to me like an ostentatious, even false, level of interest.

"What's that?" I asked.

Melissa started talking quickly, without pause between sentences. "He'll be here in a few hours. Guillermo and I have one more bake—mini-cheesecakes, we're trying a new flavor, we made this mimosa glaze—and then I have to take off. I don't know what Angelo's doing, but I think he's going to head out soon, too."

"Wait," I said. "What? Who?"

She looked up, eyebrows theatrically high. Her clipboard was the one we used to keep special-order forms, and I could see now she'd been pretending to examine something dated for the following day. She had a habit of holding things like clipboards and mail as buffers between us when she had bad or annoying news, using these items as a kind of oracle that contained information from some authority other than her, something out of her control. She wasn't a very good boss, and she knew it.

She asked conversationally, "What do you mean, 'who'?"

"The first thing you said. *Who* will be here in a few hours?"

"Oh, right," she said, as though it were so small a detail she'd already forgotten. "The carpenter. Matt Larsson." She leaned in, whispered, "He's a snack. Angelo said not to sleep with him, though."

Melissa was perennially single. She rotated through a handful of different dating apps, looking for men to take her out to brunch or a matinee, to fuck her in the early evening but not spend the night. She claimed she wasn't interested in anything serious. Her dating profile said as much; I'd seen it on rare occasions when she was feeling chummy and showed me how Tinder worked, since I'd never had occasion to use such a service myself. NOT LOOKING FOR ANYTHING SERIOUS, it read in the "About Me" section. No other information provided therein, just a few attractive photos: Melissa in full makeup with her hair down, blow-dried, her eyes relaxed at the corners. A sweet-smiling, well-kept stranger with my sister's face. Like so many people who had been partnered and settled from a young age, I was endlessly curious and eager to hear about her incidental romances. Casual sex—sex that was separate from the core of a person's existence—fascinated me. Under less irritating circumstances, I would have prodded her for information. Was she planning to sleep with the carpenter anyway, despite Angelo's edict?

I looked at the clock on the wall. It was only one in the afternoon. The bakery closed at eight. "This carpenter is coming *tonight*?" I asked. "To do carpentry?"

"Oh, no," Melissa said in a sunny voice, relieved. "He's just coming by to meet you and show his plans for the shelves." She gestured toward the cheap, wobbling aluminum racks leaned along the north-facing wall. They were packed with pans, baking sheets, and mixing equipment. The kitchen was large and disorganized, chaotic—nothing like the carefully curated dining room. Things were always going missing back there or falling on the floor and needing to be rerun through the steam sanitizer. The shelving's surfaces were sticky from years in the humid, sugar-filled room, and various spots were pocked, rusted, or misshapen.

I turned back to Melissa, my eyelashes aflutter with irritation. She glanced toward the door as though Angelo might come in and spare her this awkwardness, happy as he was to be the bad guy, to tell me to suck it up and handle my responsibilities.

"So, am I back to work because you need me to run the front-of-house, or because you need a body with keys to sit here at night with this—this—cabinetmaker? Because you guys are too cheap to close down for a day or two?"

Melissa threw her hands up. "I'm trying to be *nice*," she said. "What's the problem? You're busy? You're roasting a goat for Saint Theophilus Day? Flushing all your *toxins* and whatnot?"

I stared at her. The problem with picking a fight was that I wouldn't win. Melissa was too clever, and too willing to take the low road. "No," I finally said. "It's fine."

"Okay," she said. "If you're *sure*."

"Don't provoke me," I said. "I'll stay but Angelo should get his safety training."

Melissa was a baker. Her workday started at five a.m. She went to bed most nights around nine. I doubted her ability to stay up past then, honestly. Angelo worked all the time but rarely past seven, though he was something of a night owl in his personal life. He had a devout gym routine and a lot of friends he went out with to see shows and concerts in the city, to drink cocktails in hotel bars on the Lower East Side. I thought he was very cheesy in his fitted Armani shirts and David Yurman bracelet—an old goombah in the body of a well-exercised thirty-year-old gay man—but I was jealous sometimes, too. For all Melissa and I didn't have in common, we were both afflicted with a kind of introversion. We weren't shy, but given the choice between a party and watching television in our pajamas, we'd choose the latter. I had always wanted to be more like Angelo, who was comfortable in a group, even a crowd, and whose life seemed richer and happier because it was heavily populated. Of course, given the choice between staying late while the kitchen underwent construction and not doing that, we were all three the same. Unfortunately, I didn't have much of a say. Melissa and Angelo owned Sweet Cheeks together—they had cosigned the business loan and were paying the bank back—and I had no such stake. In fact, I had declined an offer for partnership when they'd begun the process of opening the bakery. Undesirable tasks often fell to me simply because I had less veto power. I operated at the bakery as a mostly autonomous agent; Melissa and Angelo didn't tell me how to run the dining room. I chose the companies where we purchased paper goods and cleaning supplies, I wrote the schedules and set the shifts, I dealt with customer issues and counted the deposits, which I then handed off to Angelo. Melissa baked and invented menu items, and once or twice a month she came in extra-early and waxed the floors herself. She hated being at the counter. She didn't even participate in interviews when we hired new staff for the front-of-house.

It occurred to me how many of my duties must've become part of her problem when I'd quit, things she loathed doing, and I felt a stab of guilt followed immediately by a wave of defeat. The truth was, I wouldn't have minded staying late if I had known I'd be working in the first place. If I could've come in later in the day, prepared with my own Pyrex of Radiant Regimen–compliant food.

"Whatever, it's fine," I told Melissa. "Do you know if this guy needs anything from me? How big is his crew?"

"I think it's just him," she said. "I offered to have one of the dishwashers on hand to help, and he said it probably wasn't necessary."

I scanned the long, high wall where these new shelves were supposed to go, and let out a low whistle. "Seems like a two-man job, at least," I said.

"I had the same reaction," she agreed. "But he was confident. He does this all the time, I guess." She shrugged. She pointed past the dish pit to the lowboy, where there was a stack of plastic bins, the kind David and I used for packing away our opposite-season clothing. "Angelo bought these. We're going to store the dishes in them while the shelves go up. To keep everything clean and separate. It's going to be a pain."

Melissa's face clouded with concentration. Now that we'd settled the matter of me working the late shifts with the carpenter, she could return to baking. She looked past me to Guillermo and again spoke too rapidly for me to comprehend. She glanced back in my direction. "Aren't you going to get out there?" she asked, nudging her head toward the dining room. "Athena's waiting for you; I'm sure she's going to tell you she'd like a break. Oh, and you get to meet Violet. Her shift starts at two."

IT TOOK NO TIME to get used to being back. The job was all muscle memory, intuition, a machine I could've operated with my eyes closed. Athena had only an hour left in her shift, which she spent hustling between customers and trying to get everything clean and stocked before the evening crew arrived. She was always in a rush to leave. I didn't blame her. On weekdays, Sweet Cheeks opened at six-thirty a.m., and the first few hours were grueling: making coffee, bagging up muffins and croissants, a nonstop stream of customers. There was barely time to wipe up spills, answer the phone, breathe. The rush-hour line could sometimes reach from the cash register to the door, with everyone in a hurry to get to the subway. It slowed down at about eleven, and the rest of the day was filled with idle tasks: frosting cupcakes, cleaning the case windows with white vinegar, restocking supplies and wiping off table tops, pushing in chairs.

Athena also spent a fair chunk of our hour together catching me up on what I'd missed.

"Angelo won't give me March fifth off!" she told me almost immediately. "It's my cousin's sweet sixteen! He said I ask for too many weekends. He was all, 'How many cousins do you have? You always need off.' He's mean. He knows I have thirty-three cousins—that's not my fault."

"Did you fill out a time-off request?" I asked.

"Yes! I put it in the binder by the time clock. Right where it goes!" she shrieked, offended that I'd even asked, though she often forgot to follow normal protocols.

"Then it's fine," I said, thinking of the ABANDONED RESPONSIBILI-TIES folder I'd shoved into my pocketbook. "Angelo gave me back all my scheduling stuff today, so I'll switch you out with Tiana when I make next month's schedule. She likes Saturday morning."

"I love you," Athena said, earnest and unembarrassed, as only lunatics and young people are capable of being. "Please don't ever leave us again. This has been the worst month of my life!"

"It was almost two months," I told her, tapping my nails against the bottom of the clipboard I was holding.

"Woof," she said, sucking on her plastic braces. I turned to go into the closet and call Faustina, the sales representative from the New Jersey importer where we bought coffee beans, peanut butter, nougat, and an assortment of Italian candies. Faustina had a honking laugh and a habit of clearing her phlegmy smoker's throat mid-sentence, directly into the receiver. She always wanted to spend extra time chitchatting like we were old friends. I knew all about her daughter's lowlife ex-boyfriend and his two-timing, his gambling, his late child-support payments. I knew that her nine-year-old grandson still wet the bed, and that the bed-wetting was, in Faustina's opinion, the ex-boyfriend's fault. She would be thrilled to hear from me and would want to know where I'd been, what I'd been doing. She was going to ask me if I was pregnant. She asked every time we spoke, though I had never mentioned to her any plans or desire to have a baby.

When I returned from the kitchen almost twenty minutes later, rubbing my now sore ear, Athena was talking to an attractive woman next to the espresso bar. The woman—super-slender with smooth black hair tucked back neatly, stylish black eyeglasses—appeared to only be half listening to Athena and was bent in front of the espresso machine's shiny surface, using it as a mirror to check her eyebrows, which she smoothed with her pinkie finger. As I approached, Athena went quiet and grinned in a nervous, idiotic way before scurrying off to help a customer.

"Hi," I said to the slender woman. "You must be Violet."

She straightened and looked at me. Her gaze wasn't rude, but I felt myself being assessed in the extra couple seconds of silence before she responded.

"Hello," she said. "Kit."

I smiled and it felt fake. Violet had poreless alabaster skin, and her plum lipstick and heavy eyeliner gave her a severe, almost goth look. She wore all black, and her apron was snug, revealing a small, delicate figure. Hers was the thinness—collarbones blazing weaponlike, waist a smooth, narrow wineglass stem—I'd coveted all my life. I understood, at least intellectually, that I could never exist in such a shape no matter how little I ate. No matter how skinny I got, my breasts weren't going to disappear, and while my ass could shrink, it wasn't going to tone itself afterward. I wasn't built for waifery.

Violet didn't smile back. She passed the espresso bar and pushed the ZERO button on the cash register. The drawer flew open, but inside there was only the base two hundred dollars, ones and fives organized neatly in their trays, an extra roll of quarters in the farthest left cup.

"I already did the midday drop," I said, even though of course she could see this. Then, sheepishly: "The till was even."

"Okay," said Violet. She nodded, an inward gesture. I could almost hear her telling herself to play it cool. I wondered what Melissa and Angelo had told her about me. I was sure she'd hoped I wouldn't return. I felt like an intruder on my own turf and had no idea what to say as Violet closed the cash drawer with a gentle push. I'd hired and trained every other front-of-house worker. Now here was Violet, overqualified, trained in my methods by Angelo, who made a good latte, sure, but I wasn't sure he'd ever run the cash register. And yet it looked as though she hadn't needed him much.

"Is there something you'd like me to be doing?" she asked. Her tone wasn't confrontational, but I felt confronted anyway. And confused. The problem wasn't the bad attitude about which Angelo had foretold. It was how different Violet was from the rest of the staff, all women in their early twenties. I could tell immediately that Violet lacked the latent teenage qualities so many of them displayed: crooked posture, hormonal acne, cheap manicures, and home-dyed hair. There was something sophisticated in her demeanor, self-possessed and cool. She couldn't be lumped in with the rest of them.

Oh, I thought. She's my age.

"It looks like you know what you're doing," I said. "I'm around if you need backup. I'm just going to—" I stopped, gazing at the clean dining room as though I'd never been there before and didn't have, at any given moment, a hundred things to do. "I'll be around."

Violet nodded, pleasant enough.

"My shift is over," Athena announced from across the counter, where she was digging through the drawer in which staff kept their phones. "Can I go?" she was already wearing her coat.

"Yes," I said, and she curtsied, waving with both hands and blowing kisses on her way out.

I SPENT THE REST of the afternoon in the spot where I'd met with Melissa and Angelo only a few hours earlier. Angelo had left without saying goodbye, as was typical of him. At some point, Melissa wandered in from the kitchen and shook her hair loose from its bun. It fell to her elbows, flattened by oven heat. But it was clean and thick. Melissa and I looked alike, with lightly olive skin and long eyelashes, dark eyes, and what I think of as obviously Italian-American faces: oval-shaped with a strong Roman nose and jaw, prominent cheekbones. But Melissa was taller and heavier. She had large breasts and wide hips. I was the skinny one, though I wasn't naturally more slender. My dieting showed in the bones of my face. I had lean arms and nice little breasts, but beneath my clothes were stretch marks; the skin on my ass sagged a bit from fifteen years of losing and gaining and losing weight.

Melissa's comportment overall was that of a person who liked herself. When we were growing up, our grandmother had nagged at me constantly to stand up straight, keep my head up, stop skulking away. Melissa never got such reminders because she never needed them. Her ease was apparent even in high school, and it was apparent as she shook out her hair and brushed flour off her eyebrows. Instinctually, I wrapped my arm around my side, resting my right hand against my left ribs. It made me feel better to think how I would be changed after a few weeks of the Radiant Regimen. I reminded myself I'd just started something great. Something I could control.

"What do you think of her?" Melissa asked, motioning with her head toward Violet, who, with an inured expression, was cutting cake slices for a loud family of six. She was swift but graceful, placing each generous piece on a small porcelain plate without losing a crumb.

"She's great at the job," I said, shrugging. "But I think she hates me."

"Don't take it personally," Melissa said. "She's prickly at first. She'll warm up. I'm leaving. Text me if you need anything."

"What time, exactly, is this shelf guy getting here?" I asked.

"I think around six?" She looked at the big clock above the doors. "Jesus. What am I still doing here? I gotta go."

It was four-thirty. Melissa headed for the door but stopped and turned in the middle of the dining room. The cake family went around her, taking their plates to two tables they'd pulled together, a move I found very annoying. People who were inclined to rearrange the furniture in a bakery were, in my long experience, not similarly likely to put things back.

"Hey, Kit?" she said. "Eat something. You have that crazy look you get when you're hangry."

I rolled my eyes. "Go home," I told her, and she grinned in a stupid, self-satisfied way before sweeping through the door and into the late afternoon, where two inches of fresh snow lay on the sidewalk. Through the windows, I watched her bundled silhouette cross the street before disappearing around the corner.

But Melissa was right. I hadn't eaten since breakfast. I was ravenous.

CHAPTER FOUR

I ordered sashimi—no rice, no soy sauce—from the Japanese restaurant up the block. The cooks there were used to my strange, mercurial dietary restrictions, and they sent along half a raw cucumber sliced into coins and a small serving of steamed broccoli. I overtipped the delivery person and ate in the bakery's kitchen, standing over Melissa's spotless workstation as I snarfed the raw fish like a poorly trained aquarium seal, my hands shaking, clumsy as fins.

When I was done, my head cleared. I shook off the jittering weakness my hunger had caused, stood up straight, unclenched my jaw. I vowed to be better prepared from now on, and to eat on a schedule, as the Radiant Regimen mandated. Breakfast, lunch, and dinner, no skipping. I'd been too famished to enjoy my dinner mindfully, the way Diana Spargel instructed in *Way to Glow* "Mealtime Meditations."

Time collapsed into itself after that, taken up by small chores I could've done in my sleep: changing out the espresso canister, polishing the glass with newsprint, chatting with regular customers who either welcomed me back enthusiastically or seemed not to realize I'd been gone at all. At five o'clock, Tiana, who was a senior at CUNY Staten Island and had worked for the bakery since the summer after she graduated from high school, arrived for the short shift. When she saw me, she whistled, shimmying her square shoulders without compromising her always perfect posture. She said, "I knew you'd be back soon." We hugged loosely and then went to work folding paper boxes at the far counter. She answered my questions about the health and well-being of her family and her girlfriend, about how she liked her spring classes, her professors, and so on.

Meanwhile, Violet helped the customers with efficient patience. She wasn't overly friendly or solicitous in the way some service workers can be; there was no falseness to her at all. She answered questions easily, with an already impressive knowledge of the pastries and their ingredients. At the espresso machine, she pulled shots with a calm, experienced hand. I could see people liked her. She made it look easy. Service is not easy, and it isn't intuitive. Despite how underpaid restaurant work can be, and certain classist notions about the value of service jobs in general, it is certainly not the kind of work anybody can do well. You need a good memory, steady hands, and thick skin. A good service worker has an absolutely inscrutable poker face. Violet was a natural. It was both intimidating and a comfort to see someone as self-serious and pretty as Violet doing a job that often made me feel like a slacker.

AT SEVEN O'CLOCK, MATT Larsson walked through the door and tapped his snowy boots on the rubber mat. Tiana was in the kitchen, helping the night porter finish the dishes. Outside was fully dark—a rich, viscous black—and cold. We'd had very few customers for the past hour.

Matt was tall and handsome and smartly dressed in the way of a certain type of Brooklyn man: thick black canvas trousers and a weatherproof jacket with a heavy hood, which he tossed off to reveal salt-and-pepper hair, though he couldn't have been much older than I was.

"Hi, you must be the carpenter," I said from behind the counter. Somehow I'd just known.

"Hi," he said, peeling off his gloves and shoving them into his coat pocket. His voice surprised me. It was so friendly and warm. "I'm Matt. I'm sorry—Melissa told me, but I forgot your name." He held his hand across the counter for me to shake. I took it, but the distance was awkward. His fingers were icy.

"I'm Kit," I said.

He nodded, letting go of my hand. "That's right," he said, a broad smile on his face. "Kit's a great name."

"Thank you," I said.

Looking back, I'm tempted to imbue the encounter with the energy of what was to come, to add some shock or spark lighting between us in the first instant. A crack of thunder in the unmoving February sky, the power flickering off for a second. But the truth is the snow had stopped, and it was still outside—the quietest, most unassuming kind of night. Matt had a placid, down-to-earth demeanor, a midwestern-sounding voice: the vowels slightly longer, dragged out, in contrast to my nasal outer-borough accent. At college uptown, I'd become all too aware of the way I spoke and had made efforts to smooth it over. But when we moved back to Bay Ridge in the months following my grandmother's death, I relapsed.

There was nothing extraordinary about that night or Matt's presence in the bakery. He was someone passing through, the way electricians and HVAC repairmen and health inspectors did from time to time. I met and swiftly forgot scores of people. Matt and I stood talking in the pinky glow of the chandelier light, the dining room empty except for Violet, who was organizing the cupboard where we kept paper napkins and cardboard coffee cup sleeves. Destiny's Child—the only music liked by everyone who worked at the bakery—played faintly from speakers mounted in the corners.

Matt took an oversize sketchbook and a laptop from his messenger bag, and when I came around the counter, he laid out some drawings on the glass, showing me what he planned to do. The drawings were simple, done with only brown and gray pencils and black felt-tip pen, but the details were there, and the dexterity and beauty of the design was obvious. I was impressed. I asked questions about how high he would build (almost to the ceiling, with six wide tiers), and the materials (oak for the panels, reinforced with industrial steel rods, and some iron pieces, mostly decorative, as brackets), and how long it would take (just over a week, he hoped).

"So, Melissa said she'll finish baking by three every day," he said as we walked to the kitchen, where he was going to take some photos.

Tiana and the dishwasher had finished clean up. I could hear them outside; they must've gone out the back door to smoke a cigarette, which was against the rules. The back door locked on itself, so they'd have to walk around the building to get back inside. I wondered, shivering, if Tiana had even put on her coat.

"Plan for four at the earliest," I said to Matt. "Melissa is never done on time, and it takes her and Guillermo forever to clean up. They'll have to wash and completely dry every dish, then wash the floors. It's also really hot in here for about two hours after last bake."

"Okay," he said. He used his phone to take a few photos of the crummy shelving. "I think if I come in at four in the afternoon, I can get a lot done and be out of here by midnight."

Midnight! I held my jaw still to keep myself from letting out an exasperated sigh.

"For a week?" I asked. "Every night?"

"I told Melissa and Angelo ten days, tops," he said. "For the installation.

42

The design is done, and I have all the materials ordered and precut. Angelo and Guillermo are coming with me to pick everything up from the lumber supply tomorrow and help me load—"

"Guillermo will help you," I said. Angelo wouldn't. His claiming otherwise, right to Matt's face, would've been comical if it weren't such an audacious lie.

"Right," he said. "Okay. So, then, if I need assistance during the actual build, whoever is here with me can help out. I shouldn't need much, just a sturdy hand, someone to pass me things sometimes—"

"That's me," I said, interrupting again. "I will be here."

He nodded, taken aback by this information, or maybe by my sudden rudeness, which I hadn't meant to direct toward him. I was frustrated, though. The work was happening so late, and the job was tremendous. It was typical of Melissa and Angelo to decide that the details would work themselves out, which meant the actual labor and planning and organization were someone else's problem. Mine. Did they really expect me to hang around the bakery until midnight for *ten days*?

"That's great," he said, giving me an easy smile. "We can go ahead and take these old racks apart tonight. We'll have a head start."

I wondered if he'd noticed how stressed I looked and meant to set me at ease. Or maybe he wanted to make the best of a stupid situation. Certainly, he must've expected he'd have another man to help him. At five-foot-two, I probably seemed quite small to him. He was over six feet, a broad man with wide, strong shoulders and heavy limbs. Affable, eager to please. I decided to make myself as tolerable as possible, given my unhappiness with the circumstance and my bad habit of being uncomfortably candid, especially regarding my own emotions.

"Sounds good," I said, shrugging. "I can't be here every night, though. I'll need a night or two off."

"Absolutely," he agreed. "Would you like to make a schedule?"

I am by nature an overplanner, and I've always loved to know the shape of the coming days, to sit down and do preemptive accounting for my time. This suggestion therefore delighted me.

"I would love to make a schedule," I said.

Back in the dining room, we decided to give ourselves Friday off and work the rest of the week in an attempt to hurry the construction along. Matt talked at length about the different phases of shelf installation: clearing the space, cleaning, laying the materials, inserting studs into the walls, raising the frame, the panels, etcetera. I listened, fully invested once a plan was in play. It wasn't unlike meal planning or designing an exercise routine. The decision to embark on a project has always thrilled me, and I managed to become excited for the work without actually wanting to do any of it.

"I usually have my computer," I said. "But actually, I didn't know I'd be working today." Before I could blurt out an unnecessary explanation, Violet appeared from behind the counter.

"Business is slow," she said to me. She didn't apologize for interrupting or even acknowledge that I was talking to someone. She didn't look at Matt at all. Charming, service Violet was gone, and the tight-tempered pretty girl I'd met several hours ago had returned. "Would you like to send me or Tiana home?"

"Violet," I said. "This is Matt Larsson. He is going to build new shelves in the kitchen."

She turned her head to him with robotic slowness. "Hello," she said. "We met the other day. When you were in to see Angelo and Melissa." She delivered this information, which was for my edification, in Matt's direction.

"Nice to see you again," he said.

"Likewise." She turned back to me. "I wouldn't mind leaving, if it's all the same to you."

"It's okay with me if Tiana doesn't mind," I said.

"Tiana said her bus won't come until after closing, so she'd prefer to stay. We already did all our side work except the espresso machine."

I didn't like having this conversation in front of Matt, though I didn't know why. There was nothing private about it. With any other staff person, it would've been chummy, but with Violet, it had a whiff of combativeness. It was like she could see into my soul and knew I was intimidated. It was like being in seventh grade again. She was standing, I was seated, and I was sure I looked ugly. Why my appearance would even occur to me just then was as confusing as how bad I felt about myself.

"Sounds good," I said. "Have a great night."

"Thank you," she said, and nodded at Matt.

Once she was gone, Matt grinned at me and leaned in. "She's a little scary!" he said admiringly. "Is she always so intense?"

"I have no idea," I said. "I just met her today."

"Oh," he said, standing. I was surprised how disinterested he seemed at this revelation. "Want to start packing up shelves?"

We went back into the kitchen. I clicked on Guillermo's portable radio, which hung from a lanyard off the handle of the freezer door. It was dialed to WQBU. A dramatic Mexican ballad filled the room: an orchestra and a smooth crooning voice, all the unsubtle longing of a good pop song. I swayed as we worked, taking dishes down from the racks and sorting them into "most used," "frequently used," and "less frequently used." There weren't any pans or bowls I could identify as superfluous. Melissa was too practical and Angelo too cheap for extra equipment. It was kind of fun, and as we placed things into storage containers, Matt asked me some questions about the bakery, and about working with my family, which led me to tell him the story of my recent resignation. He laughed, hard, but I didn't feel mocked.

"You're funny," he said.

"Well," I replied, "of course I know that." He grinned at me for a long minute.

I liked him. He was open in a way few people were comfortable being. I had the sense that he trusted strangers implicitly and saw the best in others without coming off as naive. I remember thinking, This is a good person. This is what a genuinely kind person is like. His niceness was charismatic, aided by his good looks.

Tiana, who had indeed walked around the building to reenter rather than knock on the back door and admit to smoking, came into the kitchen at quarter till nine and ran the espresso machine's stainless-steel grate through the steam sanitizer. She said everything was clean and covered in the dining room and asked if she could take a few mini Meyer lemon cream pies, a popular item soon to be replaced with a springtime feature.

"Melissa wants to do those rhubarb meringue tarts again in March," Tiana said, disgusted.

"What's the difference?" Matt asked. "Between a Meyer lemon and a regular lemon?"

"Meyer lemons are sw—" Tiana began to explain, but I cut her off.

"Let's give him a taste test," I said, going to the big fridge on the other side of the kitchen and pulling a Meyer lemon from the produce drawer. I searched for a regular lemon, finally finding one in a wicker basket with a sign taped to it that said MARIA PERSONAL FOODS, PLEASE DO NOT TAKE, which was on the shelf below Maria's workstation, with her weird Roshen candies and boxes of black tea. Her electric kettle was nestled against it, as though standing guard.

"I'll replace it," I said when Tiana gave me a look. "So this one is the Meyer lemon," I said, holding up the slightly smaller, more orange-gold lemon. I took a knife from the block on Guillermo's table, a slender counter that ran perpendicular between Maria's and Melissa's work-stations, and sliced each lemon on a cutting board I'd pulled from one of the "frequently used" storage bins. I handed Matt a wedge of regular lemon.

"This is funny," he said. I would learn later how often he proclaimed things to be funny without laughing. I would come to see this habit as a challenge and relish each victory I had in making him laugh, so hard sometimes he could barely catch his breath. "When I was a baby, my dad would give me lemons to see the faces I made. My mom has a whole photo album of me in a highchair, puckering."

Tiana had taken her phone from her apron pocket and was positioned to film him.

"Go ahead," she said, tapping record on her screen.

Matt lifted the lemon wedge and gave it a dainty lick, at which Tiana and I both began jeering.

"Don't be a wimp," I said. "You said you've been sucking on lemons since you were an infant. Let's see it."

"Is this some sort of bakery initiation ritual?" he said.

"Initiation is way worse than this," Tiana responded. "Are you stalling?"

Matt took the lemon straight to his mouth, biting down as though it were a lime, post–tequila shot. He pulled his head back, his eyes were closed tight, his nose and mouth were scrunched at the tartness. He was hamming it up. Tiana and I were laughing. With the radio on, I didn't hear the banging at the back door right away. When I did hear, it was loud and forceful, angry-sounding. Matt, Tiana, and I looked at each other. I moved to turn the radio off and Tiana tucked her phone into her back pocket and pulled her apron off, then dropped it into the waste basket we used as a laundry bin.

"Who's that?" she asked in a low voice.

I shook my head. I didn't know. Anyone who was likely to show up after hours had keys. The bakery's phone line had rung a few times after eight, but we stopped answering once the door was locked and the sign switched from COME IN, WE'RE OPEN to SORRY, WE'RE CLOSED. Matt stood at one end of Guillermo's table with his eyebrows raised.

I went to the heavy door. "Hello? Who's there?" I called. I realized I'd risen on my tiptoes for no reason, a cartoonish weenie afraid of a knock at the door.

A muffled response came back.

"What'd they say?" asked Tiana. I hadn't been able to hear the words, but I recognized the deep voice at once. It was David, shouting for me to let him in.

"I've been calling you for over an hour," David said before I'd even finished opening the door. "Where's your phone?"

He pushed inside the kitchen and looked around, eyes widening at the sight of the discombobulated shelves and dishes, a tall stranger holding a lemon wedge, Tiana leaning on the handwashing sink, pulling her braids out of a bun and collecting them over one shoulder to examine the ends. David looked at me in my apron, hair tied back behind a little triangle of red bandana, sweaty in my wilted cashmere. His hands flexed, balled into fists, and then fingers extended into a taut stretch—the way they did when he was mad—before he unzipped his coat with an irritated yank. Sighing, he removed his glasses and furiously rubbed fog from the lenses with the edge of his sweatshirt.

I realized I had no idea where my phone was. I had a horrible habit of misplacing it. At home, I would have noticed its disappearance sooner, because I would've been looking at it, checking for the rare text message, scrolling through social media. But today, somehow, my phone had failed to occur to me. It had been so surprising and consuming to be back at work that I'd lost track of the stupid thing. It was probably in the office closet, sitting next to my ABANDONED RESPONSIBILITIES folder.

"I'm so sorry," I said. "I forgot to text you and let you know I was here. Working."

He looked at me. I was overly aware of Matt watching us.

"I assumed as much when I got home from the office and you weren't there," David said. "But it's beyond me why you wouldn't call. Eight o'clock came and went, and then nine, and I called, no answer. I started to panic."

"Is it really past nine?" I said. "Already?"

"It's nine-thirty!"

"Hi, David," Tiana said then in a quiet voice. "We're really happy to have your girl back."

He turned to her, and his face softened. David was well liked by the staff at Sweet Cheeks. When I worked weekends, he often stopped by to have lunch with me on my break and would shoot the shit with whoever had a spare few minutes. They all knew his fondness for seven-layer cookies, and how he liked espresso shots pulled long and watery with a tiny splash of cold half-and-half.

"Hey, Tiana," he said. "Good to see you."

"Yeah, you, too," she said. "But if it's really nine-thirty, I'm afraid I have to break up the party and leave right now. I'm about to miss my bus!"

"Go, go," I said, and she grabbed her things and backed out the door, waving, wishing us all a good night, agreeing with our advice that she should get home safely, as though the choice to do so were hers alone.

Once she was gone, David turned to Matt. "Hello," he said. "I'm David." He stuck out his hand.

Matt took it amiably, but before he could respond, I jumped in. "David, this is Matt Larsson. He is a carpenter doing a commission for us—he's building new shelves."

I started to explain how the day had gone, how Melissa and Angelo wanted me to start work immediately, the spell of late hours I'd be covering while the shelves went up, how I'd set my phone down somewhere and forgotten about it, forgotten to text David and let him know.

Through this, it somehow didn't occur to me to explain to Matt who David was. I never said, "This is my husband, by the way," or made any other such claim to David. His role in my life was evident, I'm sure, but I blathered as though Matt weren't there—overexplaining, nervous without understanding why.

Finally, David waved his arm at me to stop talking. "It's all right," he said. "I was worried because Melissa and Angelo didn't answer their phones, either. I started to think this place had burned down with you all inside—I swear, I walked over sniffing the air for smoke. Your phone battery must be dead. It went right to voicemail." To Matt he said, "I hope I don't seem like a jerk."

Matt smiled, nodding. He didn't appear to know how to respond.

"So, new shelves," David said, relaxing. He hung his coat from a hook on the wall. "It's good they're finally getting rid of this crap before it gets any wobblier. I could blow these over."

"Well, you did come bursting in here like the Big Bad Wolf," I said.

"I have drawings of what I'm going to build," Matt said, moving to get his notebook. He still had the lemon wedge in one hand. He glanced at it, then at me, disoriented, as if he couldn't remember what it was or how he'd come to be holding it. I took it and fetched a plastic bag.

"I'll send you home with a mini-pie," I said.

"Why do you have that?" David asked, gesturing to the lemon.

"Oh, we were goofing around," I said. "Matt asked what a Meyer lemon was."

"Meyer is sweeter," David said. He possessed a lot of secondhand food knowledge, passed on to him through me and Melissa as well as from his own mother, an avid home cook. "You can eat them raw."

"Really?" Matt said, but David was eager to be shown the drawings and leaned on the counter, palms flat, waiting.

"Yeah, like an orange," he said in a voice Matt would have heard as perfectly friendly, but which I recognized as twinged with David's particular impatience.

"You shouldn't have taken it away," Matt said to me as he opened his sketchbook for David. "I'd have enjoyed an orange-flavored lemon."

CHAPTER FIVE

David was less interested in the appearance of the shelves than the drawings he and Matt referred to as the "detail." I had skipped over these earlier. They looked like complicated geometry equations, the rectangles of each panel laid out with a series of lines and numbers, a small table in the corner of the page labeled "quan: est.," which apparently stood for "quantities estimation." It was the kind of meticulous forecasting David did for a living on a much larger scale, using ten-thousand-dollar computer software. He was in awe of a person like Matt, who built with his own hands. Truthfully, so was I.

David asked Matt several abstruse questions having to do with the kinds of supports Matt would use to secure the shelves, where he bought his materials, the weight and grade of the wood. I returned to packing up Melissa's pans and bowls. It took only a few minutes to finish up. Matt and David were still talking in depth and with what seemed like mutual enthusiasm when I was done. I moved all the storage bins to their temporary spot behind Guillermo's counter. There were six in all, two stacks of three, and I used masking tape to label them. Neither Matt nor my husband paid attention to what I was doing.

The old racks were lightweight and easy to take apart. All I had to do was unscrew the gluey old nails holding the thing together and carry the pieces out to the dumpster. But the moment I took a screwdriver from the tool drawer, David and Matt took notice of me. They stopped talking. It was like a magic trick. All I had to do was hold an item intended for handiwork, for the kind of task men fancied themselves good at, and I had their full focus. I didn't even have to use it. The power would've been thrilling if it hadn't been so infuriating.

"Let us do that," David said, walking over and taking the screwdriver.

"Yeah, we can knock this out in no time," Matt said.

I shrugged. "The wall and the floor need to be cleaned—scrubbed—after you clear this stuff out," I said. If they weren't going to let me use a screwdriver, fine, but I wasn't going to dive back in to wash something when they were finished. I had to fill out the temperature log a final time, and make sure all the cases and supply drawers were stocked and closed up tight, the glass free of fingerprints, the espresso grinder turned off. I had to count down the cash till and run the closing report.

"Got it," David said. Matt nodded.

I went to the dining room, annoyed past the point of my own understanding. David would help speed the work up. I should be grateful. But I wasn't. I'd been excluded, and it stung. This was *my* job. I had been enjoying being around Matt. I liked him, and I liked doing something different from my normal workday. Then David had shown up and it was like I'd disappeared. Worse, I understood that my sudden irrelevance wasn't supposed to offend me; it was a given to demur when men took interest in each other. I know this kind of thing doesn't bother a lot of people. If I complained to Melissa, she'd roll her eyes and ask me why I wanted to be included in the boring, unintelligent, posturing conversations of men, anyway. And she'd be right, in a sense. I didn't want to talk with Matt and David about *wood*. But that didn't mean I wanted to be silent and ignored, as though there were nothing else all three of us might have talked about.

In the dining room, the floors shone in the low light. Tiana had done a good job, as always: Everything was neat and clean. I loved the bakery during the off-hours, the quiet peace of a place so crammed with activity during the day. But I heard Matt's voice, followed by David's wide-open laughter, then the crash of the old storage rack falling into itself, hitting the floor with a rickety clatter.

WE WERE READY TO go at ten. David and Matt had cleared and cleaned the space for Matt to start building the shelves the next day. They'd placed blue masking tape on the floor to designate where the first supports would go. We put on our coats, I set the security system, and the three of us filed out the back door to the sound of the alarm's awful warning beeps.

Matt and David shook hands with what seemed to me like a kind of desperate vigor. If they were women, they might have hugged and exchanged phone numbers. But instead they kept their enthusiasm hidden, or tried and failed to hide beneath their lame, false male indifference. We stood in the cold by the rack where Matt had locked his bike. He'd ridden, incredibly, to Bay Ridge from his apartment in Cobble Hill in the snow. Now he would get home the same way, the black, dark streets slick with invisible streaks of ice. He rode his bike in all weather, he told us. It had to be "really bad" for him to take the subway. We smiled dumbly at him in a silence I hoped wasn't coming off as impolite. David shifted his weight from foot to foot. What did "really bad" mean in this context? It had snowed half the day.

"See you tomorrow," I told him.

"Hey, tomorrow is Tuesday," David interjected before Matt could reply. "We have dinner at my parents'."

"Oh, shit," I said. "I forgot." We went to Midwood for dinner with David's parents a couple times a month.

"Do you need to skip tomorrow?" Matt said. "I can pick up all the materials with Angelo in the afternoon and wait until Wednesday to build."

"No, it's okay," I said. "Don't lose time. I can come after dinner, before the closing crew leaves."

"Are you sure? You don't mind coming in so late?"

"Yes, I'm sure," I said. "It's no big deal."

"Okay, see you guys later," Matt said, and climbed on his bicycle.

As he rode away, David turned to me. "He's a cool guy," he said. "But you'd have to be crazy to bike down Fourth Avenue in this weather."

"I know. Weird how he seemed so normal," I said. "All this time, he was a raving lunatic."

"A madman," David agreed.

"You loved him," I said. "Don't try to deny it."

David smiled. He didn't reply.

We walked home. My eyes stung from the cold, and I kept my head down and hands deep in my pockets as David told me about his day. All winter, he'd been frustrated by a project his firm was doing in Shanghai. It wasn't yet a building, only a computerized rendering of a hotel tower that narrowed so drastically toward the top, there wasn't enough room for, well, rooms. David was trying to help fix this. He was making a parametric model, rewriting a few lines of source code to configure the floor plates. I followed as best I could for several minutes before the things he said went completely over my head. In any story about David's professional life, the words eventually became gibberish. There was nothing to do but absorb what little information I could understand and make a show of listening fully. It was not a conversation but an imitation of one.

Tonight, though, David realized my disinterest. He stopped talking and let the quiet seep around us both. It was like an invisible hand had come and slapped him on the back of the head.

"So, you're back to work," he said. A cop car drove past, the emergency lights whirring blue and red over the empty block, but no siren. We paused to watch it sail up the avenue toward the Sixty-eighth Precinct.

"I am," I said.

"How was your day? Are you happy to be there?"

"It was how it always is. I don't mind being back. It feels normal. I feel pretty stupid for quitting, though."

"Melissa and Angelo are lucky to have you," he said.

"They threatened to promote this new employee to be the manager—she used to work at Magnolia," I told him.

"If you'd told them you weren't taking your job back, they'd have asked you to train your replacement," David said. He laughed. "You invented your job, and that place is a circus without you. And your sister and cousin know it. Remember our honeymoon?"

I smiled. David and I got married a few weeks after the bakery's grand opening, when Melissa, Angelo, and I had been caught up in the throes of preparation: I had to take my New York City food handler's licensing exam at the Department of Health, call the vendors, interview potential counter staff; Melissa tested recipes and met with kitchen equipment salespeople; Angelo had meetings at the bank and worked in the hollowed-out storefront with the landlord and contractors, going home every night and polishing the drywall dust off his shoes. We fought over hours of operation, hauled the dining room furniture off a rented truck into the newly tiled shop, read ten books apiece about the high-end coffee industry, which, we learned, was far more complicated than we'd imagined. I loved that part of it, all the learning, the newness, the discovery of little necessary pieces, the work that was unobservable to the rest of the world, especially if it was done well.

My wedding, a small affair held at my in-laws' house, was therefore inconveniently timed. Melissa and Angelo complained and tried to convince me to postpone. I refused. The wedding—becoming an Altmann—was the one thing I had going on apart from them, and I wasn't going to do it on their schedule.

David and I took our honeymoon, a road trip up the California coast, a month into Sweet Cheeks's existence. Throughout the ten days we were gone, I received text after text: Why was the espresso machine making that sound? How many sleeves of hot drink cups did they need to order? Was there rush delivery? We were out of hot drink cups! What day was laundry service coming? We were out of rags! We were out of aprons!

Against the backdrop of the Golden State's exotic beauty—I had never seen anything like those cliffed beaches and the fairy-tale landscape of the redwood forests—I leaned forward in the passenger seat of the rental car, or lay by the hotel pool, and texted back, telling them what to do.

"Our honeymoon was almost seven years ago," I told David.

"Exactly," he said. "You've been running that place the whole time."

"Well, except for the last two months."

"You're so hard on yourself," he said. And then, as though this thought led logically to questions about food, he asked, "Are you going to be able to stick to the Radiant Regimen at Sweet Cheeks?"

"I'm going to try," I told him. "What did you have for lunch today? Was it hard to find something Radiant-compliant?"

"I had a salad from that chain salad restaurant that's on every city block. It was sixteen dollars."

"Was it good?"

"Actually, it was quite good," he said, nodding methodically, slow to answer, as if remembering a meal he'd had long ago rather than only a few hours earlier. "It had avocado. What about you?"

"I got sashimi from the sushi place."

"Was it good?"

"No," I said. "I hated it."

He chuckled. "You aren't going to be able to survive off a few pieces of raw fish every day," he said.

"We couldn't afford that, in any case," I replied. "I'm going to pack my meals. I can pack yours, too."

"Nah," he said. "I need to go out, break up the day. And there are plenty of options in the city."

Before we turned off Fourth Avenue, we passed a Mexican restaurant that had recently opened—one of those tiny steamed-up storefronts with fluorescent lighting and a couple of Formica-topped tables. Inside, a short, round person was rolling out tortillas. The only customers were a young couple—very young, maybe only a few years out of high school. I peered at them through the foggy window. David was reading the handwritten signs on the other side of the storefront.

"Two-dollar Corona," he said, delighted. "That's a great deal." David adored cheap yellow beer. Beach beer, he called it, referring—I suppose—to the way the beer was advertised on television. We hadn't been to the beach in several years.

The restaurant was called Verde Taco's. A lime-green awning hung above the doorframe, opulent in contrast to the poster-board menus written in black marker at the windows, the paper already curling and damp at the corners.

"Ah, the unnecessary apostrophe," I said. "A final, disappearing vestige of the Brooklyn of our childhoods."

"Well, doesn't the restaurant ultimately belong to the food it serves?" David asked, grinning at his own stupid joke.

"You're an idiot," I said admiringly. "I love you so much."

He leaned his chin on my shoulder and smiled goofily. The desire to go into the restaurant entered my mind: a soft, wobbly thought. We could sit in the bad, bright light and scarf delicious, salty tacos, gulp cheap beers, and take churros home for dessert, eat them on the sofa with chamomile tea and the syrupy old Sambuca in the back of our pantry. We could stay up late, not worrying about being tired or hungover the next morning, not worrying about the insalubrious meal corrupting our insides and slowing down our bodies, making us dehydrated and sluggish. We could just have a good time. If I said, "Fuck the Radiant Regimen, let's quit, let's cheat," David would be overjoyed to oblige. I knew this. The friendship David and I felt in the moment—the reminder of our sweet, familiar comfort with each other—could have been extended if we stayed out past our usual bedtime. The change in my routine, the late night at the bakery, might bring us some new energy. I could relax about food, he could forget about work. Just for a couple hours, even.

We could. We might. It sounded easy. But we didn't.

The urge didn't disappear, but I walked through it. David took my hand, bone-cold inside my flimsy glove. We turned onto Eightieth Street—our street—and once we were inside our apartment, I reheated the previous night's lamb. It was still a little cold in the center, but neither of us mentioned this as we ate at the counter.

Afterward, I got in the shower while David checked his email.

Woogie started pawing at the door. I cracked it open so he could lie on the bath mat while I rinsed off, a thing he liked to do and which I always appreciated.

I let the water get so hot it stung. Sometimes I liked the feeling of barely being able to stand it. Under the faucet, my face directly at the base of the stream, I almost didn't hear David tap on the door and let himself in.

I turned to look at him through the shower door and began to shampoo my hair. He started brushing his teeth. I rubbed the steam from the glass to get a better view of him. He put his toothbrush back in the holder and turned to me, looked my nude body up and down in an obvious, cartoony way.

"Do you want to come in here with me?" I asked.

David didn't respond but removed his clothes all in one motion. He lightly tapped Woogie with his bare foot. Woogie made a small noise of displeasure but moved off the bath mat, and David stepped into the shower. I moved so the water could hit him enough for us both to be getting wet.

"This is scalding," he said, laughing. I turned it down a little. If he weren't in there with me, I would've waited until I couldn't stand the hot water anymore and swung the lever the other direction, until it was freezing. Cryotherapy. I liked to see how long I could be miserable.

"The couples shower," David said, cupping his hand beneath the showerhead and splashing more water onto himself. "So appealing in concept, so difficult to pull off in any satisfying configuration."

"You don't like this?" I said, bumping him out of the way with my hip so I could rinse the shampoo from my hair. "But it's so cozy."

"I like *this*," David said, running a finger down my sternum, between my breasts. "And this." He leaned himself against me, our wet bodies making a gross slapping sound, and squeezed my ass. "Promise you won't get too skinny doing this program."

"Is this conversation foreplay?" I asked him, turning my face to his neck, where I gave him a few wet kisses and then bit his ear lightly. He loved that, and shuddered.

"My God, aren't you clean yet?" he said. "Let's go do something else."

Our sex had become playful in recent years; we knew each other's bodies so well, and what we liked, how to make each other orgasm quickly, how to make it happen slowly, so that the chumminess of the rest of our relationship had made its way into the one thing we'd initially been careful and serious in undertaking. David kept grabbing my naked butt on our way up the stairs to our attic bedroom, and I kept turning to slap his hands, pretending to be scandalized. Then I had to suppress the inappropriately timed urge to tickle him as we slid under the sheets, our hair still dripping, giggling and getting right to it. All told, we probably took ten minutes from when we got out of the shower to when we both came.

Afterward, I put in my earbuds and listened to a podcast about how a person might train her metabolism to burn more calories. David fell asleep immediately, and Woogie circled the bed looking for a place to sleep, finally settling on the small strip of space between me and David.

It was a nice night—comfortable and quiet. It was exactly what I'd expected.

CHAPTER SIX

"So, you're really going to work tonight?" my mother-in-law, Rebecca, asked.

"Yeah," I said, smoothing the creases from my sweater. Once again I would be overdressed in the bakery.

Before sitting down at the long rectangular table in the Altmanns' cheery kitchen, all warm yellows and glass-door cabinets, I leaned over to hug David's younger brother, Benji. He was a supremely intelligent and goofy man who looked very similar to David. They both had strong, symmetric bone structure, deep-set eyes, full lips, small white teeth.

"Hello, *Katerina*," he said, wiggling his ears because he knew I found his ability to do so delightfully fascinating.

"*Benvolio*," I said. "Tell me what's good in your life these days."

He pretended to think. "Nothing comes to mind," he said.

Rebecca set a heaping plate of deep-fried matzo balls on the table in front of us. They looked like falafel and were accompanied by a dish of tahini dipping sauce.

"Last time you made these, I got terrible gas," Benji complained. "I sat through a deposition the next morning with the worst stomach pains of my life." But as he said this, he was already using a fork to pierce one of the golf-ball-size hors d'oeuvres. Steam poured from its hot, soft center.

To say I needed willpower for dinner with my in-laws would be an understatement. I was never so tempted by food anywhere—not even the bakery—as when at the enormous Victorian house on Eighteenth Street where David had grown up. I loved this house, with its homey, lived-in furniture and its constant music. I loved my mother-in-law's adorable, chirping laughter, and most of all, I loved sitting at their big table over wine and Rebecca's Mediterranean-style comfort food.

David was late, but the rest of the family was there. My father-in-law, Hiram, was, as usual, in the den adjacent to the kitchen, playing his old Baldwin piano. A ragtime number floated through the house.

"That's impossible," Rebecca said to Benji. "If you had gas, Benjamin, it's because you drink too much beer."

"Beer doesn't cause gas," Benji said.

"Of course it does," she replied, unblinking. "Kit, what's the matter? Eat up, honey."

Before I could remind Rebecca that I was doing the Radiant Regimen— I'd told her about it last week on the telephone, at length—she flitted back across the granite floor. She rustled about, talking to herself in a cheerful way. She checked the oven, stirred the big pot on the stove, rummaged through cupboards in search of the right chopping board or measuring spoon.

"What was I doing? What was I doing?" she muttered. "Ah! The celery salt!"

I cleared my throat.

"Rebecca," I said. "I think I told you? David and I are doing a new food program. I can't eat these right now. They look great. They smell amazing. I'm sorry."

Rebecca looked up from her little shaker of celery salt. "I forgot," she said. "What's this new diet? I know you told me," she added sheepishly. I felt the familiar wave of embarrassment that came over me in any social situation involving food. It didn't matter how well a person knew me or how long we'd been eating together. Besides Melissa's naked derision, most people in my life reacted to my fluctuating dietary restrictions with awkward politeness. Rebecca and I called each other at least once a week, and last Wednesday I'd gone on for longer than twenty minutes about the Radiant Regimen. I realized now she might have tuned out the details, been unable to keep her mind from wandering. She couldn't be blamed. I'd known the Altmanns for nearly thirteen years, and in that time, I'd probably done twice as many diets or programs. I was grateful to Rebecca, who was so sweet and accepting, for finding me merely somewhat tedious, especially given my own sister's downright contempt for my habits.

My grandmother had lived in the kitchen. Melissa and I were superbly fed children, three hearty meals each day—heavy baked chicken with pasta, orecchiette with hot sausage, veal and pork ragù, everything high in carbohydrates and fatty meat. We were each given a lobster over linguine as children on Christmas Eve and taught by Angelo's father, our uncle Nicky, how to use metal crackers to extract the meat from the claw, to swirl each forkful in the rich sauce at the bottom of our dish, to get the most pleasure out of every bite.

I cannot say why Melissa went on to understand our oil-soaked, dough-flaked upbringing as a normal, if somewhat hedonistic, way of life, seeing food as a kind of ordinary luxury everyone could and should enjoy, while I used food as integers in a math equation I was always in the process of solving, a highly scientific controlled experiment.

"It's not really a diet," I reminded Rebecca. "It's more like a program."

"What's the difference?" Benji wanted to know.

"Well, for one thing," I said, "the goal isn't weight loss. I mean, you *can* lose weight. Inevitably, people on the Radiant Regimen do—" I saw Benji holding in a wince. It was embarrassing. I fumbled through my explanation, phrasing everything as a question like a nervous teenager.

"It's about changing your relationship with food? Like, there's a lot of additives and toxins in processed foods. Some of them are addictive. Sugar is addictive."

"I've heard that!" Rebecca said. "It seems true to me!"

"Right," I said. "So, the premise of the program is basically, like, when you eat only pure, whole foods, you cleanse your body of those toxins."

"Interesting," Benji said kindly.

"So what's the typical meal?" asked Rebecca. "What did you eat today?"

"Well," I said, pausing with a slow tilt of my head. "At breakfast I had this grain-free porridge made from coconut milk and these seeds, chia seeds? Have you heard of them?"

"Yes," said Benji, and at the same time Rebecca said, "No."

I explained the gluey texture of antioxidant-rich chia seeds soaked in coconut milk. "For lunch I had pan-seared salmon and some steamed broccoli."

"Sounds wonderful!" Rebecca said with too much enthusiasm. "Now, are you doing all organic, too?"

"I'm trying," I said. "The hardest part is that the food can be kind of bland. Plus, now that I'm back at work, I'm going to be tempted by sugar all the time."

"I can imagine," Rebecca said. "You'll just have to bring us your rations!" She laughed dorkily and hooted. I loved her so much. "We'll eat Kit's sugar on her behalf, won't we, Benji?"

"What about alcohol?" Benji said, noticing for the first time that I wasn't drinking. He put his hand over his own glass of wine protectively, as though the discussion itself could force him to give up alcohol as well.

I shook my head solemnly. "No alcohol," I said.

"None?"

"None."

He and Rebecca sucked in air loudly.

"Woof," Benji said, raising his glass to me.

Our eyes drifted to the bottles lined up on the counter. I blinked and reminded myself how good it would feel later to have drunk only water all day. My skin would be so clear this time next week. *Glowing.* My stomach flat. In a few weeks, my mind would be razor-sharp, my memory boosted by all the clean blood pumping through my heart. I'd be in control—over my size, my moods, my circadian rhythms—and everyone would admire and envy me for my improved appearance and ironclad willpower. This was the hard part, the days before results. I took a long swig from my glass of water.

"Well, you always impress me," Rebecca said. "How you keep learning and how curious you are about all the different options . . ." She drifted off for a moment, and we listened to the piano music wafting faintly from the den. Then, coming out of the brief trance and remembering where she'd left off, she added, "It's amazing, especially in your line of work! That bakery! Oh! Everything there is divine. How is Melissa, by the way? Happy to have you back?"

I said, "We hired a carpenter to do our shelves, so everyone is focused on the construction in the kitchen."

"When is that happening?" Benji asked.

"Tonight, actually," I said. "That's why I'm heading over there later."

"You are, that's right!" Rebecca said, essentially shouting as she remembered what I'd just told her. She shook her head so her wiry hair swooped around, ghostlike. "Hiram!" she shouted toward the doorway. "Stop playing. Come say hello to the kids. Kit has to leave early tonight."

The music stopped and David's father walked into the kitchen, his glasses low on his nose and his thick head of white curls a little outgrown, flipping out at the base of his neck like a small slide. He kissed the top of Benji's head and then mine. Rebecca headed back to the oven to check her brisket. Then she began to empty the dishwasher. I would've offered to help with dishes, with cooking—anything—but Rebecca never let me. It was an odd position to find myself in. My grandmother had imbued my childhood with a steep sense of myself as a participating citizen in and out of the house. No matter where I was, I felt responsible for helping. I wonder if this was why I landed in service. At age five, I made my own bed, put my toys away. By ten years old, I did laundry. I came from a household where sheets were ironed, shoes came off in the vestibule, and no one ever sat on the good sofa (and no one wanted to; it was adorned with a stiff plastic slipcover). The Altmanns were different. They had college educations and retirement accounts, and I wondered if something about this kind of security allowed people to fuss less over their possessions. Rebecca and Hiram's house was clean enough but disorganized. There were always little messes around: shoes and unopened mail on the staircase, towels in a pile on the floor in front of the washing machine, and no one could ever seem to find their keys when it was time to go somewhere.

Without taking a seat, Hiram reached over my and Benji's shoulders and grabbed a fried matzo ball with his fingers.

Rebecca shrieked, "Sit down! Utensils! This isn't a bowling alley."

Hiram sat at the head of the table but continued to eat with his hands, no plate. I watched him pull the dumpling apart and pop one warm half into his mouth. I'd eaten my sparkling clean lunch six hours ago. My stomach was a kettle, almost empty and using the last of its steam to torture my insides.

DAVID WAS LATE. HE was often late, and his family maligned him for it. Individually and as a unit, the Altmanns were a breed of friendly bully, picking on one another without anyone ever getting upset. They were aggressive teasers, laughing through raised voices and fingers pointed in faces. My family was similar, especially when my grandmother had been alive and everyone gathered at our house; but the shouting was more self-serious and sometimes consequential. The arguments I frequently witnessed as a child were vitriolic. Doors slammed in faces, grudges held for long stretches—years, in some cases—brought up again and again at inappropriate times: a christening party, Thanksgiving dinner. I remember Uncle Nicky half out of his chair and leaned over his ricotta pie on the Feast of the Immaculate Conception, red-faced, shouting in a murderous tone at my second cousin Daniel Jr., whom Melissa and I called "Big Uncle Danny" for reasons I either no longer remember or never knew in the first place.

"This is not even about this *particular* three hundred dollars you owe me," Uncle Nicky said, his red track jacket a painful effulgence against the pale rose and ivory wallpaper of my grandmother's dining room. "This is about *who you are.*"

Big Uncle Danny argued back, though he didn't shout quite as loudly, saying Uncle Nicky was coldhearted and smug, that he was too cheap and selfish to do family—his own mother's cousin's son—a favor. "One little favor," he said. "And you begrudge me that. Because you're such a big guy, huh?"

Through these confrontations, Melissa, Angelo, and I ate our food, silent, semi-interested, as though observing a tennis match or some other sport whose rules we didn't fully comprehend. My grandmother watched with a solemn, annoyed expression, her eyes turned up and her jaw pointed down, so it was as though her face were being pulled by an invisible string in opposite directions. Every now and then the screaming got to be too much, and she threw somebody out, telling them they could finish eating after they'd walked over to Holy Visitation and said some prayers in front of the statue of the Madonna.

I almost never knew what anyone was fighting about. This example involved a debt. But, like Uncle Nicky said, the rifts were bigger than any single circumstance.

The Altmanns didn't owe one another money. Their disagreements appeared personal in the moment, but afterward it seemed as though the whole thing had been theoretical. Nothing worth getting upset about, at least not more upset than everyone already was at their baseline. The Altmanns viciously argued—over someone's rude tone or someone's bad manners, over whom they should support in local elections, over whether or not Woolite was really worth the price—because that was the whole point of having a family. Family was a theater in which one explored and exercised personal anxieties without fear of real-world consequences. Their bond was unbreakable, so they went ahead and slammed their fists on tables and hurled over-the-top, hyperbolic insults: shithead, tyrant, *sociopath*. It didn't really mean anything.

"I'm sure whatever he's doing is *so* important," said Rebecca sarcastically of David. "He can't be bothered."

"I'm sure whatever he's doing is incredibly important to the oligarch on whose behalf he's doing it," Benji replied. Benji was a lawyer with the ACLU, specializing in housing discrimination. There was never enough time to comment on David's and Benji's conflicting ambitions: brothers raised in the same middle-class home by caring, left-leaning parents; now one helped to produce skyscrapers, and the other sued skyscraper developers.

"Oh, don't be theatrical," said Hiram to Benji. "He's late because he's self-centered and slow. It's not part of some evil conspiracy."

"I'm not being theatrical," Benji said. "The situation *is* dramatic. Safe and affordable housing is life-or-death."

"Oh, here we go," said Rebecca. "Another lecture. I blame David for this."

"Blame me for what?" David said, appearing in the doorway so suddenly that we all jumped. He'd come into the house through the side door, silent as a cat burglar, his black coat over his arm, his forehead shining with sweat. He must have run from the subway.

"For being late," Rebecca said. "As usual."

"Oh, give me a break." David draped his coat over the empty chair next to mine and went to the sink for a glass of water. "It's rush hour, and this house is on the two worst subway lines."

An uproar ensued.

"The Q train is an excellent train!" Hiram basically screamed.

"Honestly," said Benji, "I cannot believe someone who lives on the R line would have the audacity to complain about the B/Q."

David didn't answer. At the sink, he bolted a full glass of tap water in what seemed like one incredible swallow and then refilled it. "I'm parched," he said as he sat down next to me. He gave my shoulder a little squeeze.

"Maybe your new diet makes you thirsty," Benji said.

"You know, when I was a kid," said Rebecca, who was still stuck in the previous conversation, "the Fourth Avenue line—the R train—connected to the Sixth Avenue subway from Thirty-sixth Street to Ditmas Avenue."

"That's right!" said Hiram, thrilled, always, for a chance to reminisce about the Brooklyn of his youth. "The Culver Street Express."

"It's not a diet," I piped in, addressing Benji. I couldn't help myself.

"Sorry. Maybe your new program makes you thirsty," Benji said.

"That's not it," David said. "Speaking of, though, what's for dinner, Mom? Did Kit tell you we're surviving on our wits for the time being?"

"The cemetery had to be expanded," Hiram said to no one. "That's why the city got rid of the express connection."

"A nice, comforting pot roast," Rebecca said. "So good on a winter night, don't you think?"

"Can we have pot roast?" David asked me.

"What could possibly be in pot roast you couldn't have?" Rebecca said. "It's brisket, onions, garlic, olive oil, salt, and pepper."

"You don't know what's in a roast?" Benji asked.

David rolled his eyes. "Mom makes all kinds of weird stuff." He gestured to the fried matzo balls. "Last time we were here, she gave us chicken soup with curry."

"That was good," Hiram said. I agreed and wondered if Rebecca could do a version of the soup to comply with the Radiant Regimen, without the noodles, the thickening flour, the vegetable oil.

Rebecca said, "Kit told me about your program."

"Too bad you can't have dessert," Hiram said.

"Or booze," Benji added.

"It's not so bad," David said, likely feeling defensive on my behalf.

I looked around the table, sinking into my shame. I was always talking about food and pleasure in the context of everything I wasn't eating and enjoying. My ever-shifting, entirely self-imposed dietary limitations were a burden on everyone else's leisure, and I knew it. Rebecca constrained her cooking on my behalf, working around my restrictions no matter how often they changed. My own family gave me so much grief—for over a decade I'd had a reputation with them as a bad eater, a killjoy, a dupe who fell for every fad—so that the Altmanns' patience, their unexamined acceptance of these habits, was somehow mortifying. Melissa was right, and my in-laws were wrong, and worse than that: I knew it, but I couldn't change.

"It's not bad yet," I admitted. As I said this, my chest tightened with a familiar pang of disappointment. Certain realities about who I was— my essential wet-blanketness—always felt worse beneath my in-laws' gaze. Sitting back in my chair, I observed the conversation without fully listening.

Benji began to talk about the many investigations and minor, boring scandals plaguing the mayor's office, and everyone started to talk over one another in a debate over who was the bigger bozo: the mayor or the governor. It was a close contest, and opinions shifted from one moment to the next. I absently twisted the cloth napkin still lying across my lap, turning my mind away from this pointless argument, wandering into the memory of when I first met David and all these people with whom I now shared a surname. I thought about it a lot lately, about how I used to have a different life, and how easily I might never have arrived at this table at all.

CHAPTER SEVEN

David and I met at City College when I was twenty-one. I still lived in Bay Ridge with my grandmother and Melissa, who'd done an eight-month course in pastry and baking arts at a culinary institute downtown. By that time, she'd cycled through a few crowded dessert stations at fine dining establishments and had just landed a gig as an assistant to a pastry chef in the main kitchen of a brand-new luxury hotel. I was a full-time student with a part-time job waiting tables at a café on Manhattan Avenue, just a block over from Morningside Park. The café was popular with Columbia students who often left insultingly small tips. But the café's management treated me well, and the place was close to a stop on the subway line that got me to Brooklyn quickest and offered the most reliable transfer onto the train I took home from the crowded, sticky-floored hell-mouth that was the Flatbush Avenue station.

It was autumn of my junior year. I had seen David on campus, in one of my classes that semester—a history elective called American Labor and Capitalism, one of those huge auditorium seminars all students end up taking, regardless of its relevance to their major, at least once in college. But David was just a face—one of many attractive, studious-looking boys—I sometimes passed and noticed without much thought.

Then one day in early October, he came into the café during my shift. We had three sections in the evening, and mine was the busiest. Five loud graduate students, all men, were lounging on the sofa and armchairs in the farthest corner of the café, a somewhat private nook where the ceiling sloped. My least favorite demographic of customer: male, white, mid-twenties, either a goatee or ponytail or both—an atrocious combination—often garnished with scarf. Every now and then such a person was pleasant, or at least unassuming, but this look also happened to fit the description of ninety percent of the customers who gave me a hard time.

This particular group of men really sucked. Smoking had been outlawed inside New York City restaurants and bars earlier that year, and one guy kept relighting his gross little hand-rolled cigarette to take one puff at a time and then clip the end with his fingernails. He wasn't as discreet as he seemed to think, and I kept having to ask him to go outside if he was going to smoke. He told me, a loose, smug smile on his face, that he wasn't smoking. His friends agreed. What was I talking about? Was I crazy? I stood, dumbfounded, amid the thin cloud of tobacco and clove smoke he'd released only a moment ago, and told him, Okay, fine, but, well, if he *was going to* smoke the cigarette concealed in his fist, he needed to please go outside.

"The health department could shut us down," I said, though I could tell my appeal was a wasted effort.

"Well, then, I hope you aren't letting anybody smoke," he said.

"We aren't," I said idiotically, and his friends erupted into hyena laughter, like this was the funniest thing they'd ever heard.

I hadn't seen David come in. I was so mad, I didn't even glance at my other tables as I went behind the pickup counter to discuss with my coworkers—one making drinks and the other serving the front section and sidewalk tables—how to deal with the smoker and his posse of obsequious douchebags. If I told them to leave, they likely wouldn't pay for their PBRs. Worse, they might refuse to go, and it would turn into a whole thing.

It didn't matter, anyway. After a minute of talking, we all had to get back to work. It was a Thursday, and Thursday nights were always busy during the school year. The sun had almost set. The place was filling up.

I approached David's table with the coffeepot in my hand. He was with friends—a stern-faced, pale redhead and a heavyset kid with short dreadlocks and a lot of freckles. All three of them were good-looking in dissimilar ways while appearing self-assured in exactly the same way: good posture but soft, open expressions. The redhead dealt playing cards amongst the three of them.

"Hey, guys," I said. "Sorry for the wait."

David looked up at me. "Oh, hey," he said. "I know you. You're in my history lecture."

His friends looked up with interest.

"You go to our school?" asked the redhead, whose name, I would soon learn, was Ryan.

The other friend, Darshawn, added, "I think I've seen you around, actually."

As I relaxed into conversation, leaning my weight on one foot, opening my mouth to answer, I felt eyes from one of my other tables bore down on me. I remembered they'd asked for their check before I'd stopped at the sofa to talk to the smoker. That was where I was going, in fact, when I saw him take a drag, and the encounter had flustered me so much, I'd forgotten.

I held up the coffeepot, gave an apologetic, tilted smile. "Yeah, I'm—uh—I'll be right back to take your order. Unless you want coffee?"

They shook their heads, and I scurried to top off some coffees and grab the delayed check. Just as I made my way back to David's table, someone tapped my arm.

"Excuse me," said a girl when I turned. She looked to be my age, wearing heavy eyeliner and red lipstick. She had on opaque black tights and ballet flats, a black slip over a leopard-print blouse I recognized from the window of the Betsey Johnson boutique on Columbus. She tucked a piece of platinum hair behind her ear. This was one of the regulars, an undergrad who came in a few times a week and drank espresso mixed with seltzer while she drew in her sketchbook. I liked her a lot. She didn't spend much money, but she was polite and tipped well. "That guy is *smoking.*" She whispered the last word haughtily as she nudged her head in the direction of the sofa.

I groaned. "Thank you for telling me," I said.

"I saw you talk to him already," she said. "It's illegal, and he's rude. You should call the police."

I didn't have the heart to tell her what a stupid suggestion that was. It wasn't her fault she didn't know what she was talking about; she was just some cool-looking rich kid who lived in Ivy League student housing and probably hadn't ever had a job, any job, let alone in Manhattan, waiting tables in a place where the bathroom floors were sticky and the best thing on the menu was grilled cheese.

But I didn't have to do anything, because at that moment, David's friend turned in his chair.

"You can't smoke in here, man," Ryan said loudly. Some of the noise in my section stopped as others turned to watch the confrontation.

The smoker frowned, put a hand on his bright blond mustache. His friends looked a little stricken. They assessed Ryan, and the smoker looked to David and then to Darshawn and then back to Ryan. He let out a dismissive laugh, but he couldn't ignore the confrontation. Too many people had noticed.

David added in a somewhat more subdued tone, "The waitress already asked you to go outside." His voice was deep and smooth. A grown-up voice. A radio voice. I was immediately attracted to the way he sounded.

Now the smoker glared. David's confidence was obvious; it must have been threatening to him. "No one was talking to you," he said prissily. "Don't worry about me."

"I'm not worried about you," David said calmly. "No one here cares about you at all."

From somewhere at the front of the café, someone shouted, "Just stop fucking smoking, dude!" There were a few murmured agreements throughout the room. None of the smoker's friends said a word. Mostly, they looked mortified.

The smoker laughed lightly. "All right, fellas," he said. He was staring at David and his friends without blinking, humiliated, resentment coming off him like sewer heat. "Thanks for looking out."

"No problem," Ryan said, and he, David, and Darshawn turned back to their card game.

I looked at the girl on the sidebar. Her thickly mascaraed eyes sparkled, delighted.

"The beard-o is cute," she said. She grinned at me. "The beard-o" was David, with his short-cropped, neat facial hair. All this time later, I've seen him clean-shaven only a small handful of times. It's like seeing his skeleton, a good-looking but unwelcome ghost. "You should get his number."

THE SMOKER AND HIS friends paid their bill, leaving what amounted to a seven percent tip. David and Ryan drank IBC root beer; Darshawn had several cups of tea. After they played a few rounds of cards, they all read in congenial silence. They were polite to me and asked about school, taking what felt like real interest in my answers.

When they were ready to go, I put the bill on their table and David said, "Thanks, Katrina."

I balked. "It's Kit," I said. I probably sounded defensive. "I mean—I go by Kit."

"Oh," David said. "Okay. Sorry." I could see the wheels turning in his mind, adjusting, reordering.

"How'd you know my—my *Christian* name?" I asked. The minute the words left my mouth, I felt like an idiot. I remembered it for days afterward, and each time, a rush of embarrassment would heat my face.

"Um, I saw it on the attendance sheet," he said. "In history seminar. Sometimes you pass it to me after you sign in." Ryan and Darshawn put down their books and observed us. David's own book already lay closed on the table. It was called *War in the Age of Intelligent Machines.*

"Oh," I said. "Well, anyway. It's Kit."

"I'm David," he said.

"Hi," I said. Like an imbecile. And then I kept standing there.

He smiled and picked up the bill. His friends watched, amused. The girl at the sidebar, drinking her fourth or fifth espresso with seltzer, waved me over.

"I just made an ass of myself in front of beard-o," I said as I approached her, like she and I were old friends.

She looked at their table. "They're definitely talking about you right now," she said. Instinctively, I started to turn. "Don't look!" she loud-whispered, grabbing my hand. "They're putting down money. They're leaving. Oh!" Her mouth formed a circle, as though she were about to start whistling. "He's coming over here!"

"Beard-o?" I whispered.

She nodded vigorously but then snapped her head back to her drawing, pretending to be engrossed.

"Hi," he said in his low, soothing voice. I turned, and there he was. "I wanted to know if you wanted to hang out sometime."

A COUPLE DAYS LATER, David and I ate bodega fried chicken on splintery picnic tables at the base of St. Nicholas Park's steep hill. We hung out for a few weeks, taking walks between classes and my shifts at the café. We had a route, starting at campus and heading east, then a long trek down Columbus Avenue.

I would learn over the course of these walks: David was a year older than I was and at CCNY earning his architecture degree. He lived with Darshawn and Ryan in a tiny apartment on 130th Street and had grown up in Midwood, had gone to high school at Stuy. He was a fourth-generation college student, if one counted the yeshiva his great-grandfather had attended in Eastern Europe a hundred years ago. David was interested in architecture from an engineering, rather than design, standpoint, and he was literate, obsessively absorbed, in a number of computer coding and software programs not taught in universities but which he believed—rightly, it would turn out—would be lucrative expertise for industry professionals by the time he entered the workforce. The moments when I learned and relearned these particular details are strung together by the thousands, across years, in precise and seamless embroidery, stitched with invisible thread, to make one thing, one David.

Sometimes we went to his apartment and drank canned Miller Lite on his living room windowsill. Ryan and his boyfriend liked to sit on the fire escape, talking to us through the open window. Darshawn spent half the week out late at stand-up comedy open mics, but he hung out when he was home, slumped comfortably on his special bean bag chair that no one else was allowed to use. They played the same Wu-Tang album over and over, the one that had come out the year before, the one adored by every college boy I'd encountered in New York City all through undergrad. Ryan and Darshawn approved of my presence in the apartment immediately. The first time I came over, I brought them a pre-rolled joint and a paper box of green-tea tarts and mille-feuille—all of it procured from the kitchen where Melissa worked.

On one of our walks, David brought me a cookie from Levain Bakery, and I shoved half of it into my mouth in a disgusting, marauding manner. It took great effort to chew with my mouth closed.

"There's chocolate in your teeth," David said when I'd finished.

"I *know*," I said. "I'm *savoring* it." He laughed. I made David laugh a lot, his square teeth shaking inside his handsome head, his face made imperfect by a carefree, somewhat dorky laugh.

I wondered why he hadn't kissed me or even held my hand.

For nearly two months, we just hung out. Ate sweets and drank with his friends in his living room. He picked me up from work sometimes. I had a hard, dense crush on David, and for the life of me, I could not figure out what his motives were.

The week after Thanksgiving, he got me a ticket to the Pixies reunion tour, a show happening at Hammerstein Ballroom over winter break.

I was in Cohen Library waiting for him when he arrived with the news. We'd discussed how badly we both wanted to go, but I assumed he understood I had no plans or money to actually buy tickets.

"Oh my God," I said when he brandished the small envelope containing two general admissions. "Was it expensive? Did you get them from a scalper?"

He shrugged.

"I might have to pay you back in two parts," I said, embarrassed. I was already doing the math in my head, without even knowing how much I owed, and feeling a little sick.

"But I bought your ticket," David said. "I'm inviting you."

I stared at him for a moment. He paid for my food sometimes, but only when he showed up with it. Otherwise we split everything down the middle.

"Okay," I said. I'd become exasperated. I had the pull of feelings for David in my belly, a desire to be around him all the time, to tell him things and hear the things he said, to lie next to him and listen to music in bed at night, to run up and press my face into his chest when I saw him on campus. In other words, I wanted to be his girlfriend. I was getting kind of mad about it. "Listen, I have a question," I said. "What is our deal?"

"What do you mean?"

I swallowed. "You must know that I'm attracted to you. And we hang out a lot. But I have no idea, like, why."

David stared at me for a long minute. I stared back. Nobody blinked. I waited for him to say whatever bullshit thing: He had a girlfriend at another school or down in Midwood, a high school girlfriend. Or—worst-case scenario—he was available, just not to me. He thought we were *friends*—he was one of those awful guys who liked to lead women on, just for the sick thrill of feeling attractive and powerful.

"Would you like to go for a walk?" he said.

"I guess," I told him. I gathered my books and shoved them into my backpack.

Outside, it was getting dark, and the streets were mostly quiet. The air was crisp and smelled of trash and fallen leaves. David took my backpack by its strap and lifted it from my shoulder, carrying it for me, and he held my hand, gripped my pinkie and ring finger in the sweetest way. My heart pounded.

"Say something," I said.

He turned to me. We were at the south side of the library, between streetlamps.

"I want to kiss you," he said. "Would that be okay?"

I exhaled noisily. "Yeah," I said. "This is a weird way to go about this, though. I'd just like to point that out."

David nodded. "I'm sorry you think I've been weird. I kind of thought we were dating already."

"But you've never even kissed me," I said.

"I've been enjoying getting to know you. I didn't want to start off by assuming you want to, like, make out all the time. I don't want you to feel, you know, forced."

"Did you get accused of raping somebody or something?" I asked. I wasn't serious. I was just nervous and blurting things out.

"Oy," he said. "No. Of course not."

"Well, I really do want you to kiss me," I said. "I have been wanting you to kiss me for two months."

"Well, I don't know if I want to, now that you asked if I'm a *rapist*."

"I asked if you'd been *accused* of rape," I said. "And fine. Don't kiss me. I don't care. I changed my mind, too."

He looked at me, his big eyebrows arched.

"But how about this," I said. I sucked in air. "We'll go to your apartment and you can go down on me." My wheels were spinning. I was escalating—*intensificazione*. There was heat coming off every part of me, I so badly wanted to have sex with him.

David laughed. "You really are so goofy, you know that?" he said. "You are excellent—beautiful, smart, and so fun to talk to—but you are also the goofiest person I have ever met."

I stood there, my arms hanging at my sides. David still had my backpack.

"Let's go," he said, and we walked to his apartment in a fugue of college-kid horniness, squeezing hands, tripping over each other's legs because we kept pushing the sides of our bodies together, leaning like drunks.

At his apartment, David kept his gaze down as we walked hand in hand past Ryan and Darshawn, who were playing *Tony Hawk* in the living room. In David's bedroom, I took off my shoes and jeans and underwear in a single pull.

David laughed, but then he came close and took the back of my neck in his right hand, gently placed a finger, barely touching, on my clit. I shuddered in anticipation. It was so exciting.

"Is this okay?" he whispered, and I said yes, and he kissed me. I remember thinking he was a forceful kisser for how long it had taken him to make a move, but I liked it. I liked it a few minutes later, when he laid me down on the bed and said, "This is okay?" before he moved between my legs, putting his mouth in the wrong spots for a little while as I wiggled and maneuvered his shoulders, placing him eventually where I wanted him to be, his mouth right in the center of my body, his tongue pressed firm against my wet skin.

AFTERWARD, AS I WAS getting dressed, David asked, "Are you really leaving?"

"It takes me an hour to get home," I said.

"You can sleep here."

"I need my toothbrush," I said. "If I sleep here, I have to go to class and work tomorrow in the same clothes—the same underwear. I'll feel grimy all day."

"Okay," David said, disappointed. "Let me walk you out."

The walk to the subway was chilly. As we were saying goodbye, David asked, "Do you want to come to Brooklyn and have dinner with my family on Wednesday?"

"This Wednesday?" I said. "Wow, everything is zero to sixty with you, huh?"

"I cannot wait a moment longer!" he said jokingly. "If my mother does not approve of you, it is a time-honored Jewish tradition to continue to date you and bring you around my family and pretend I don't notice her passive-aggressive comments until, finally, she asks you if you like your new haircut without first complimenting it, and says something about how the color of your dress is *hard to wear*, and you reach your breaking point and dump me. I believe we should begin this process as soon as possible." He grinned.

"That's a clever joke," I said. "A terrifyingly specific but nonetheless clever joke."

"It's more of a bit than a joke," he said. "Darshawn is helping me with my timing."

He reached for my arm, pulled me toward him. We kissed nearly to the point of full making out, until a dog walker with a big pack leashed to the belt at her waist told us to get a room and whistled, causing several of her smaller charges to howl mournfully as they passed.

INSTEAD OF GOING STRAIGHT home, I went to Columbus Circle to wait for Melissa. All her coworkers—including the bellmen and other lobby employees—loved Melissa, and they let me wait for her outside the employee lockers on the service floor. She came out a little before one a.m.

"I have the worst stomachache of my life," she said. She said this a lot. It meant she had to poop. "Let's get a cab."

"You have to pay for it," I said.

"Okay, whatever," she whispered. "The subway will take two hours. I'll end up having to shit off the side of the platform."

"Just go here," I said.

She tilted her head, giving me a wary look. "This," she hissed through her teeth, "is a private job."

"Ugh, you're so gross. You're going to give yourself colon cancer," I said as we got on the elevator, because it was what our grandmother was always telling her. Sometimes we went for a nightcap with her coworkers at a dive-y sports bar on Ninth Avenue, and it was a bummer to be heading home. I'd slept with David. I had a boyfriend. I felt like celebrating. I wanted to tell Melissa what had happened over a drink, not in a hush from my childhood bedroom, like a teenager.

IN THE CAB, ALL I told Melissa was that I was going to meet David's family.

Melissa paused Lamaze breathing through her abdominal discomfort. She asked, "What's he do again?"

"He's going to be an architect."

"Huh," she said, incredulous. "I'm surprised."

"Why?"

"Because usually you like the dum-dums. That's, like, your type."

The only real boyfriend I'd had up to that point was Carlos Ortiz, a good-natured, handsome pothead with big white teeth and a high laugh. We'd dated for two years in high school. Everyone called him Lolo. He was a lot of fun. By the time I met David, Lolo was serving his first of three tours in Afghanistan. He'd been in basic training down in Georgia on September 11.

I said to Melissa, "Lolo wasn't dumb. He was—I don't know— unassuming."

"Listen," she said. "I have nothing but love for Lolo. He's a great guy. But I was reading *The Hunchback of Notre Dame* senior year, for language arts class, and he comes into the kitchen and goes, 'Hey, I've heard about that book.' And we get to talking and he asks, 'So is it a true story or just a legend?' Like, are you fucking kidding me? And you're such a smarty-pants, and you love books, so you know. I've always just kind of assumed you *preferred* bozos. There's nothing wrong with want- ing to be the smart one." She shrugged. The taxi sailed from the West Side Highway into downtown, pulling up to a stop sign on Chambers Street.

After a minute went by and I hadn't responded, she asked, "He's cute, right? This guy."

"Yeah," I said, even though I was annoyed. Why did she have to say everything she thought? Why wasn't she excited for me? I added, "He's got a really cute face. He has a beard. A nice one."

"Oh, right," she said. "You told me that."

We didn't say anything as the cab went past Ground Zero, street cops guarding the fences, the barbed wire glistening against the spot- lights. Behind that, the hole in the city was pitch-black.

In the tunnel, Melissa looked at me with wild, flickering eyes. She said she didn't know if she was gonna make it.

"You *will,*" said the cabbie, suddenly animated. I had no idea he'd been listening to us. "Nobody's shitting in this cab tonight."

DAVID HAD BEEN RIGHT about his family. I loved them.

He and I took the train to Midwood in the afternoon, and when we got to his house, Rebecca was on the porch with groceries, fumbling through a tote bag for her keys. We rushed up the steps to take her heavy bags—one of which held a pumpkin—as David introduced us. "This is Kit, who I told you about," he said, slinging one of her canvas bags over his arm.

Rebecca said, "Hi, Kit!"

"Hello," I said, and leaned in to kiss her check. She gasped, as though I were winding back to slap her, and got out of the way so fast I nearly fell over.

"Are you okay?" she cried, hand to her heart.

I wanted to die. David burst out laughing.

"Ma," he said. "She was trying to say hello. She's *Italian.*" He said Italian in a low voice, like it was a secret.

Rebecca blinked, realized her confusion, and said, "Oh, I'm sorry, dear. I wasn't trying to reject you! You surprised me. Here, do it again."

I liked her immediately. She was self-deprecating and set me at ease, erasing my humiliation without hinting at my awkwardness.

BECAUSE WE'D HURRIED TO help Rebecca, I didn't have as much time as I really needed to process that David's house was a mansion. A pale blue Victorian with a huge mahogany door. The porch wrapped around the south side of the house and felt only a little smaller than the entirety of the first-floor apartment I lived in. There were big fancy homes in Bay Ridge, but I'd never been in one of them.

I attempted to take my shoes off in the foyer when we got inside. Rebecca's laugh was enormous, charmed.

"If you do that," she said, "you're going to have to throw away those socks."

The place was cozy but not fancy whatsoever. The Altmanns weren't rich. The house in Midwood had been purchased at the right time— the late seventies—in relative disrepair. Hiram and Rebecca spent the majority of David's childhood renovating it bit by bit. It looked as nice as it did because it was well loved. Benji and Hiram arrived a few minutes later, shouting at the top of their lungs about what a waste of money David Weathers had been. Baseball people! Mets fans! I was thrilled.

"Shut up, shut up," Rebecca said. "David's friend Kit *DeMarco* is here, and she gives *the best* air kisses I've ever had in my life."

"Prove it," Hiram said, turning to me. I pressed my cheek to his and then to Benji's. "Pretty good!" Hiram said. David stood aside, shaking his head as though embarrassed, but I could tell he was loving it.

"Absolutely top-notch," Benji agreed, and then went to dump his schoolbooks and backpack on the living room sofa. "I'll have to work on mine. Come here, Mom, help me practice." Then they all went around pressing their cheeks to each other's.

"Start on the right cheek," I said. "And you don't have to do both sides. Italian Americans don't do that."

"You from Bensonhurst, hon?" Hiram said.

"Bay Ridge."

He looked excitedly at Rebecca. "I was close!" he said triumphantly.

As someone who'd grown up under strict rules regarding neatness and noise, I appreciated the homey disorder of the Altmann house. I smiled and looked around that first day at the ornate floral wallpaper and the dark hardwood floors.

If I ever had a house, I thought, maybe it would look like this house. Maybe someday I'd have a family like this one.

CHAPTER EIGHT

Now we said good night after what might've been my ten thousandth meal with the Altmanns. David and I rode the bus back to Bay Ridge. It was a long trip—forty-five minutes—down Coney Island Avenue and then Seventy-seventh, straight into the heart of the neighborhood. We sat toward the front, facing a Hasidic woman and her three children: two little girls on each side of her and a baby in a stroller. David always took the first available seat. Other riders were scattered behind us, heads down, full attention on their phones.

The Hasidic woman was reading a small prayer book. Her daughters were quiet, well behaved. They looked exactly the same, one slightly smaller than the other, in their starched, old-timey skirts and cardigans. The woman wore a thick, dark wig and a pillbox hat. It was a nice wig made of real hair. I might not have been able to tell if she and her kids weren't so identifiably Hasidic: their clothing, their hushed Yiddish, the neighborhood we were in. I tried to guess how old she was. Younger than me, surely, but I couldn't have said if the difference was five years or fifteen: Her face was sweet and young but tired, lined from constant work. Three kids in a row, all those nights up with a newborn, early mornings washing and dressing and feeding toddlers. All the laundry, all the cooking and shopping and cleaning.

I turned my attention to the infant, a soft creature whose thin layer of hair was so red, it looked magenta against his pale skin. He was on his back in the stroller, head turned in my direction, and he appeared to be watching me. We held each other's gaze, or at least I imagined we did. I'd heard somewhere that tiny babies can't see much. He blinked slowly, sucking his pacifier. I felt in my core the familiar longing for a baby of my own. It occurred to me, more and more often, that if we were going to have kids, we needed to start. I had an IUD to remove, and we had money and my job and David's long, busy work schedule to renegotiate. All the business trips his work required, two weeks or more overseas several times a year to look at job sites and meet project managers. There was a tiny room to clean out and paint, a musty daybed to discard, thousands of dollars' worth of new furniture to acquire. It all scared me, the practicalities of having a child, not to mention the incredible science of the thing itself, the physical transformation and the demand, the upheaval of my body. I wasn't ready. But what if I was never ready? Neither David nor I had brought it up in over a year.

I could practically smell this baby, his delicious, tender, powdery skin.

I doubted Melissa would have kids of her own, even though (or perhaps because) we'd never discussed the matter. Melissa remembered our mother. It was different for her. Our mother died when I was a baby, and maybe this had nothing to do with my prolonged childlessness, and maybe it was the root of it and of every other thing about who I was. Now my hormones smacked against my ambivalence with blunt force. My stomach hurt a little. I felt suddenly adrift and alone. The baby had fallen asleep; his mother pulled down the stroller's retractable canopy, covering him from view. I turned to look at David, who was, like everyone else on the bus, basking in front of his cell phone. I watched his eyeballs crawl down the screen. I watched him fail to notice my gaze; I watched him fail to see me wanting something from him; I felt myself failing to name precisely what it was.

I GOT OFF THE bus a stop ahead of David, telling him good night in a casual way.

"Do you want me to come meet you later?" he asked.

"No," I said. "Go to bed—you can't keep the same hours as me through this renovation."

"I don't like the idea of falling asleep before you get home," he said.

"I know what you mean," I said. "I do it all the time." I kissed the cold top of his car.

"I like the carpenter," he said then, just as I was turning to go. "He's cool."

I nodded. I said, "I like him, too."

AT THE BAKERY, TIANA was sitting at the front table in the dark; she'd turned out the dining room lights and was wearing her coat, pocket-book in her lap. She stood when I came in. Twin tunnels of light spilled from the small windows of the swinging doors, and there was music playing faintly from inside the kitchen.

"Hi, thanks for waiting," I said, though I resisted making an apology. I was hardly late. There were still an acceptable ten minutes on the closing shift, which was padded with an extra half hour in case things ran late.

"I normally wouldn't be in a rush, but I have an exam tomorrow," she said, embarrassed to have been caught looking so impatient. I wished her good luck on the exam and said if I was a few minutes late next time to go ahead and leave, but to make sure Matt locked the doors behind her.

In the kitchen, Matt was playing a Fiona Apple record I'd listened to every day in college.

"I haven't heard this in forever," I said, tossing my coat on a column of storage bins.

Matt was standing over Maria's workstation with a pencil in his hand, making small marks in his sketchbook. He wore dark brown work pants and an ivory short-sleeved shirt with a collar. There was a pencil behind his ear.

"It's good music for working," he said. "How was dinner with your boyfriend's family?"

I waited a beat and considered not correcting him. Finally, I said, "Husband."

"Huh?" he asked.

"I'm married," I said. Why did this feel so strange? I told people I was married all the time. I'd been married long enough. But it was like when a customer called me Kat or Kate, and I'd let it go a few times, until we were past the point of it being appropriate, and I realized I had to correct them. This situation had the awkward embarrassment of those conversations, as though I'd previously misrepresented myself by not wearing a name tag: MARRIED.

Matt smiled in a confused way, like he was trying to hide being taken aback by this information. "How was dinner with your *husband's* family?" he said in a funny way.

I just looked at him. "It was fine," I eventually said.

"I wish there were a Borat-esque joke about the word 'husband,'" he said good-naturedly.

"Mey *hus*-bandah," I said in the Borat voice. "Yeah, it really doesn't have the same ring to it."

He laughed, and that was it. "This afternoon I went to pick up materials with Angelo and this guy Richie?" he said. "Do you know him? He wanted to drive my cargo van, like it was a carnival ride. He was kind of a hoot."

94

Richie Bolognese worked for his namesake father—the revoltingly named Rich Bolognese, who was called "Big Rich" for simplicity's sake—at Prestige Plumbing. Richie—"Little Richie"—had a loud, weaselly voice and wore a tracksuit everywhere. A man out of time, Melissa called him. When we saw each other, Richie called me sweetheart in an avuncular tone. He'd been in my kindergarten class at P.S. 264, in 1987.

"He and Angelo are an unlikely pair," Matt said. "It's funny to listen to the two of them talk."

"Richie must get Angelo a discount at the lumber supply," I said. "They don't hang out that much."

"They were arguing like an old married couple."

I let the phrase hang in the air for a moment, until finally, I said, "Any two people from this neighborhood, confined in a smallish space together, will start to argue like an old married couple."

He laughed in a hearty, appreciative way. His laughter delighted me, made me feel taller, lighter.

"I'm kind of jealous of you all," he said. "You and Melissa and Angelo. It's like you get to be from New York City and from a small town at the same time."

I asked, "Where are you from?"

"Cincinnati," he said.

I nodded, as though I could conjure an image of Cincinnati. "The Reds," I said, like an imbecile, and felt myself blush.

"That's right." He was smirking a little. I wanted to crawl under Melissa's workstation and die. "Do you like baseball?"

"I love baseball," I said.

"So, are you a Mets or Yankees fan?" he asked.

"Mets," I said, offended. "Do you need my help?" I realized I could allow the conversation to wander, far, if I didn't pay attention. He was easy to talk to, and a good listener, and had a sweet, funny way of speaking. He was an excellent and artful flirt, so unobtrusive I didn't even notice he was doing it.

I looked around the kitchen, which was immaculate, as usual—
the floors spotless, the counters polished, the sink scrubbed—but
marred by the disorder of the construction. The eight-foot ladder Angelo
brought out only to hang holiday decorations leaned against the brick
wall. I could see spots Matt had marked for studs and the holes he'd
drilled. The supplies were piled in neat rows on the floor where the old
racks had been. The new wood, several bundles of varying shapes and
sizes, was shrink-wrapped together in thick green plastic. Lined up next
to it were several small boxes full of pavers and nails and other practical
pieces, then a collection of large tools, including an electric sander, and
an oversize toolbox with Matt's name engraved on the handle.

I knew how designers worked: toward strict deadlines, tapping
at computers in remote, windowless offices far from a predetermined
or hypothetical construction site. They rendered images digitally on a
bright monitor. Matt's notebook, open on the workstation, had full-
color drawings. His method looked like some atavistic fantasy of a design
process, one I viewed with equal parts admiration and skepticism. That
Angelo and Melissa had hired him at all was still a point of confusion.
I guessed they wanted the cachet of working with someone like Matt
instead of hiring one of the many contractors we knew, who could've
copied something from the pages of a trade magazine. It was overwhelm-
ing to see Matt's work spread out like this, and to wonder how it would
come together with no crew in such a brief amount of time.

But Matt had a plan, of course, and the work was intuitive to him.
He had all sorts of setting up left to do, he said. He had to proof and prep
the wall, which I found funny, but he didn't seem to realize "proof" and
"prep" were also baking words. I drifted in and out, spending some time
restocking the dining room but substantially more time wiping down
the stainless steel—the fridges, the sinks, the steam sanitizer—at the
other side of the kitchen. We listened to Fiona Apple in a comfortable
quiet, besides the occasional sound of Matt's drill. I wanted to talk but
couldn't think of what to say.

The album ended, and Matt was sitting on a low stool packing up certain tools, retrieving others. After a moment he said, "How'd you guys get into the bakery business?"

"Oh, well, I'm not really in the bakery business," I said, and he raised a skeptical eyebrow. "I just mean—it's kind of complicated. Melissa is a pastry chef. She always loved to bake and worked at a bakery in high school. Not a bakery for sweets but a *forno*. It's closed now, but she, I guess, apprenticed with the owners before she went and got her culinary certification in pastry."

"Aforna?"

I laughed, then blushed again. "*Forno*. A fresh bread store," I said. "It—um—*forno* means oven? There used to be a lot of them."

"They all closed down?"

"Yeah, for the most part. Then Melissa worked at restaurants in the city for years before she and Angelo opened Sweet Cheeks. I just kind of—oh, I don't know—I fell into this because Melissa had the plan, and she and Angelo asked me to come on board."

Matt said, "What do your parents do? Are they nearby?"

I balked, blinking at the wall behind his head for a moment. Melissa and I had always lived at our grandparents' house, even when our mother was alive. She'd been a young mother, and—though I still don't know much—troubled for most of her adolescence. After I was born, she'd been so depressed that she went in and out of treatment, but she never got better. That's how both my grandparents always talked about it. She committed suicide before I was six months old. Melissa was two. We knew her always from her absence, and from our grandmother's deep and scary grief, the photos of her around the house, a girl in a frilly yellow prom dress, 1979, grinning to reveal the braces she still had when Melissa was born a year later. Our dad wasn't in our lives in a meaningful way. My grandfather died from a rapid, evil stomach cancer when I was in second grade.

Melissa and I were always close with Angelo and his younger siblings, and Uncle Nicky—our mother's big brother—and his wife, our

Aunt Tina. They, along with a heap of others, were always around. It never occurred to me to think of myself as abandoned or orphaned until I began having to explain my upbringing as an adult. I avoided doing so as much as possible. I hated people's dramatic expressions, the way they seemed to treat me like a rare and fragile animal when they found out.

"They aren't nearby," I said, trying not to be curt. It wasn't Matt's fault. He'd asked a perfectly normal question, I reminded myself, and softened. "We grew up with our grandmother, but she passed away."

"Oh, I'm sorry."

"Thank you. It's been some years now. Do you need help?" I asked. Matt had begun opening the lumber packets, slicing off their green plastic coating with a pocketknife.

"That would be great," he said. "Can you cover this table?" He gestured to Guillermo's counter. I covered it with long sheets of brown craft paper ripped from the industrial cutter, then a big sheet of painter's plastic. I helped Matt lift the largest slabs of oak, and I held things still as he sanded and measured, the distance between us closing as we talked. Sometimes he leaned so near me to make a pencil marking, I could smell the cinnamon gum he was chewing and the briny, woodsmoke smell of his skin. He gave off warmth. My mouth twitched whenever the conversation paused.

I asked about his family and what had brought him to New York, what year he'd moved here, and what his plans were. He talked about himself easily but without too much pleasure or self-involvement. I admired his openness, the genuine way he spoke with love for his parents, who were both accountants, and his younger brothers, who were twins in college at Ohio State. He was close to his family and thought Cincinnati was a fine town. But he loved New York and had always wanted to live here.

"I'm fascinated by people who have been here their whole lives," he said. His earnestness was somehow comfortable. "I've lived here for eight years and rarely come across native New Yorkers."

"That's certainly untrue," I said. I was holding a slab of oak in place as he drilled small holes into the other side.

"It feels true," he said. "It's true in my neighborhood."

He lived on Henry Street, in a part of the borough I thought of as downtown, though he seemed to disagree. He could barely afford his place, he told me, even though his rent was undermarket for the neighborhood. I imagined Benji rolling his eyes, playing an invisible violin, but I was sympathetic. In the months following my grandmother's death, when Melissa and I were deciding what to do with the house, David and I were living in Alphabet City, in a decrepit fourth-floor walk-up on East Tenth Street. It was a glorified studio, listed by the sleazy broker as a one-bedroom. When we actually went to see it, he didn't argue as we accused him of lying about the place's size. "But the location!" he'd insisted. "Just look at where you are!" Five minutes to the subway, so many restaurants, so many bars, so many places to buy a fourteen-dollar jar of kimchee at eleven p.m. The apartment was narrow and damp, with paint peeling off the kitchen cabinets. Its two rooms smelled faintly and mysteriously of licorice, there was an outline of mildew around the shower, the window screens were coated in permanent grime, and the rent went up each of the three years we lived there. Our decision to come to Bay Ridge and live above my childhood home had been predicated on our disillusionment with a *great location*.

But Matt told me how much he liked his apartment, and his neighbors, and the new riverfront park under the Brooklyn Bridge. He didn't mention a girlfriend or partner; he mentioned his friends with clear specificity, even naming them. I decided he must be single. He talked about his experience of New York City in a way that made me want to go there someday. It didn't sound like a place I knew or understood, let alone the city where I had lived my whole life. Whizzing around on a bike, drinking at bars in Red Hook, seeing stand-up comedy in some residential loft in Bushwick, of all places. I watched his hands moving at his work while we talked. They were big and sturdy. He caught me looking at one point, and I darted my eyes to the space over his shoulder. When we were finally ready to quit for the evening, it was past midnight, and I was sad. Matt offered me a ride home in his van, a black Ford Transit parked on the street behind the bakery, but I said I wanted to walk. He asked if he could give me his phone number.

"Text me if anything comes up," he said as we covered the supplies with tarps, duct-taping them to the floor so nothing would mingle with the bakery operations in the morning. "If you need to change our schedule or move any of this equipment. I know it's kind of a health inspection nightmare."

I handed him my phone and he entered his number, listing himself as "Matt Carpenter."

After he walked out the back door, I stood alone in the kitchen's mammoth silence, phone in hand, and counted to one hundred.

Once I was sure he would be driving, I texted: **This is Kit Bakery. Here's my number, too. Just in case.**

CHAPTER NINE

I don't know if I'm explaining myself quite right. Let me be clear.

I loved my husband. David's very being was attached to everything I had, our marriage a spaghetti smothered in thick tomato gravy. There was no separating out any one part of it without making a big mess. And: We'd been together for what felt like my entire existence. But also: We'd been together for what felt like my entire existence. I wasn't on a diet; I was doing a program. And: I thought about food all the time. But also: I thought about food all the time.

Matt Larsson was tall and smelled nice. He was a good talker, he had a handsome face, a nice laugh, a one-bedroom apartment, and no roommates. He made things. Besides his brief job at the bakery, he had nothing to do with the rest of my life. When we met, we had no friends in common, none of our circles overlapped.

Listen, I wasn't some idiot. I'd studied Romance languages in college and read a hefty number of nineteenth-century novels. I could read English, Italian, and French. I was particularly acquainted with Russian translations. In basically every single book I'd ever enjoyed, somebody's listless, repressed wife—the hero of the story—ran off with some mustachioed guy who did manual labor. Matt didn't have a mustache, but he did have a number of expensive tattoos. I knew the embarrassing, anachronistic trope I was in danger of becoming as I leaned over this broad carpenter and inconspicuously sniffed his scalp while he sanded oak panels in my sister's commercial kitchen.

But I wasn't trapped, was I? I wasn't going to end up as Anna Karenina, throwing myself in front of a train, or debt-ridden Emma Bovary, drinking arsenic and dying on a cache of illicit letters. I wasn't somebody's listless, repressed wife at all. I was a modern woman who happened to be listless and repressed *on my own terms*. I was married to a man I really loved. But for some reason, in the company of Matt Larsson, I felt my unhappiness—and my constant hunger—subside, and so I followed those moments, chased time alone with him, pressed his words and then his body closer and closer to the center of who I was until, eventually, I had a real problem. I was obsessed with my size, sure, but that didn't mean the Radiant Regimen was more than one choice in a million I could make. On all fronts, I had options. The problem, then, *was* my options. I could explode my life and survive. My days were full of decisions, and whatever I did—or didn't do—I had to live with the consequences. I had to see everything through.

THE NEXT NIGHT, I closed with Violet. As had been the case on Monday, she was diligent and professional in her work but somewhat standoffish when there weren't customers around. When she went on her break, she asked if I wanted anything from the bagel shop.

"Oh, no, thanks," I said. "I brought food from home."

She raised her eyebrows slightly. "Okay," she said. Her voice was higher than usual, and she smiled in a knowing way.

"What?" I asked. "You're smirking."

"Nothing," she said, gliding out of the bakery.

I slammed through the kitchen doors. "Did you say something to Violet about me?" I asked Melissa. She was writing on a cake, stooped over, and didn't look up or answer. She had a hairnet on, and her white cotton shirt was cut so that I could see her strong back muscles, tensed to match her concentration. I waited.

Finally, she stood up and observed her work. "Eh," she said of her perfect cursive. She pointed her piping bag at me. "Don't interrupt when I'm doing this shit. You know I hate this."

"I could write on cakes, and you could hang out with your friend Violet out there," I said, pointing into the dining room with my thumb. "What did you say to her?"

"Many things," Melissa said. "What's your problem?"

"Did you say something about how I eat?"

Her upper lip curled, a look somehow both uninterested and vicious at the exact same time. "Probably," she said. "Sorry—I didn't know it was some big secret that you're a fad dieter. To be fair, you talk about it a lot."

"But I barely *know* Violet. I don't talk to her about it," I snapped. "And I'm not a fad dieter! I'm health-conscious."

"It probably wasn't even me," Melissa said, wagging the piping bag in my direction in an obscene way. "One of the Girls probably was making fun of you."

"But Violet isn't one of the Girls," I said. "They don't talk to her the way they talk to each other. She's our age."

Melissa rocked back on her heels, her clogs clacking when she righted herself. "Ha!" she said. "You want to impress her. You don't want her to know what a douchebag you are."

"That's not it," I said. Of course it was. It was embarrassing to be doing the Radiant Regimen in front of someone as effortlessly cool as Violet, with her worn-in leather jacket and black nail polish and bagel dinners. Earlier in the afternoon, I'd wanted to tell her how much I liked her eye makeup but was afraid she'd receive my compliment coldly or assume I was being insincere.

Angelo came into the kitchen then. "What are you doing back here?" he shouted. "Don't leave the counter unattended."

"It wasn't unattended," I said. "You were sitting at a table right next to the counter. *Now* it's unattended." But I went back to work, glad for the opportunity to storm off.

Behind me, I heard Angelo say, "*Somebody's* hangry," to which Melissa answered, "She's worse than usual."

Sometimes I hated them so much.

WHEN MATT ARRIVED, HE worked alone during the hours the bakery was still open. At 7:55, Violet came back from the kitchen, where she'd been washing the grate of the espresso machine. She clipped it back into the base and started polishing it with the little microfiber cloths Angelo made all the Girls carry around, lest they find themselves unprepared to wipe a random smudge.

"Do you guys need help tonight?" Violet asked me. Her voice was casual—friendlier—than usual. "I don't mind staying."

"Oh, no," I said. "It's not much work at all."

Violet said, "Huh." She went off to the basement to get paper cups and napkins.

I crept to the kitchen door and peered through the window. At the same moment—precisely the worst possible moment—Matt looked up from his work and surely saw me, my bandana'ed head bobbing in the Plexiglas rectangle, then disappearing like a house elf. I went back to taking inventory of expired pastry. I dumped half a tray of stale cupcakes we called "the Paisano" into the black Hefty bag at my feet.

"Why does Melissa keep making those?" Violet said behind me, unloading an armful of paper products onto the counter.

It was a good question. I looked into the bag. The Paisano was almond cake with honey nougat frosting, a semisweet chocolate drizzle, and a piece of imported *torrone* on top. They sold well at Christmas but hardly at all the rest of the year. Sweet Cheeks didn't make traditional desserts; rainbow cookie cake and the Paisano were the only menu items inspired by Italian pastries.

"I think they remind her of our grandmother," I said, surprised by my own candor. I looked at Violet, and she cocked her head at me, her face softening.

"My grandma lived with my family, too," Violet said. "My dad brought her over from Korea when I was a toddler." I realized Violet knew that Melissa and I had lived with our grandmother but not that she had been our sole guardian. I didn't correct her.

"I think Melissa still wants our grandmother's approval," I said. "She does certain things in some sort of spiritual exchange, as though Nonna's watching." Our grandmother had been an incredible cook but not an enthusiastic baker, and from our middle school years onward, she was happy to have Melissa prepare desserts on holidays and birthdays. Our grandmother never got to see the bakery; she'd died a year before it opened. She would've been so proud, though I wonder if she would've been affronted by our most popular items: Melissa's gourmet version of the Hostess Snoball, her Mallomar icebox cake, the funfetti pieces in the banana pudding.

"I feel that. I find myself doing things now that embarrassed me about my family growing up," Violet said. "I make my roommates take their shoes off in our hallway. Last week I used a movie coupon while I was on a date."

"Melissa has plastic covers on her furniture."

Violet laughed. "Speaking of turning into our elders, is any of the stuff you're throwing out salvageable? Because I'll take whatever's somewhat edible."

"These are all broken," I said, pushing a paper bag of full cookie pieces toward her. "But they're fresh."

"Nice," Violet said. "You don't want any?" She crouched in front of the cups-and-straws cabinet and began to restock.

"Nope," I said.

"Tiana says you never eat any of the pastries."

"Well, that's an exaggeration," I said.

Matt swung in silently from the kitchen and turned down the basement stairs. Violet pulled the cordless mini vacuum from its charger and started to suction crumbs out of the display case I'd just emptied. I went to close out the cash register for the day. I could've counted money in my sleep after so many years breaking down drawers, pulling bills through my fingers without needing to concentrate. I stuffed the cash into an envelope, writing the totals in the top corner. I dropped it into the safe slot under the register. Violet finished vacuuming and went to the closet/office next to the basement stairs. I saw her check out her face in the mirror that hung from the door. She removed her glasses and took her hair down. I wanted to ask how it stayed so sleek after eight consecutive hours smothered inside a net. My own hair was surely oily and flat beneath my bandana.

"You and the carpenter really don't need any help?" Violet asked. "I don't mind staying."

"There's not much for us to do except clean up in here," I told her.

This was a lie. UPS had delivered supplies that morning, Richie dropped off another bundle of lumber, and Matt would need help lugging stuff upstairs, plus someone to hold the foundation pieces while he mounted them into the wall.

"Well, I can help with cleaning," she said. "I need the money."

"Okay," I said. "Fine."

Matt appeared at the top of the stairs carrying a three-slab bundle of wood. "That looks like a two-person job," Violet said, going to him.

She took one end of the bundle and walked backward with enviable ease, not looking over her shoulder, her feet assured in their reversed motion. Violet's back was straight and her toned arms flexed above the elbows. Working together, she and Matt fell into immediate ease. It wasn't just their dexterity while doing physical work, or their look of hip, curated shabbiness, but also how they gave off the same self-assurance, a tenacity I encountered only in people from suburbs and small towns. I watched them slide into the kitchen, my hands useless at my sides.

I trudged down the basement's concrete steps. There were only a few boxes I could carry myself, so I chose the biggest of those and heaved it upstairs.

"Don't lift with your back like that," Violet said when I got into the kitchen. She and Matt were looking at his sketches. "Use your legs."

I ignored her and shoved the box in Matt's direction. He took it, smiling distractedly. The closeness Matt and I had the night before was still there, an exciting new heat, but Violet disrupted our chemistry. Her presence pointed to the weirdness of our overfamiliarity. I did not return Matt's smile as I narrowed my eyes and walked away.

THE NEXT HOUR MOVED along this same embarrassing trajectory: Violet and Matt did the work together, and for a while I tried to include myself with small offerings, carrying the lightest, littlest things up. Finally, I abandoned my attempts and brought out the Hauskeeper, went about the arduous, arm-toning work of waxing the dining room floor.

Around ten, I looked up over the din of the Hauskeeper and started at the sight of Matt standing at the back wall, grinning in a cute, foolish way. I shut the Hauskeeper off and felt it pulsating in my hands.

"You scared me half to death," I said. "Where's Violet?"

"She left," he said. "She said to tell you good night, but I think she was kind of annoyed you polished the floor without warning her first; she had a hard time getting her coat."

"Poor Violet," I said bitterly.

"Were you annoyed that you didn't get to be alone with me?"

I let the question, and my astonishment at Matt's frankness, hang between us for a moment. His eyes were playful and his slight smile wonderfully confident. He looked so sexy standing there, daring me to answer honestly, knowing already I wouldn't be able to lie.

Finally, I said, "Yeah, I was."

He went back into the kitchen, and I followed.

"I was thinking about you, Kit Bakery," he said. "I almost texted you this morning." He took a step toward me.

"To say what?" I asked, but I already knew. It was incredible how, the instant we began speaking openly, this was the way we talked now, making the whole of our attraction to each other available for mutual examination. A curtain was being drawn back, revealing a wide-open space where pretenses had been. Maybe we'd never had any pretenses in the first place, had merely believed them to be there. Attraction, after all, speaks its own language.

"Nothing, really!" he said. "It sounds dumb, I guess, but I just wanted your attention."

"It doesn't sound so dumb," I said.

He was only a foot away from me now, and I could feel us teetering on the edge. I could mention David, bring out the biggest, best reason we shouldn't be standing this close, or I could pretend David didn't exist. Those were the two choices. Matt certainly wasn't thinking about David.

I let out a sharp breath, said nothing.

He leaned his face into mine, his breath against my mouth. He kissed me. I kissed him back and let him grab my waist and pull me onto the counter. We pushed a clipboard and a can opener out of the way, knocking them into the empty garbage bin. The whole bakery smelled like floor wax. Matt's lips were warm and smooth, and the relief of them against my lips, and against my neck, felt exactly how I wanted it to feel. He pressed his hand to my breast. I couldn't believe what I had: the pleasure of knowing I wanted something, wanted to consume it whole, and just doing so, putting it directly into my mouth. I didn't feel hungry anymore.

It was like being drunk, like the first few minutes of drunkenness. The world was emptied of anything outside the kitchen. There were no other people, or noises, or thoughts. I wasn't aware of myself doing anything wrong, because it barely occurred to me that I was at work. It didn't occur to me to pull away, to get my coat and my bag and rush home to David, who was surely waiting. It no longer even occurred to me that I was married.

PART TWO // Easter Sunday

CHAPTER TEN

"Join us or don't," Angelo said. "I don't care." But his bitchy tone implied how deeply he did care. Melissa and I stared at him. He wanted us to come to five o'clock mass with Uncle Nicky and Aunt Tina.

It was Easter Sunday. The three of us were locking up the bakery. I tossed the garbage into the dumpster, checking out my reflection in the shiny surface of Angelo's black car on the way. I was thin in the early spring sunshine, wearing the new jeans I'd bought the day before because everything else was finally too loose. I put my hands around my waist to feel and appreciate its narrowness, resisting the urge to press into my ribs. I was six weeks through the Radiant Regimen now, over halfway done. This was the longest I'd ever maintained a dietary program. I was hungry all the time, even though Diana Spargel claimed I wasn't supposed to be hungry at all by now.

"I'll go to mass," Melissa said in an annoyed tone. "Jesus Christ, I said I would go already. Just because I said I don't *want* to go doesn't mean I won't."

Angelo patted Melissa on the cheek. "Nonna would be very pleased," he said.

Melissa rolled her eyes. "Don't drag her into this."

As was typical for a holiday, we'd opened Sweet Cheeks on reduced hours, giving the staff the day off, so it had been just the three of us working the sales floor. We shuttered the bakery only on Christmas. Angelo worked the espresso bar, I worked the counter, and Melissa, useless in a retail situation, stood at a table topped with pies and handed them out to customers who'd ordered in advance. She checked their names off a list I'd compiled in Excel.

"Look, I'm you!" she'd said to me during a lull in customer traffic, and she held the clipboard in the crook of her arm, straightened her spine importantly, spread her feet apart.

"That's not how I stand," I'd snapped.

"Of course it is," she said. "You always stand like this, with your hands on your hips. Just like Peter Pan. Now you even have the same body."

"I *don't*," I said childishly, in a whining tone.

"You do!" she insisted cheerfully.

"Hey, idiots, no fighting," Angelo said. He took a sip of espresso from a tiny porcelain cup, holding it by the handle in an exaggeratedly dainty manner. "Today is a *holy* day. Jesus *died* for us. Show a little respect."

He was smirking, and Melissa snorted in response, because Angelo was exactly as religious as she and I were, which is to say Angelo never considered whether or not God existed.

Easter was what Melissa referred to, with dismay, as one of the "candy holidays." She made and sold a fair number of preordered ricotta pies to devoted crowds of old-timers and people we'd known in the neighborhood our whole lives. Cupcake sales spiked the days leading up to Easter, too, but as a whole, the holiday didn't touch the breakneck business we got over Christmas or on Mother's Day.

"Kit, do you want to go home and fill up on Kentucky bluegrass and raw steak or whatever you consume these days? There's not going to be a thing for you to eat at Uncle Nicky and Aunt Tina's."

I checked my watch. It was only two-thirty in the afternoon. David was still at home, probably, but he had plans to play racquetball with Darshawn. I could go home and have lunch with him and say I was going to mass with my family. And then, once David was on his train and headed into the city, I'd go to Matt's apartment. We could have a few hours together. But racquetball wouldn't provide a long enough window. David would come straight home afterward. He might even want to meet me at Uncle Nicky's, and I wouldn't be there. He might text Melissa or Angelo, who'd say I'd told them I had a headache (I'd been getting a lot of headaches lately) and needed to stay home. To pull it off, I'd have less than two hours with Matt.

This was the kind of calculus I performed all the time now.

"I don't want to go home and then come back out," I said. "I'm sure *somebody* has *something* I can eat."

"I have some chicken breasts in my fridge," Angelo said.

"Organic chicken?" I asked.

Melissa made a pained, exhausted noise, like she was riding a bicycle up a very steep hill.

I DIDN'T SLEEP WITH Matt that night in February, when we'd spent some time making out on Melissa's work counter. He'd pawed around beneath my shirt, and I'd unclipped his belt, but we'd stopped, breathless and red-faced, before anything more happened.

Panting, I'd said we should cool it.

Matt had leaned in, kissed me one more time, bitten my lip lightly, and licked the corner of my mouth in a way I should have found crude but which sent a shiver through me.

115

"That's true," he said. We stood a short distance apart, rearranging our clothes. I buttoned my blouse back up; he fixed his belt. Glancing over, I saw the outline of his hard penis inside his jeans and didn't look away immediately. He caught my eyes and, without embarrassment, smiled, as if to say, *Pretty great, right?*

We cleaned and organized the kitchen in jittery silence. I was on edge, giddy. After I set the alarm, we went out the back door and into the cold night. I pulled down the gate and locked the padlock while Matt tossed two black garbage bags into the trash.

"Okay!" he said with what seemed like hysterical cheer as we stood under the security light, kicking gravel beneath our feet. "I guess we are both going to our homes now!"

"Bye," I said. It was surreal, confusing. We didn't touch again. He lingered another moment, looking at me, before heading to the rack where his bike was locked up. A few days before, I'd thought he was insane to bike in the winter, but now a ride in thirty-degree darkness looked appealing, pent-up energy spent usefully.

AT HOME, DAVID WAS half asleep in front of cable news: a press conference from the Republican primary campaign trail.

"Because I'm a nice person, I didn't want to say it," said the worst of the candidates, the reality television star with the red face and the inhuman rings of white around his eyes. "But then I had to say it. I said, 'Excuse me, Jeb, we aren't safe. Iran is taking over Iraq.' I was against the war in Iraq, by the way. And then when they went in, I said, 'Take the oil,' they didn't take the oil. This has fueled ISIS! ISIS now has so much money because they had the oil. From Iran. Iran has the oil, too. So."

Abruptly, he stopped speaking, as though he'd expressed a complete idea or even a fraction of an idea that made sense on its own, and turned to take the next question.

I groaned. David said, "That guy is a clown."

It was still funny at that point. It was funny all year, almost, until the election came and went, leaving behind a waking nightmare, and we were left stunned, bereft, to realize our own smug lack of imagination.

I said, "Turn off this circus." Then I took the remote off the side table and shut the television off myself.

David reached for me, and I hesitated a moment before coming closer, letting him rub the back of my leg with a sleepy hand. I worried that Matt's smell was on me. My heart had been beating fast the whole walk home and was only now slowing to a normal rate. I took in a deep breath.

"How was work?" David asked.

"It was fine," I said. What did I usually say? "I waxed the floor."

David giggled. At what? I realized he wasn't awake enough to bother talking, and relief washed over me, and then a tide of terrible guilt.

"I'm taking a shower," I said. "You should go to bed."

"I will, once this is over," David said.

"I turned it off, David."

"Oh," he said. "I see that now."

He looked up at me, puppy-faced in his exhaustion. He said, "I waited up for you."

I left him there. When I got out of the shower, he was still in the living room, snoring in the IKEA armchair, Woogie curled on the ottoman by his feet.

"Come on," I said to the cat and made a clicking noise with my tongue. Woogie rose and stretched before following me up to the bedroom. I didn't wake David. I lay in bed a long time, going over in my mind again and again what had happened with Matt. I was both horrified and exhilarated. Eventually, David must have come up to bed, but I'd fallen asleep.

* * *

THE NEXT MORNING, MATT texted early and invited me to see an exhibition of early-twentieth-century chairs at the Brooklyn Museum. I stared at the text for a few minutes before responding.

—**When? Today?**

—**Yeah. How about 1pm?**

When I arrived at the museum's enormous lobby several hours later, he was standing beneath the curved glass and steel pavilion, his head high, his gaze soft and open, which I took to be a practiced demonstration of his patience.

"I'm only ten minutes late!" I blurted out, and he raised his eyebrows. "For me, that's basically on time. This is actually the most punctual I've ever been."

"Well, congrats!" he said. It was exactly what Melissa would have said, but Matt didn't sound sarcastic. We didn't hug or really greet each other at all. I wondered when we'd acknowledge the events of the night before.

At the ticket counter, Matt elected to pay the full price of admission. I considered doing the same so as not to look cheap, but I couldn't bring myself.

"I'll pay half," I told the kid at the counter before she could even ask.

We walked to the elevator. Matt hit the button.

"Are your parents New York natives?" he asked me.

I tried not to stiffen. "Yeah," I said. "My mom grew up in Bay Ridge. She died when Melissa and I were babies. I'm pretty private about it. I mean, it's not a secret or anything. But it makes people act weird, whenever I tell them."

Matt was quiet for a moment. I could see him wanting to ask how my mother had died and, to my relief, deciding to let the question go. He nodded with solemnity. I became embarrassed for divulging so much and couldn't wait to get out of the elevator. I didn't want to talk about my family or my childhood. My interest in him had nothing to do with my real life.

On the third floor, we stood at the entryway to the exhibit: a wide-open room, high ceilings. No one else was around. Several dozen chairs were displayed on white pedestals.

"Let's get a load of these chairs," I said.

Matt examined the chairs the way I might watch a movie, his eyes following some invisible narrative having to do with the construction—a story I was excluded from truly understanding—each tiny detail a careful, handcrafted task. The curved beech and cherrywood were steamed, he explained, to make them more malleable under the carpenter's carving tools. It was delicate work, difficult beyond anything computer-programmed machines did on the mass market. Everything we had was hideous in its clunky simplicity, he said. Everyone's house was crowded with the same cheap IKEA crap.

"I put my IKEA chairs together," I said. "It wasn't simple at all. It took the entire afternoon, and I had to call a hotline for tips. Twice!"

He looked at me, his head tilted down to meet my gaze. "I like you," he said. It was a firm statement, and immediately, we were both awkward, standing in front of each other in a fugue of sexual tension.

I shifted my weight, felt my neck and chest turn pink, the blush climbing toward my face. "Well," I said. "We've seen all the chairs, and it's only three o'clock. Do you want to go outside and take a cold walk through the park, or do you want to go somewhere private?"

"The second option, please," he said without pausing.

"Let's go."

It was amazing to discover how irrelevant David could be. His existence didn't come up. I hadn't known I could put David away like that.

I still wonder if the afternoon might have gone differently if Matt had not revealed himself to be a kind of antidote to David. I don't mean merely that Matt was available to cavort through museums on a weekday. My job in food retail was usually a hindrance to normal adult fun, which was relegated to weekends for many other people my age. That was part of it, I think. And there was Matt's tallness and broad physicality stacked in front of David's compact frame, my husband's respectful tendency to keep his hands to himself. But it was the chairs, too. Matt was a builder, a maker. He didn't live his life under the terrible reign of emails in need of swift reply. He wasn't chained to a computer at all, and if he had been, he'd have hated it. He was someone who loved his work deeply, and he could explain to others what he did. He was something different, and I just wanted to try it, to taste this new offering.

In the taxi headed to Matt's apartment, I was almost unaware of the monumental decision I was about to make. The thing I could, for another fifteen minutes, still undo. My heart wasn't beating wildly, my palms didn't sweat.

Once out of the cab, through the vestibule and up the stairs and, finally, inside Matt's living room, we remained silent as we removed our clothing, our skin flushed and slippery, our mouths tenderized by the gruesome, teeth-knocking way we went at each other; the next day, my lips would be sore. His body was large and pale, and his skin smelled like something I wanted to be wrapped up in, consumed by. His pubic hair was a surprising shade of light, reddish brown.

"I've never met someone whose pubes were lighter than the hair on their head," I said.

He replied, "I'm sure that's not true."

I said, "You know what I mean."

It was clear through the assurance with which his hands cupped my ass, his one-handed unsnapping of my bra, the expert unrolling of the condom, that Matt had touched many naked women. I decided to stop wondering how many, exactly, as he guided me by the hips on top of him and held my waist, rocking my body in exactly the right way. Once I stopped thinking about it, I came. My breath must have been loud in his ear as I collapsed, and then he finished, too, his torso and legs trembling beneath me.

Sitting at his kitchen table in our underwear, we shared a few glasses of tap water and I explained that I'd never cheated on David, and I promised I wasn't lying even though I knew it sounded like a lie. My fingers ran across the fabric at the waist of my panties: black bikini briefs, the nicest pair I owned. I suppose the panties were a sign that I'd been prepared for this. The afternoon's events hadn't sneaked up on me; I hadn't been merely overtaken by passion in the moment.

"It's all right," Matt said. He leaned forward, took a tendril of my hair, and moved it away from my face. "You don't have to explain. I like you. I told you that."

"I like you, too," I said. "Obviously. But I feel like you're acting really cavalier for having just slept with a married person."

"I admit my first choice is sex with an unmarried person," Matt said after a pause. "But you're an adult. Look, David seemed cool. I'm not trying to be a dick. If you're not square with your conscience right now, I'd understand that. And I would understand if you said this was a one-time thing. But I'm not responsible for what goes on between you and your husband."

In my memory, I gulped audibly, like a nervous cartoon character. I was nearly certain Matt had been involved in something like this before. Maybe he'd never slept with a married woman or maybe he'd slept with five. Either way, he had no doubt cheated and been with cheaters. What was more, he didn't seem to think it was such an enormous transgression. I know that for plenty of other women, this might have been a red flag, the sure sign of a promiscuous and callous man. But for me, it was a comfort.

When I think about that late afternoon in Matt's sun-streaked kitchen, my sweaty underwear stuck to the seat of his lovely handmade chairs, my lips reaching for water from a spotty glass, it seems like another life, like someone else's memory.

"So, we both have to go to work in a few hours," Matt said.

I sighed. "Oh, right," I said dryly. "Work."

"We should probably arrive separately," he said.

"Are you kicking me out?"

"I was actually wondering if you wanted to order some food," he said. The sun was warm coming through the window—the golden hour lighting up the branches of the leafless tree outside.

I was careful with how I looked at him. "What kind of food?" I asked.

"Pizza?"

I opened my mouth to say I couldn't eat carbs, but I stopped, sucked the words back. It would be easier if I never brought it up. "I live in Bay Ridge," I said. "Not to brag, but my pizza access is pretty much unparalleled."

"Okay, well, what is rare in Bay Ridge? What do I have that you don't?"

"Healthy food," I said. "A nice piece of grilled salmon. And some asparagus."

"Wow, boring," Matt said, but he'd already reached for his phone and was scrolling through the delivery app, quickly finding what I'd asked for.

"Okay, this place has your lame, healthy food and a triple-decker club sandwich, which I would very much like," said Matt. "Do you want french fries?"

"No, thanks."

"Great, more for me."

His apartment on Henry Street was a true one-bedroom with high ceilings, huge windows, and a nonworking fireplace where he kept a record player and its accompanying large speaker. He had an extensive, ornate collection of antique housewares—lamps on every surface, mirrors and paintings leaned against the wall, several crates of porcelain dishes and crystal wineglasses—plus some vintage furniture.

"My friends have an online resale business," he explained. "They pay me to store some of their stuff."

"So, is this your sofa or theirs?" I asked, languishing across an orange velvet midcentury sofa that was more attractive than it was comfortable.

"Theirs," he said. "Once it sells, they'll bring in a new one or I'll be on milk crates."

"Weird!" I said, yawning. "Rotating decor. I like that. Never boring."

My head was heavy, and I knew as soon as our lunch came, as soon as I'd eaten, I'd fall asleep. In *Way to Glow,* Diana Spargel claimed the Radiant Regimen would bring me levels of energy like I'd never known, but so far, I was more sluggish, especially in the afternoon. These recent odd work hours didn't help my fatigue, and afternoon sex, of course, had a similar lulling effect. I liked the feeling, though. I decided I was going to let myself take a nap in this carpenter's house. I think I already understood, in some languid, ill-formed way, how I hoped to be invited back here soon, and then again after that.

When Matt's doorbell buzzed, flat and loud, I jumped in surprise.

"Food's here," he said, pulling a T-shirt over his bare torso before opening the door to go down the stairwell. "Be right back."

He returned a moment later with a paper bag. Though there were several tables to choose from, we ate on the floor at the coffee table, our knees touching. My salmon was fine, exactly what I'd asked for, and I liked knowing I could carry on with the Radiant Regimen no matter how else my routines were broken up, altered, defaced. It was a good sign. After lunch, Matt put *Frasier* on Netflix, shocked when I admitted I'd seen only a few episodes and wasn't sure I liked it. I fell promptly asleep and didn't wake until Matt shook me hours later and told me it was time to go to the bakery. I'd take the subway, and he'd ride his bike. We'd meet there.

CHAPTER ELEVEN

Since February, I'd become an adept liar. It wasn't just the untrue things I said, unflinching, to David and Melissa and Angelo and anyone else who might have wanted or needed to know where I was. I was always lying. My presence in my own home was a lie, my presence at work was a lie, walking down the street in Bay Ridge was a lie. Because everything I did, I did as though nothing had changed. My life, which remained ordinary despite its new element of constant duplicity, exhilarated me. I felt more thrilled than terrified or ashamed, at least during those first weeks.

My deceit was further complicated by the acceleration of David's career. In early March, he was promoted to director of design technology—whatever that meant—and began to work even longer days, spending extra hours in front of his laptop when he was home. It seemed he hardly had time to spend with me, which, contrary to what I'd hoped, made my own busyness more glaring than it might have been. Usually, when David was overloaded, I used the flexibility I enjoyed, as author of the Sweet Cheeks staff schedule, to make sure we got to see each other.

But now, I, too, was preoccupied.

The morning after Easter, David was rushing around the house in a panic to make it to work on time. I sat on the sofa drinking a cup of black coffee. Woogie had climbed into my lap and was demanding that I pet him, taking his paw and pressing it hard into my chest, releasing his claws just the smallest amount.

"Cut it out," I said, and Woogie looked into my eyes, offended, and made a small mew of displeasure. "That hurts," I told him. But I gave in.

I was studying the jumble of cords in the corner of the living room, where the cable box and Wi-Fi router were plugged in. I'd strung up some lights above the media stand. I'd never noticed what a mess the ball of cords was, how ugly and dormlike it made the apartment feel. I noticed it now because Matt had built an attractive cabinet for his own living room; it had a false drawer and a hole in the back, so all the wires were hidden from view. Spending so much time in Matt's apartment, full of beautiful accent pieces and his own handcrafted furniture, made me want to pay more attention to my own decor, a thing I'd rarely thought about before.

"I call this piece *The Preconscious*," Matt had said one day when he opened up the back of the cord-hiding cabinet to reset his Internet. I was jealous and impressed.

"You should sell those," I said. "I'd buy one." I'd been serious, but he laughed. He made all sorts of things I thought he should sell, things I myself would have liked to purchase, though most of it would've been too expensive for me, and neither David nor I was all that interested in interior decorating. I liked useful furniture, items that didn't take up too much space or cost too much money, and David didn't care about furniture, which, due to the nature of his work, he saw as ephemera: inconsequential and deciduous. If we'd sat around on folding chairs and kept our clothes in cardboard boxes, our books stacked on the floor, that would've been fine with him, so long as we had a fast Internet connection. I knew this for certain; it was how he lived when we first met.

David's footfalls sounded heavily in the bedroom above me, and then he came pounding down the stairs. Woogie and I looked at each other. I rolled my eyes.

"I'm out of shirts," he said, coming into the living room.

I lifted my gaze slowly. I said, "I'm sorry to hear that." He breathed out loudly. I'd always dropped off and picked up our dry cleaning. I was the one who had the time and stayed in the neighborhood. I was also the one who usually kept track of these things, knew when the work shirts were nearly all in the hamper, made sure to keep up with the laundry, along with most of our other household chores.

"I have a meeting," he said, nearly whining. "I need a shirt."

David was working on a tower in Seoul. It was going to be sixty-two stories, all glass. He'd been talking about this building—or, rather, he'd been talking about digital renderings of this prospective building—for a long time. I was ready for him to talk about something else, but I'd felt bad about how uninterested I was. Now I was annoyed.

"Is it my responsibility to make sure you have clean shirts?" I asked. "Is that why you came down here with no shirt on?"

"Well, no," he said, surprised. He ran his hand down his bare stomach, looked around, like he'd been struck by amnesia and didn't recognize where he was. "Of course not."

"Because it kind of feels like I'm being accused of something," I said.

"It's just, you always get our laundry," he said. "Which I *really* appreciate. I don't expect you to do it—or, I guess—" He paused, at a loss. "It's just, you didn't mention you *weren't* going to do it. I didn't know I needed to take care of it myself." He sounded so weak as he said this, like a scared child, and guilt flooded me, my moment of righteousness passing before I really had the chance to enjoy it.

"Sorry, Woogie," I said to the cat, and gave him a delicate shove off my lap. He righted himself and glared at me before moving to the other side of the sofa, tail twitching. I went upstairs to the bedroom and opened my dresser. In the bottom drawer, beneath my clothing, were three brand-new men's dress shirts, still wrapped in the tissue paper from the day I'd purchased them. I took one, shook it out. Sometimes, when I went shopping, I bought extra things and hid them from David. He went through laundry like it was disposable, wearing fresh socks to bed, changing his shirts before meetings, leaving dirty underwear in his gym bag for weeks. The hamper was always full.

I shut my dresser quietly and grabbed an undershirt from David's drawer before I went back downstairs, where he was standing in the living room, bewildered.

"Here," I said, handing him the shirts. "I'd been holding out on you."

His face went slack with gratitude. "You're the best," he said. He rested the undershirt on the arm of the sofa.

"No, David," I said. "You have to wear an undershirt."

"But I hate it!" he cried. "I get overheated."

I blinked, exasperated. These domestic arguments were the trenches into which our marriage had disappeared and was festering.

"You get armpit stains on them," I said. "And Sunny can't get them out." Sunny owned the dry cleaner's. "And it's weird not to wear an undershirt. You know, your nipples probably show, in the fluorescent lights at the office."

"Well, I have my vest," David said.

Oh, the vest. The Midtown Uniform. A sleeveless North Face vest with special windproof fleece. I fantasized about burning it in a ritual sacrifice. I hated it, I hated myself for buying David one several years earlier. If only I'd known the dorky ubiquity to come.

"I can't believe this is where I am in the world at this moment," I said. "What's that quote on our fridge magnet? 'What is it you plan to do with your one wild and precious life'? I never thought, Someday I plan to beg a grown man, a man I *married,* to wear an undershirt in case his business-bro vest doesn't cover his nipples. It's kind of a shame. I had a lot of potential."

David put the undershirt on, rolling his eyes. "I didn't think I'd marry someone who quoted poetry off fridge magnets," he said good-naturedly. "But I'm glad I did."

I smiled at him. I wished he'd leave so I could call Matt.

"I know it's totally not your responsibility," he said. "So if you say no, it's fine—I'm just asking so I can plan to do it myself—"

"I'll do the laundry," I said curtly. There was no need to be rude. I was nearly out of underwear myself.

"You don't have to," he said. "I was just asking."

"David," I said. "When is the last time you did laundry?" It was an unanswerable question.

"I appreciate everything you do around here," he said. "I know I don't say it enough. But I'd be lost without you."

"Don't say that," I said.

"Why not? It's true."

My heart lurched, and I felt sweaty at the back of my neck.

"You're going to be late for your meeting," I said. "Get out of here."

AFTER DAVID LEFT, I sat around the living room with Woogie, playing a word-scramble game on my phone. I'd texted Matt, but he hadn't responded; he probably wasn't awake yet.

Moseying into the kitchen, I thought about what meals I should put together for work that day. The Radiant Regimen required more assemblage than actual cooking. Half the recipes were described as "salad"—even ones wherein the main ingredient was something salad-antithetical: wild-caught swordfish or organic grass-fed ground beef or, oh, I don't know, unshelled sunflower seeds. My copy of *Way to Glow!* was dog-eared by now, the back cover stained with splatters of unrefined cooking oil, the whole book softened somewhat from being near stovetop heat so often. I pulled up the Radiant Regimen app on my phone, leaning it against the counter wall, and tapped my finger on the "exclusive subscriber content" tab.

Here were the extra videos, updated a few times a week. Diana Spargel or someone from her handful of personally selected brand ambassadors ("the Regiment," she called them) shared new recipes and program survival tips. Less often, a Regimenter talked about wellness in some nonfood capacity, like "banishing negative self-talk" or "how to reclaim your power and stop caring what people think." This content was not interesting to me. I told myself I would get around to becoming mindful, but first: I wanted to be thin.

Diana's videos were shot at the Radiant Group Headquarters. The stage kitchen had beautiful sand-colored porcelain tile and glass-doored cabinets. They were filled with shallow bowls and tall vases, things no one really kept in the kitchen. Diana was calm and spoke in a soothing, confident way. When she laughed, her crow's-feet showed. You could tell she was right where she wanted to be. She never talked about anything but food. She wasn't full of lame truisms about self-love and the cosmos, like Jess Rain, the astrology Regimenter who posted "spirituality for secular souls" talks in the paid content tab every Sunday. When I'd first started the Radiant Regimen, I'd defended Diana Spargel to David and Melissa, who thought she was a phony, even though I'd secretly agreed with them. But after a few months of watching her videos and following her on Instagram and reading her blog, I'd started to like her.

Before the newest video started, the app played an ad for the Radiant Retreat, a three-day all-inclusive symposium in Wyoming. I'd already read about it in Diana Spargel's newsletter and, for a brief moment, had entertained the idea of spending a hefty chunk of my savings to attend. I'd gone so far as to imagine myself, preposterously, participating in a horseback ride which included an aura reading under a waterfall and a "foraging session" with a professional mycologist. In the end, of course, it was only a kind of digitized window shopping. I didn't want my aura read, and I didn't want to roam the forest in search of my own food.

I'd never ridden a horse, and my strongest association with horses were NYPD mounted units, which had terrified me as a child. Diana Spargel could make things look appealing whether or not they actually appealed to *me*. I was at a precipice, looking into the vast esplanade of the Radiant Group's online wellness empire, but something about who I already was— my education? Melissa's influence? my own self-centeredness?—kept me from falling in.

Diana's newest recipe was for a three-salad medley—one of her "power packs"—meant to be eaten slowly over the course of an hour in the late afternoon, designed specifically for those who had successfully completed the first half of the Radiant Regimen. These were great if one wanted to incorporate intermittent fasting into the program, combining lunch and dinner into one super-meal meant for lasting satiation. I wasn't sure what intermittent fasting was, but I was on board.

"This one is easy," Diana said, looking into the camera. Her hair and skin were soft in the studio's perfect light. "You're going to take your choice of protein—pick from the list on the right—and combine that with this simple vinegar-free vinaigrette."

I paused the video to get some cooked turkey breast out of the fridge. I chopped the turkey into small cubes. Then I found the ingredients for the vinaigrette and set them out. I watched the rest of the video through one eye—mostly listening—as I followed along and made the protein pack, then the green pack (a pound of arugula with fresh herbs, tossed in walnut oil), and finally, the true root pack, the worst one (roasted carrots with chopped celery and daikon in a turmeric brine).

Afterward I went upstairs and put on my work clothes, even though I didn't have to be at Sweet Cheeks for another five hours.

—**Thinking of riding down to yer neighborhood,** Matt texted. **It looks pretty nice outside.**

I peered through the curtains at the bedroom window. The sky was gray and heavy with rainclouds.

—**It doesn't,** I responded. **It looks like it's about to rain.**

—**Sure, but it's warm! In the fifties!**

I checked the weather app. It was fifty-one degrees Fahrenheit.

—**We have very different definitions of good weather,** I wrote.

—**Haha. I'd still like to take a ride,** his next message said. And then: **I want to see that bike path.**

Matt and I had been circling around this conversation for a couple weeks, since I'd off-handedly mentioned the greenway that started at the entrance to the Sixty-ninth Street pier and ran the entirety of Bay Ridge's waterfront and beyond, under the Verrazzano Bridge and past the VA hospital, finally ending down at the Belt Parkway tennis courts. It was a solid five miles of unimpeded bike path. I'd been surprised he hadn't known about it.

I regretted bringing up the greenway, though, because now he tried to get me to come with him, not necessarily for a bike ride (a thing I would never do) but for a walk. The problem with accompanying him down to the Shore Road greenway, or to Cannonball Park, which was on the hill just before the highway and had an impressive view of the bridge, was the same problem I had with every part of my neighborhood and the surrounding sections. I'd see people I knew. As spring turned milder, the pressure to be outdoors with Matt increased.

—**I could come up there & when it's time for me to go to work, you can ride down here. You can stop into the bakery afterward and say hi to everyone!**

Sometimes he asked after Melissa, whom he'd liked, and some of the staff. He hadn't seen any of them since he'd finished installing the shelves a month earlier.

—**Wouldn't it be weird to pretend we haven't seen each other?** he responded right away.

—**Extremely!** I admitted.

He didn't write back for a few minutes. I put my hair into tight French pigtail braids. I remembered our grandmother teaching Melissa and me to braid our hair when we were in high school—she was sick of doing it for us—and how I'd stood over Melissa while our grandmother demonstrated and then watched. When it was Melissa's turn, I'd sat on the upholstered bench at the base of Nonna's bed, and the two of them had taken turns braiding my hair and then undoing it, braiding it again until it was perfect. We'd complained of sore scalps later, and she'd laughed at us, called us a Barese insult that essentially meant "bird skull." It was strange now, knowing I'd once been so close to someone who fixed my hair for me several days a week. I was filled with sadness, thinking of it, of the way her strong hands felt, how she held the front of my skull with an open palm, tilting my head downward while she used her rose quartz comb to draw a clean part.

In my periphery, my phone lit up with a text. I twisted a clear rubber band onto the end of each of my braids and moved to check the messages.

—It's going to full-on rain this afternoon. And: **That's why I want to get out of the house now.**

Matt had never been to my house. I always went to his apartment, usually in the morning before work. I looked around my bedroom, at the queen-size bed, still unmade, at David's rumpled pillows, his flimsy nightstand with its knock-off Anglepoise lamp and an academic-looking book called *Digital Design: Readings from the Field.* The thought of sleeping with Matt in my own bed made me queasy. This had little to do with the shame and sleaziness of betraying David on his own turf, among his own belongings. Nor was it fear of being caught, of somebody noticing the tall stranger on the bicycle coming in and out of the house, how such a thing might be mentioned to David, to Melissa, or—worst of all—to me directly. These possibilities scared me, but what bothered me more was the idea of Matt seeing the inside of my home. I didn't want him to pet Woogie or look at the photos in their frames, pictures of me and David over the past decade, photos of Melissa and me as children, smiling on either side of our grandmother. I didn't want to discuss growing up in the apartment downstairs or my ownership of the property. I didn't want him to see my dog-eared copy of *Way to Glow!* on the counter, along with the various other specialty diet cookbooks and personal transformation literature I had all around.

I decided not to respond. Matt knew David wasn't home in the daytime, and I knew he was hoping I'd invite him over. I was anticipating how the one-sidedness of our arrangement would become irritating to him as things progressed and the thrill of what we were doing wore off.

I started to go through the hamper, which was overflowing. I separated out what needed to go to the dry cleaner, and then the semi-delicate things I dried on a rack. It was several loads. I couldn't remember the last time I'd let the laundry pile up like this.

I was packing everything into an enormous vinyl bag to take to the Laundromat when my phone pinged with another message from Matt. I nearly ran over to the bed where I'd left it.

—So, since you aren't interested in getting a little fresh air with me, what are the chances you want to come over and get naked?

My heart went into my throat. I responded immediately.

—100%

I held my phone in my sweating hand, surveying the laundry on the floor. I could drop off the dry cleaning on my way to the subway and beg Sunny to have it ready the next day. But what about everything else? The Laundromat offered regular wash-and-fold drop-off in addition to the coin-operated self-service I preferred. The idea of giving my laundry over to a stranger to deal with bothered me. I'd inherited from my grandmother many little idiosyncrasies in how I did the wash. A few favorite pairs of socks I didn't put in the dryer, the load of David's gym clothes I washed twice on the cold/delicate cycle in order to get the smelliness out with minimal damage to the spandex and Lycra. No one else could get it right.

I checked the time. It was maddening to choose. I sent Matt another message.

—**I have to run an errand, then I'll be over.**

—**See you soon.**

I gathered the dry cleaning in a tote bag and grabbed my house keys. The rest of it, I'd do after work. The Laundromat was open until midnight.

CHAPTER TWELVE

Matt had propped open the door to his building with a brick so he wouldn't have to buzz me in. When I got upstairs, his apartment was unlocked, and I could hear the shower running inside.

"It's me," I called into the bathroom. Dr. Bronner's scented steam poured from the crack in the door.

Matt shut the water off and came out into the living room wearing only a towel around his waist. He offered me a cup of coffee from the French press on his table.

"I'm already wired," I told him. "I had a lot of coffee. I actually have to pee so bad."

"Watch your step," he said as I went into the bathroom. I shut the door behind me. Matt's bathroom was the best reminder I had of his essential bachelordom. The floor was pocked with his wet footprints; he had no bath mat. While the rest of his place felt cozy and well curated, and in many ways was more adult than my apartment, his bathroom was pretty gross. There was dried toothpaste in the sink, and mildew in the caulk between tiles, even on the walls outside the shower. I don't think he ever cleaned his toilet bowl. The floor was usually dusted with the tiny stubble that flew off his electric razor. I peed quickly and went back out to wash my hands in the kitchen sink. Matt had pulled on a pair of baby-blue boxers but otherwise was still undressed, standing in the middle of his living room, looking at a piece of mail he'd picked off a big stack of unopened letters.

"Anything good?" I asked.

"Oh yeah," he said. "A medical bill for two thousand dollars."

"Jesus Christ, what for?" I asked.

"I got a spider bite last fall," he said. "When I was home over Thanksgiving." He always referred to Cincinnati as home. It made me a little sad, but I wasn't sure why.

"A spider bite?" I said.

"Have you ever heard of a brown recluse?"

I admitted I hadn't, and he put down the bill and picked up his phone to show me a picture of an absolutely vicious-looking spider, and then a few grisly photos of skin afflicted by a brown recluse bite. I wasn't afraid of spiders or vermin in general, but the wounds were horrifying.

"You got a bite like *that*?" I asked.

"I *thought* one bit me," he said. "It's embarrassing. I got bitten by something—probably just a harmless wolf spider—and had a big red welt right here." He pointed to his throat. "I made my brother take me to the ER on Black Friday, convinced—irrationally—it had been a recluse." He ran his hand through his hair and smiled as if to himself. I found him so attractive when he did that, the way he absently pulled back his hair, his amusement with his own story.

"Turns out it's incredibly rare to get bit by a venomous one, but I had been smoking weed with my brothers in our parents' attic since the moment I stepped off the plane. I was paranoid."

"That's an expensive mistake," I said. I wanted to ask if he had health insurance, but we never talked about money. Outside of my strong physical attraction to him, what I relished most about my time with Matt was our lack of need to justify ourselves. He didn't pry into my life. I was alone with him; we had no plans.

"Indeed!" he said. Then he tilted his head to the side and asked jokingly, "Aren't you happy you came over to hear the idiotic story of my hysterical spider bite?"

I took a step closer to him and put three fingers into the elastic of his boxers, moving slowly between cloth and skin. "Oh, that isn't why I came over," I said. All the things we might have said to deepen the conversation fell away. I put my mouth, open, on his chest. He was so much taller than I was; it was as close to his neck as I could reach unless he bent down. He let out an almost inaudible moan of pleasure as I slipped my hand all the way inside his underwear. Then he leaned down to kiss me. We kissed for a long time before moving to the bedroom without speaking. I went to climb onto the bed, but he took my arm and gently turned me back toward him. He shut the bedroom door with his foot; even though he lived alone, he always closed the door when we had sex. His fingers trembled as he undid my polka-dot button-down top, a shirt I kept only because Melissa hated it and complained with real exasperation every time I wore it. It was a horrible mustardy-brown shade, and the black polka dots were, in her opinion, ostentatiously large.

Matt unhooked my bra and kissed the top of my chest. We were both shaking by the time he'd fully undressed me, and in the bed, I thought I was going to come right away. I asked him if we could stop for a second. He said okay, and I could tell how difficult it was for him to slow down. We lay there, kissing and breathing directly into each other's mouths until I said we could keep going. It was always like this, instinctual and visceral. Afterward, we'd hang around Matt's apartment. He liked to run his hands over my skin, down my back and legs. His hands were large and calloused from his work, and the roughness of them was strangely comforting. Later, I'd think about the sex and feel equal parts thrilled and embarrassed.

"I have to leave soon," I told him. We were at a low table in the small alcove made by the bay windows at the front of his apartment, playing cards and looking out onto the street. I was wearing one of his T-shirts, which was so large it came nearly to my knees. Rain had started to fall heavily.

"I should go into the shop, too," he said. Matt had a shared workspace in Gowanus with a collective of other builders and a few installation artists. When he didn't have a large in-house job like the one he'd done at Sweet Cheeks, he made commissioned furniture. I'd gotten the sense that he didn't have a lot of work at this point in time.

"I wish we could stay here," I said.

He reached out and took my bare foot in his hand. "I don't know what you mean," he said, laughing. "It's so nice out." We looked out the windows, where the rain was heavy now, splashing against the glass.

I groaned. It would be slow at the bakery, and the customers who did come by would be cranky from the weather, and the Girls would be just as cranky from boredom, and Angelo would behave like a maniac about people tracking wet shoes through the dining room.

"Do you have time for lunch before you go?" he asked, but jokingly. Besides delivery from the restaurant with the grilled salmon, which Matt didn't like very much, I refused offers to join him for meals.

"Do you want to share mine?" I asked, pointing toward my canvas tote on the floor where I had my prepacked Tupperwares inside an insulated lunch bag. The thought of that food now, with no Diana Spargel video to accompany it, was appealing only insofar as I was already pretty hungry. "I have three kinds of salad."

"How tempting," Matt said, climbing to his feet and heading toward the kitchen. "But I think I'll pass."

I got dressed and brushed my hair while he stood in the wide doorway between his living room and little galley kitchen, eating a piece of cold pizza.

"How old is that?" I asked, grimacing.

"Honestly, I'm not sure," he said. "Hans brought it over yesterday, but I think he and Allie ordered it on Saturday." Hans and Allie were Matt's closest friends. They were the married couple who owned the vintage and antique resale business; it was their lovely inventory that populated Matt's apartment. It seemed they were around whenever I wasn't. Matt peeled a slice of pepperoni off and pretended to inspect it before popping it into his mouth. "I never would've guessed a person who owned a bakery would be such a health nut," he said.

"I don't own a bakery," I said, and he made a dismissive face, as if to say *Don't split hairs,* but he dropped the subject and started talking about a movie he wanted to see at Film Forum, some dark comedy from New Zealand based on a comic book. I got the sense that I should have heard of it, but I had no idea what he was talking about.

"I think you and I belong to different subsets of the Internet," I said. "I get, like, blender advertisements. I never get movie trailers."

"Never?" he asked.

"I mean, maybe I do and I just don't know it because I scroll right past them."

"What movies do you see?"

"I used to see all the scary ones," I said. "And I still think horror movies are the best. I especially like when there's a serial killer. Something to make my heart pump—otherwise I feel like my heart is racing over nothing all the time."

"I see," he said, and shrugged without much interest.

THE PREVIOUS SATURDAY, DAVID had gone with me to the supermarket. Food shopping was an ordeal on the Radiant Regimen; there was so much to buy. In the beginning, I'd tried to stay in Bay Ridge, cobbling together our program-compliant grocery list by going to the halal butcher, the fish market, so many different produce stalls, and the health food store up by Leif Ericson Park. It was too much. Now we went to Whole Foods. It was alarmingly crowded for eleven a.m.

"Why do I feel like I'm at Columbus Circle during rush hour?" David said as we attempted to shimmy our shopping cart around the produce section.

"Because there's a Whole Foods in Columbus Circle, too, and it's always packed," I said. "Remember when Melissa used to work up there? My God, I thought it was all so fancy."

"It *is* fancy," David said. "This bunch of radishes is three-ninety-nine? Am I reading the sign correctly?"

"I'm afraid so."

David rolled his eyes. He was still doing the Radiant Regimen with me, and for the most part, he was a good sport. But I could tell he was over it.

"Why is the program seventy-five days?" he asked. "Whole30 felt endless—this is over twice as long and even stricter."

"That's how long it takes to fully cleanse the blood of toxins," I said in an ironic way. "Seventy-five days and you've got liquid gold running through your veins!"

"Do you really buy that?" David asked. "I'm not trying to be a downer, but— Well, I guess when you say things like 'cleanse the blood,' it doesn't sound like you."

We rounded the cart into the meat department, took a number at the counter.

I was quiet for a minute. I said, "I don't know. I know that preservatives and processed foods are bad. And I know that I like to eat as healthy as possible. But, like, do I think root vegetables are some sort of magical elixir? No."

David said, "But you always want everything to be so exact."

"Well, I'm a good student," I said. "I love an assignment."

The butcher called our number and we ordered a hundred dollars' worth of meat, then moved on to the seafood counter.

"You know, you don't have to finish the Radiant Regimen with me," I said. "I get it. It's a lot to ask. I wouldn't be mad if you wanted to have a beer with your friends after work and do all the things socially that Radiant Regimen ruins."

He didn't respond and looked pensive as we walked through the dairy section, where there was nothing we could eat.

"When this is over," David finally said, "let's go to Clinton Street Baking Company. Chicken and waffles. Blueberry pancakes."

"Biscuits and gravy with poached eggs and bacon," I found myself saying, entranced at the thought.

"Then we'll spend the rest of the day bar hopping. Champagne toasts all over the city."

"We'll see. Maybe the Radiant Regimen will have transformed us by then. We won't be interested anymore in waiting on a two-hour line for breakfast or drinking until we're cross-eyed."

"I really hope not," David said.

We checked out and waited for a cab in front of the store.

"Hey," David said. "Isn't your yoga studio close by?"

"Hmmm?" I said, distracted. "My what?"

"Where you go to yoga—didn't you say it was up here somewhere?"

"Oh," I said. I tried not to blush. "It's Pilates. I've been taking Pilates."

"You've been taking *a lot* of Pilates," David said. "What is Pilates, anyway?"

My heart sped up. "It's, um, well—there's a machine. And you stretch on it. You work your core."

"What kind of machine?" David said, his interest piqued by the introduction of equipment.

"It's—it's kind of hard to describe. Google it when we get in the car," I said as our ride pulled up. The driver popped the trunk, and as we loaded our exorbitant groceries, I remembered something I'd heard about Pilates and said, "It's supposed to make your muscles long and lean."

"You can check the lean part off your list," David said, squeezing my skinny arm. I followed him into the backseat of the car, said hello to the driver, confirmed our address. "I don't think it's doing much for your muscles, though."

David took out his phone and looked up the Pilates reformer machine and, thankfully, repeated everything he learned during the ride home.

The thing was: I kept meaning to go to Pilates. I didn't want Pilates to be just a lie I told David about where I was when I was with Matt. But I never went because Matt was always available. He was easier.

I WAS FIFTEEN MINUTES late to work and came in drenched. Matt had offered to let me borrow an umbrella, but the one he had was too nice— an enormous windproof contraption with Teflon coating and vents— and I wouldn't have been able to explain where I'd acquired it, and everyone would certainly ask, incredulous, about the price and when I purchased it and where.

When I walked into the bakery through the back door, Melissa and Angelo were in the kitchen and dropped whatever petty argument they'd been having to join forces in giving me a hard time.

"You're soaked," Melissa said, agitated, as though it weren't raining and I had no excuse for such unprofessionalism. Behind her, Matt's impressive shelves already held too many dishes. The design had been perfect; nearly to ceiling height and sturdy, the wood treated to the nicest shade, sanded to smoothness. There were industrial grates and fasteners between each eave, giving the whole thing a steampunk feel. The interior panels were sturdy and deep, cubby-like, and on each end, he'd installed ladder-style shelving with ingenious swinging storage space. We stuck random pantry items—sprinkles, food dye, piping tools— inside. It was distinctive as well as functional.

"You're dripping all over the floor," Angelo said. "Someone is going to fall and sue us."

"I guess you'd better get the mop," I said, peeling off my jacket. I opened the empty oven doors and turned on the fan, let the stored warmth blow over me. Melissa and Angelo immediately complained, their loud voices knocking over each other so it was a cacophony of useless "whoas" and "are you kidding me right nows."

"That's dangerous," Melissa said.

"Just let me dry off," I said. "If you cared about me not getting soaked, you could have come and picked me up," I snapped at Angelo, though of course if I'd wanted that, I should have asked, and I hadn't asked because I hadn't been home.

Guillermo, who'd been ignoring us from the dish pit, came over with the mop and began to clean up around me.

Melissa picked up a card from her workstation. "We got some mail," she said, holding out the envelope. She had a smirk on her face, and so I knew who it was before she said. "Eddie and Jaclyn."

"I could tell," I said. "Just by the way you're looking at me." We both laughed.

Angelo looked over and rolled his eyes at us in a sympathetic way. "That fucking guy," he said, shaking his head and grinning.

EDDIE EMIDIO WAS OUR father. Jaclyn was his wife. They lived in California, in the desert, and we didn't know them very well. They were kind of a joke to us. Eddie had been nineteen years old and shipped out to the marine recruit center in San Diego when Melissa and I were toddlers. He was still in the service or somehow associated with it, maybe a defense contractor? They lived by a huge base. Jaclyn was tan in a leathery way and had absurd hair—overbleached chunky highlights cut into a fried-looking bob. They had two daughters of their own who were teenagers now. Our half sisters had idiotic names: Brylee and Kaylin. They competed in beauty pageants. We'd met them a handful of times, when Eddie brought them to visit his parents, who lived in New Jersey, but the relationship existed mostly through social media. Melissa and I enjoyed making fun of things all four of them posted online, including their recent enthusiasm for the whole MAKE AMERICA GREAT AGAIN thing. ("So creepy!" Melissa had said the week before, holding her phone to show me a photo Jaclyn had posted of Eddie in his red hat.)

While I experienced a kind of permanent grief about my mother-lessness, a dull but manageable sadness like a low-grade fever, my prevailing feeling about Eddie Emidio was one of enormous gratitude for his having been too young and dumb and maybe even bereaved to have stuck around and helped raise us. He had not petitioned for visitation rights when our grandparents had taken guardianship of us. Eddie was a superficially nice enough man who was, as Melissa liked to put it, just not our cup of tea. We knew him well enough to know not to grieve his absence.

I'll never forget being sixteen and looking at Eddie over my laminated menu at the TGI Friday's where we'd all met for a post-Christmas gathering. We did something like this every few years. Melissa and I dreaded these occasions, saw them as a socially awkward waste of our precious teenage time. Eddie felt my eyes on him and looked up, smiling in a way that pained me, and said, "You guys want to start with some of them *yalo-peno* poppers?" and Jaclyn had said, "Ooooooh," and raised her eyebrows at us like we were imbeciles, or like we'd never been to a chain restaurant. Now I realize she was just incredibly nervous, but at the time it seemed like she thought Melissa and I were space aliens.

I'd thought, How? It was obvious he'd been involved in my and Melissa's creation from a genetics standpoint; we had inherited Eddie's pronounced jaw and serious, dark eyebrows. But it was difficult to imagine our mother—our idea of our mother, which was really a collection of ideas we had about ourselves—in a serious relationship with *this* guy, in his golf shirt and wraparound sunglasses. I'd turned to Melissa and made a wide-eyed *kill me* face, and our grandmother had given us a stern look before returning to her menu; I could tell she was struggling to find something that looked like food. Nonna had invited Eddie and his family to Brooklyn for a home-cooked meal, but he'd claimed his parents wanted to see Melissa and me as well, and for some reason this resulted in all of us, a party of nine, seated around a huge table in a restaurant attached to a New Brunswick shopping mall. There was just no reconciling this person—a military man with a barbwire tattoo and a wife who referred to all varieties of soda as "Coke"—with the kind of people Melissa and I were even as teenagers: sarcastic and border-line urbane, food snobs, progressives. I thought grimly that my mother must have been so depressed to have been with this guy. Honestly, his own parents seemed baffled, especially by Jaclyn, who was from Orange County originally but had a twinge of inexplicable southern accent. Eddie's parents were suburban versions of my grandmother. None of this made any sense.

NOW I TOOK THE mail from Melissa and saw an invitation, printed in glittery gold ink, to Brylee's high school graduation.

"Holy shit," I said. "Is she really a senior in high school?"

"Apparently!" Melissa said. "And she's smart enough to make sure we get the memo, too. Education pays! How much should we send her?"

"Ugh," I said. "A hundred?"

"I can't believe you send them gifts," Angelo said.

"Mind your business," Melissa retorted, but truthfully, I think we sent gifts—always money—to our half sisters only to preserve our sense of superiority. It was difficult to think of Brylee Emidio, basically a stranger, as a real adult person out in the world. Would she attend college? If not, would she move away from Twentynine Palms, California? I'd never visited, but it looked in their online photos like the kind of place a person escaped after turning eighteen. Of course, I'd thought the same thing about Bay Ridge when I was a teenager, and I'd only ever moved a few miles away. Anyway, I was still here.

Violet busted into the kitchen just then, her half apron falling down her narrow hips. She moved to adjust it.

"Do you need backup?" I asked.

"Not unless you're willing to tell Marian and Babe they're banned for life," she said, rolling her eyes. Marian and Babe were two octogenarians—sisters—who came in a few times a week and played cards or scratched off stacks of lottery tickets for hours at a time. They were always crabby and complaining. Once Marian had advised me to purchase concealer to cover my under-eye circles, which was the kind of rude, weird shit you never really get used to when you work in service. People, even people you see so often you know them, think they can say whatever they want. Things they'd never say to an acquaintance in any other setting. But I always just laughed them off, especially Marian. In her twenties, she'd won the New York City handball championship five times. Now she lived with Babe, and they walked with canes and tested their blood sugar and played tedious lotto games all day, and everyone treated them like they should be invisible. I forgave them.

"I'm afraid not," I said.

"What's that?" Violet asked, gesturing to the invitation in my hand. "Catering job?"

"I wish," Melissa said. "Our father's kid is having a graduation party in the California boonies. Want to go?"

"You have a father?" Violet asked, and in unison, Melissa, Angelo, and I answered, "Not really."

"Okay, well," she said. "Does anyone want anything from the pizzeria? I'm going on break."

"Kit does," Melissa said, and everyone laughed at her hilarious joke. I didn't bother defending myself.

When Violet was gone, Angelo said, "She's mad nosy," but his tone was more objective than condemning.

"She just likes us," Melissa said, batting Angelo's appraisal away with a dismissive gesture. "Everyone's been around so long, or is from the neighborhood, we forget when somebody has to get to know us. If you two weren't so in love with yourselves, you'd ask her questions, too."

"Oh, please," I said. "I know way more about Violet than both of you put together, and you met her a month earlier."

"Are you bragging about that now?" Angelo asked. "About how you quit your job the busiest week of the year and left us high and dry?"

"I have work to do," I said, because I was never going to apologize.

"We all have work to do," Melissa said. I handed back Brylee's graduation party invitation, and Melissa dropped it, without fanfare, into the wastebasket.

CHAPTER THIRTEEN

Not long before sunset that night, when the rain had finally slowed to a sprinkle, a pale double rainbow appeared across the edge of the sky, ghostlike. A customer told us to make sure we got a look, so Violet and I stepped outside for a few minutes, leaving Athena, who relished any chance to sneak her phone out while I wasn't looking.

On the sidewalk, the smells of wet pavement and ozone were my first premonition of true spring that year. Violet and I were still underdressed without jackets, but we stood arm to arm in our cotton shirts rolled to the elbows, and looked, like everyone else on the street, at the spectacular rainbow over the bridge.

"I miss being in nature," Violet said, turning to me. She shivered. "I miss seeing the stars." I kept my gaze on the sky. An airplane appeared from the ether, as though birthed by the clouds, and began to descend. Then another airplane, and another, in the endless chain to JFK, Newark, and LaGuardia. All the airports had flight paths over the neighborhood.

"For some reason I thought you were from a city," I said.

Violet let out a wry laugh, like the first note of a song. "I mean,

Centreville's not the sticks or anything. It's an hour from D.C.," she said. "But it's ten minutes in another direction from, like, three different state forests. Have you ever been camping?"

"I haven't," I said. I honestly wasn't sure I'd even been in what Violet called a forest. David and Benji had gone to sleepaway camp upstate as kids. Sometimes David reminisced about camping and fishing and getting a stiff neck from looking up at the hundreds of stars in the black night sky. I always listened respectfully, even though none of it sounded so great to me. It sounded like the absence of being anywhere, like being lost. The idea of going so far from the road that you couldn't hear the cars made me anxious. True wilderness, to me, was a mythical place, a setting for historical events and stories about demons and murderers. It was "Hansel and Gretel," Stephen King novels, *Deliverance*. I told Violet this. I did not tell her the closest I'd ever come to considering being in nature, as it were, was the Radiant Retreat in Wyoming.

"You might like camping," Violet said. Matt had said something similar a week earlier, telling me about a bachelor party he was helping to organize for a friend from high school. Matt had wanted to wait until Memorial Day weekend, when the group of guys could rent a cabin at a place in Kentucky 150 miles south of the Cincinnati suburb they were from. He was disappointed the timing wasn't going to work out; the wedding was in June, and varying schedules had resulted in a choice to go to Nashville instead. I remembered that trip was soon. Was it this coming weekend? Next weekend?

Matt, like Violet, had made a passive case for me as a potential nature lover. ("You love to talk about the weather and the sky," he'd said. It was true but irrelevant. The sky was everywhere.) What they saw in me—a person who ate only organic food and couldn't drive a car—was not something I myself was able to find, no matter how close I tried to look. I thought how it would be nice to confide in Violet about Matt. That was the hardest thing about how chilly Violet was. Out of pride and, to a lesser extent, sense of professional boundaries, I kept my distance from Violet. But I wondered what it would be like to have her as a friend. I wished she liked me. With a true friend to confide in, my affair with Matt could be a point of mutual fascination, free of judgment or scorn.

I HADN'T MADE A new friend in a long time. Not a real one, at least.

Right around the time I'd met David, I'd befriended Vanessa Cohen, my verbal assignments partner in Advanced French Conversation. She was a Long Islander with one of those archetypal Long Island girl voices: deep but subdued, sounding bored all the time. She could be funny and charming, but I remember her best for her exceptional rudeness.

"Wow, I really got the shaft," she told me about a month into the term, while we were supposed to be practicing for a presentation. "I'm not even supposed to *be* at CUNY."

We were at a vegetarian restaurant in the Village, one of those tiny fern-filled places with green-painted floors and beaded curtains that were all over lower Manhattan back then. The air was heavy with the scent of nag champa, so much so that all the food kind of tasted like incense. Vanessa had insisted we meet on Eighth Street because she had plans nearby after we were done studying. This was inconvenient for me, as I had to go back uptown for work, but I hadn't wanted to tell her that.

She frowned over her cucumber salad. "My two best friends are studying abroad in Paris right now," she said. "For a whole year. They go to NYU. I was supposed to go to NYU, too."

"Oh," I said helplessly. I'd been kind of excited about practicing our French and was growing increasingly troubled that it didn't seem like that was going to happen. The moment I'd sat down, I had taken out my notecards and laid them conspicuously on the table; a week earlier, Vanessa had chattered on during the other practice session we'd had, and our presentation was scheduled for the end of the week. It was now Tuesday. I had studied my part at home and knew it by heart, but I was pretty sure Vanessa hadn't so much as looked at her lines.

"It's bullshit," Vanessa said. "And now I only get to go to Paris for one semester, because CUNY's French exchange program doesn't have a whole-year option."

She paused expectantly, and I realized I was supposed to inquire further.

"So, why aren't you?" I said. "At NYU, I mean."

"Because the admissions people are *retarded*," she said. I looked around, ashamed, to see if anyone had heard. "Like, I had *two* C's in high school. I didn't get *bad* grades! I got straight A's in, like, half of my classes. But here I am"—she gestured inexplicably at the couscous dish I was eating—"at City College, which isn't even a *real* school."

She rolled her eyes dramatically. To this day, I have trouble imagining what Vanessa expected me to say in response to this insulting opinion. I was the first person in my family to be getting a bachelor's, and City College had been my top choice.

"So you didn't get in?" I asked. As in: *Is this just a story about how you were rejected by a prestigious college?* She'd made it sound like some kind of scandal had taken place.

"Thank God I had applied here for my safety," she said, not answering me.

I was twenty years old and in awe of young people like Vanessa, who wore clothes from the dELiA*s catalog and smoked American Spirit cigarettes and, as a consolation for not spending the year in France with her two best friends, was subletting a studio apartment on the twentieth floor of a Lincoln Square high-rise. It belonged to an elderly couple from her family's synagogue in Oyster Bay. I had been to the apartment the week before, for our first rehearsal attempt, and she'd made a point of complaining about how much her parents were paying for the place. "They don't even *use* it," she'd said of the owners. "They bought it when

Mr. Bernal worked in the city. That was, like, the eighties. He's retired now. All they do is go on cruises."

My body sank ever more cozily into the Bernals' leather sofa as I listened. There was a view of the Hudson from the windows. We were drinking chardonnay that I was pretty sure belonged to the old couple; Vanessa had rifled in the back of the fridge for it, then examined the label for several minutes before finally uncorking the bottle.

Our presentation, delivered in front of the class, was to be the first and easiest of the semester's major assignments. All we had to do was recite a few lines from a French film, novel, or play of our choice. It didn't make sense to me why I even needed a partner for this particular task. We'd chosen *Amélie,* which I owned on VHS. I'd come to Vanessa's apartment with the tape, assuming we'd watch our scene, wherein Amélie defends Lucien when Old Man Collignon calls him a vegetable. I was going to be the narrator, and Vanessa would say Amélie's lines, which were brief and relatively simple.

But when I'd arrived, Vanessa seemed to be under the impression that we were going to watch the whole movie, because she hadn't seen it in two years. I didn't protest. In fact, I had been excited to realize suddenly that we weren't just studying, we were *hanging out.* But then Vanessa had talked through the entire movie and hadn't shown particular interest when our presentation scene came on and I asked her to turn up the volume.

"So," she said when the movie ended. "Tell me what we're doing for this. Like, did you write down what I'm supposed to say?"

For our lunch meeting in the Village, I had indeed copied down her lines for her. Besides the looming presentation, something about Vanessa made me uneasy. From the distance of my bona fide adulthood, I can see that my uneasiness had to do with how much Vanessa sucked, but when I was a college junior, I wanted to impress this rich girl who had her own credit card.

We started hanging out. Vanessa bombed all our French assignments, but it didn't affect my grade. In her shoes, I would have been embarrassed to be fumbling through each presentation, reading her part off notecards while our classmates gave each other looks, but she was unfazed. The professor told me once, in office hours, that I was generous to have partnered with Vanessa. In actuality, I'd had no idea we had a choice. The 1 train had stalled, so I had arrived, breathless as usual, about ten minutes late to the first day of class. When I sat down in the back next to Vanessa, she'd turned to me and said matter-of-factly: "You're my convo partner, FYI."

I had been apprehensive to tell Vanessa I worked in a café, because I assumed she'd think I was poor, but she was actually impressed when she found out. "Like Rachel," she'd said, referring to Jennifer Aniston's character on *Friends*.

Sometimes Vanessa came by and hung around during my shifts, getting me in trouble with my tables and my coworkers, as she had no respect for boundaries. She'd call me over to talk about her bad grades and her anxieties over her friends studying in Paris without her. She had a paranoid side, and her feelings of jealousy and inadequacy over not being with them manifested as wild, highly unlikely scenarios in which they were plotting to exclude her forever. I always listened and expressed sympathy, flattered to be included in her drama while simultaneously bored and worried about my job.

IT WAS VANESSA WHO introduced me to my first diet, Weight Watchers. Vanessa was always on a diet, constantly counting and configuring, talking about her body in derogatory terms—her big thighs, her fat ass— even more than she talked about her traitorous friends or bad grades or overpriced sublet. Vanessa was short and compact, her shoulders square and her back muscled from playing volleyball in high school. None of the things she said about herself made any sense. Perfect student that

I was, though, I took an interest. Vanessa carried around a branded FlexPoints calculator in her mini backpack and used it at every meal. She did Tae Bo tapes on Saturday mornings and ordered Salad Shakers when we went to McDonald's after class.

"There's really no other way to get the dressing even," she'd say, shaking furiously. "And you burn calories doing this!"

I hadn't thought much about dieting but quickly became hooked. When I try to think of any real thing I said to Vanessa, any moment of true intimacy outside of her long monologues, all I can remember is how I started to talk with her, daily, about calories and which low-fat snack foods were the best-tasting. I liked the game of it and how much control it gave me. I felt an ownership over my body and my brand-new adulthood.

VANESSA AND I CYCLED through each other's lives for the next few years. Senior year, when she was back from her semester abroad, we hung out in the afternoons. She still wanted help with her coursework. But her friends, her *real* friends, were back at NYU, and she spent most of her time downtown. It didn't seem to occur to her to invite me along. After graduation, we became close again for a few months while she was applying for graduate school to be a teacher ("You get every summer off") and wanted help studying for the GRE, someone to proofread her statement of purpose.

She was the last new friend I'd made, really. I hadn't seen her in over a decade. In our mid-twenties, I turned down her invitations to meet for a drink, and after a couple of attempts, she didn't ask again. Sometimes I Google her name, but "Vanessa Cohen New York City" is a long shot. Even on Facebook, I was never able to find her. I guessed she—like I had—had gotten married and had a new name.

The fact of the matter was I'd become intrigued by Violet during our first couple months working together. She was no Vanessa Cohen. For one thing, Violet *had* attended NYU. But my admiration for her was similar. Violet was smart and wry and plain-speaking. Unlike Vanessa, she had a clear handle on the subjectivity and sensitivity of others. Her style was really good—she was the kind of person who understood what clothes looked best on her and purchased the right things. Not like me, snapping the hangers across the racks at Century 21 without a mission or even an inkling of whether some trendy tulle skirt or mid-length linen tunic would flatter me. And Violet was so perfectly thin. In private, I studied her social media profiles. She was very good at social media, especially photo sharing. Her Instagram account was a pale gallery of photos she took of herself in particularly photogenic spaces, like the art deco–y bathroom of a cocktail bar on Atlantic Avenue, and under the perfect diluted light of the American Wing café at the Met, and aglow beneath a pink floor lamp in an apartment filled with large leafy plants: her spine arched, shoulder blades revealed like wings in a backless jumpsuit, hands clasped at her waist. She took photos of meals, of art, of herself. She was neither an overposter like Athena nor a lurker like me. Angelo had given her the password to the bakery's social media pages and told her to post at least once on each platform whenever she worked. She'd had no formal photography experience but nonetheless was quite good at making GIFs and videos of goings-on at the bakery: cakes being frosted, egg whites as they were beaten to meringue in the electric mixer, steam whistling from the espresso machine. I thought she was so cool. I was annoyed by how much I liked her and would have denied it to anyone.

"My *halemoni*—my grandmom—loved to go hiking," Violet said. "We took a long walk around a big lake in the woods every Tuesday until I left for college." She sniffed the air. "I miss her."

"I miss my nonna, too," I said. "So much." My grandmother had not, to my knowledge, ever been hiking.

"I'm sure it's even harder for you," Violet said. "Since your grandmother was like your actual parent." I wondered how much Violet knew about my and Melissa's upbringing and who had told her these things; certainly not Melissa and probably not Angelo. Tiana or Athena—one of the staff members who'd been working at the bakery a long time— though I struggled to imagine either of them finding me interesting. Maybe the staff all gossiped about us, and Violet was simply the one comfortable enough to reveal she'd been doing so. Hiram often told David and Benji that it was none of their business what other people said about them. It was a good point, though impossible to believe and put into practice. I was flattered by Violet's apparent interest but also sure I had nothing interesting I could actually reveal. If I had a life like the one Violet showcased on Instagram—or, even better, the skills and self-efficacy to make my life look a certain way—I imagined I'd be more comfortable talking about myself.

Violet and I looked at the sky another minute. I felt at ease with her, as comfortable as I had been earlier at Matt's apartment, when he was undressed and no one could see us. The way I'd felt with Melissa when we were kids. And then David, for years, until I started lying to him all the time. It was an ease I never had anymore.

Violet took a deep breath. The sky's purple deepened more with each passing minute, and I wanted to stay there and watch it. Finally, though, Violet turned to look into the dining room and said, "Oh, there's a line at the counter. I think Athena's pissed."

WHEN I GOT HOME from work that night, David was in the shower with the bathroom door closed. He was certainly masturbating. I stood at the door for a moment and then walked on tiptoes up to the bedroom, where I took off all my clothes and put on my bathrobe, leaving it open. I sat on the bed, reading the news on my phone.

Sometimes David and I had sex early in the morning, after Woogie woke us up, warbling in our faces like a starving stray, demanding to be fed. Coming back from the kitchen, I'd slide my body against David's bare back, pressing my hand against his warm skin, beneath the waistband of his boxers until he stirred. Once roused, he'd turn over and pull me close, yank my panties away from my hips and down my legs with a kind of groggy efficiency. He'd ask, "Is this okay?" and when I said yes, we'd fuck in silence. Then we both fell back asleep. Along with a few quickies in the shower, these morning encounters were the only way we'd had sex for over a year.

The water finally turned off, and I heard the shower door squeal as he opened it. With undoubtedly wet feet, David climbed the stairs up to the bedroom, towel around his waist.

"Hi!" he said. "I didn't hear you come in."

If he noticed my nakedness beneath the open robe, he didn't mention it. I couldn't blame him. Every night before bed, he stripped off his clothing and walked through the apartment to the shower with his firm ass and strong, hairy legs in full view, but the sight alone did nothing to arouse me anymore. For each of us, the other's nudity had lost its eroticism. Sometimes I'd get out of the shower and spend a full fifteen minutes sitting naked on the edge of the bed, scrolling through my phone before I finally started getting dressed. We'd done this to ourselves and to each other; we'd let sex become just another thing to do.

David put on his underwear, asking me how my day was. I watched him. He was aging well and not just because he was a man. He was in good shape, far stronger and sturdier than when we'd met in undergrad. His muscles were larger now and firmer; his beard was full, and he kept it cropped close so his features were visible, defined; his hair was still thick.

Instead of answering David's inquiry about how my day was, I said, "Do you want to have sex?" I blurted it out in an unappealing way, not moving to touch him—no seduction, no desire in my voice. It was rough. An accusation, a challenge. I was really saying: *I know you just jerked off.*

He picked up his phone from the nightstand to check the time. "It's late, baby," he said. He looked embarrassed. He kissed me several times. His kisses were soft and reassuring. David knew exactly what I liked; he'd had years of practice.

I wondered: Is this why people have children, even if they aren't sure it's the right thing for them, even if they don't feel ready? So they can feel something intense or new again? Or to distract themselves from the fact that they don't?

"It's okay," I said. "Just thought I'd ask." I kissed him back. I was friendly about it, a good sport.

We got under the covers.

"Guess who I was thinking about today," I said.

"I give up."

"Vanessa Cohen."

"Oh, man," he said, a wistful smile across his face. "Your problematic fave. I wonder what happened to her."

"I doubt much of anything," I said. "She probably married a doctor and had some really cute kids, lives back on the Island. In a big house on the water, even bigger than the one she was raised in."

David laughed. "I bet she's miserable."

I thought of saying more about Vanessa, asking David if he knew how much she, with her persuasive calorie obsession, had changed my life, but I could see he wanted to retreat to the privacy of his phone.

I got my own phone out, snuggling up with it. Next to me, David scrolled through Twitter. Every few minutes, he laughed at something, but I'd stopped bothering to ask what was so funny a long time ago. Even if he showed me something that was indeed funny, that was a huge waste of time. If it was good enough, it would float into my own feed soon.

I was distracted, anyway, wondering how my cheating would eventually play out. I'd started thinking lately about how it couldn't just go on forever.

I found myself Googling "How to get over a broken heart." I wasn't sure why I chose this particular question. Did I fear a breakup with Matt would break my heart? Not really. Maybe I was thinking about David, about what it would be like to lose my marriage when David found out about Matt? Or was my heart already broken—was the heartbreak from the present moment, the moment of having too much, of feeling so empty anyway, of knowing myself to be a liar, of not knowing what I should do next?

The first link was from a women's magazine promising expert advice in eight simple steps. I clicked. Step one was "Embrace Your Heartbreak." *Don't try to ignore the hurt,* the article said. *Don't distract yourself with meaningless rebound sex or gallons of ice cream or drunken nights out clubbing. Those are cowardly approaches. It takes courage to be sad and to focus on your sadness. Ask yourself what your sadness can do for you.*

I thought: Okay, well, there's a load of poorly reasoned horseshit. These weren't clear steps, just a list of what *not* to do. There weren't any actionable suggestions for what the heartbroken might do *instead.* Should I embrace my sadness at the gym? The mall? On vacation? At a Heartbroken Anonymous meeting?

The next step was just as vague. "Know the Difference Between Grief and Depression," it said. I was so mad I could've screamed, right there under my covers.

I went back to the search results, but every link led to more or less the same article: a condescending list of inapplicable truisms or unrealistic, bossy "don'ts." *Don't engage! Block your ex's phone number and unfollow him on social media.*

Most of these silly suggestions didn't apply to my situation. I was being proactive. This was heartbreak-preparedness Googling.

So I Googled: "How to get over an affair."

The first link was: "How to Survive Betrayal." The second: "Forgiveness and Infidelity: Can Couples Move Past It?" Number three: "The Phases of Recovering from Your Husband's Cheating." The fourth, fifth, and sixth each explored various answers to questions around whether it was worth trying to save a relationship with an unfaithful spouse.

"I'm going to sleep," David said, putting his phone facedown on his nightstand.

"Me, too," I said, closing my browser.

"Good night, Kit. I love you."

"I love you, too," I said, and we kissed again: a simple, perfunctory peck. Nothing was revealed in our lips coming together for the millionth time, none of our secrets or failures or disappointments. It was a thing we might as well have stopped doing if it weren't for the fact that kissing still felt good, put us as close to each other as we could get.

CHAPTER FOURTEEN

A chasm was opening up between me and David. I started to pick fights.

We rode the train together one morning at rush hour, when he was going to work and I had a dentist's appointment. We'd gone only a few stops when he began to dig through his coat pockets, then the nylon sling pack in which he carried his computer and gym clothes.

"What's wrong?" I said. "Did you lose something?"

"My phone battery is dead." He looked distressed.

"Don't you have that portable charger I bought you?" I asked. Then I saw the object in question was already in his hand. "You don't have a cord?"

"No," he said. "I have no clue what happened to mine."

I opened my pocketbook and removed my own lightning cable, wound carefully around a rubber loop that fastened with a snap. Melissa had bought a pack of six and given Angelo and me each one along with some advice: "Get your lives under control."

"Neato," David said dorkily, taking the cable from me. As he unwound it, he began to laugh. "This looks like you let rats chew on it." He held up the top of the cord where the rubbery sheath had frayed, revealing the braid of stringlike wires inside. He was smiling like this was charming or sweet.

My heart sped up with a sudden infusion of anger. "Why are you picking on me?" I snapped.

"What?" he said, confusion rippling across his face. "I'm not."

"You always have some little dig," I said, folding my arms across my chest. "Like everything I do is some big joke to you. Meanwhile, you don't even know *where* your cable is."

He stared at me, baffled. "I know that," he said. "I wasn't criticizing you—"

I cut him off. "Yours could be in the goddamn trash, for all we know, but you have the gall to criticize mine for being well used."

"I swear I didn't mean to criticize you."

"Then why bring it up?" I said loudly. Someone sitting near us was eavesdropping. I saw her take an earbud out and lean in our direction. It was one of those embarrassing subway arguments, where strangers judge you for losing your cool but it's too late; you don't care and carry on as though in private. "You always have some taunt that's pointless except for the purpose of needling me and implying there's something wrong with me."

"Okay, I'm sorry," David said, the hurt falling from his expression. "But this seems overblown."

I didn't answer. I pretended to listen to a podcast, ignoring him until it was my stop at Eighth Street–NYU. My dentist's office was on Christopher Street, in the basement of a big apartment building with long marble floors.

"Have a good day," David said as I stood to push my way off the train. He sounded uncertain and sad. I nodded meanly and left without looking back, knowing he'd probably think about my accusation all the way to Fifty-seventh Street.

* * *

MY PHONE RANG AS I took a seat in the dentist's waiting room. It was Rebecca. I hesitated but then answered at the last second.

"Hi," I said.

"Hi, dearheart," she said. "Is this a good time? What are you doing?"

I sighed. If it had been a couple months earlier, I'd have told her about how David pissed me off on the subway, and of my embarrassing overreaction, and she would have taken my side and told me David had always been a teaser—that's just how eldest children are—and assured me he had no idea what he was talking about. We would have laughed.

But how could I complain now?

"I'm at the dentist," I said. "But I have a few minutes. What's up?"

"Oh, I hope everything's fine with your teeth," she said.

"Just a cleaning."

"That's good—I had a crown fall out in the fall—I was brushing my teeth and it went right down the drain; it was a disaster—did I tell you about this?" She had told me the story several times, going so far as to show me the hole where her second molar should have been, as well as the fourteen-hundred-dollar bill she'd received after its replacement. I let her tell me again. I liked to listen to Rebecca; her voice was so kind.

"Listen, enough of me going on and on," she said after a minute or so. "You're humoring me. I've told you all about the damn crown. I'm calling because I want to talk about Italy."

"Okay," I said. For several years, the Altmanns had wanted to take a family trip to Italy, to Puglia and the Adriatic Coast, where my grandmother was from. Rebecca and Hiram always got really excited in conversations about us all going. Even Benji would join in and read Tripadvisor tips and look for the best hotels. After so much talk, it always seemed like a lot of hype. No one could ever settle on dates that worked for all of us, commit to the expensive airfare, take the actual necessary steps to make the vacation happen. I didn't begrudge them the fantasy, but I'd stopped looking forward to a trip that seemed not to be real.

"I finally got a book—one of those Rick Steves guides. It has a great itinerary I think we would all enjoy, we just have to decide which city to fly into. Because we'll have to take the train to Bari"—she pronounced it "Barry"—"and the other towns on the east coast. So, Hiram and Benji can commit to September third through tenth. I just need you to work on David."

"This September?" I asked. "Seriously?"

"Yep," she said casually, as though this development shouldn't be surprising. "If we book plane tickets this week, we'll get the best deals, according to something Benji read. It will be nice to skip a week of American election season, won't it? Especially *this* election—ugh!"

"Um, yeah," I said. "Okay."

I felt disgusting, sitting there talking to my mother-in-law like I had nothing to hide and deserved a vacation, knowing she and Hiram would insist on paying for most of it.

"Are you okay?" she asked, hearing the doubt in my voice. "What's the matter?"

"I just don't know," I said, "if this September is a good time for me."

She was quiet. Then she whispered, "Are you pregnant?"

I said, "Oh my God—no. It's not that."

She exhaled, not knowing what to say and probably not wanting to betray her certain disappointment.

"I will tell you if I'm pregnant," I said. "I won't wait until the second trimester or anything, so don't worry."

"I'm not worried!" she said in an overly friendly, worried tone. "Listen, please just see about these dates for Italy. I really want to do this. Will you ask Melissa if she wants to come with us? I think the two of you traveling to Italy could be wonderful."

"No," I said. "She'd say no. She wouldn't want both of us to be away from the bakery at the same time." Melissa had been to Italy, anyway, to

Rome and Milan. If she'd had some burning desire to see Puglia, she'd have taken the complicated trip on the high-speed rail.

"That's okay," Rebecca said. "So it'll just be us Altmanns. What do you think about flying into Naples? We'd have a layover at Heathrow. In London."

"Sure," I said. And then, as though in a daze: "September."

"It's so exciting," Rebecca said. "I'm excited. And, you know, you aren't pregnant *now*, but who knows how long we can keep putting it off? This might be our last chance to do something like this for a long while."

"Right," I said, my heart pounding and my palms soaked with sweat. "That's a good point."

Rebecca started to say something else, but—to my enormous relief—the dental hygienist called my name. I hung up, promising my mother-in-law I'd let her know about September.

AFTER I HAD MY teeth cleaned, I went to a fast-casual salad restaurant. I ordered three, one to eat immediately before heading to work and another two for David and me to have for dinner later. I asked for beets on David's, even though he hated them.

When I got back to Bay Ridge, to the bakery, I shoved them in the lowboy, hiding the stamp of the restaurant's logo inside a plain white paper bag so no one would make fun of me for wasting so much money on uncooked vegetables.

I WORKED IN THE kitchen with Angelo through the afternoon, our laptops facing different sides of Guillermo's counter. Guillermo had the day off. Melissa and Maria were at Maria's workstation, moving a three-tiered cake around on a lazy Susan and examining photos on Maria's phone.

"She really wants green?" Melissa said. "With gold glitter?"

I couldn't hear Maria's answer. I could almost never hear anything Maria said.

"Kit, come see this cake wreck Maria has to do. It looks like something a leprechaun drag queen jumps out of to do a striptease."

"No offense to leprechaun drag-queen strippers," Angelo said. "It's really the worst cake we've ever had to make."

Before I could join them, though, Athena burst into the kitchen. "That bitch is here," she said.

"Which one?" Angelo asked, sounding bored.

"The one with the little dog," Athena said. "She brought it in again."

"Two bitches, then," I said, and Maria surprised me by laughing.

"What dog?" Melissa said, her body angling, menace in her tone. "There's a dog in here?" She moved toward the doors, peering through the Plexiglas window. "Aha!" she said, turning to me. "It's Angelica Corrado."

"Ugh," I said. Angelica Corrado was someone we'd known our whole lives. She and Melissa had been close friends as children, but the relationship had died in middle school, when the gel of who each was becoming began to cool and it was clear Angelica and Melissa had nothing in common because Angelica was a jerk. Her father owned a black car and limousine rental company. She "worked" for him in some capacity, but I always saw her out during the day. She came into the bakery in a combative mood, often smuggling her overanxious teacup Pomeranian in a big leather handbag, tapping her acrylic nails against the glass to indicate what she wanted from the pastry case. She talked on her cell phone at the cash register, ignoring whoever was helping her, including me. Other times I'd noticed her car double-parked outside the dry cleaner or witnessed her yelling at an employee in the post office or bank about something over which the person likely had no control. She had princess hair extensions and some obvious-looking lip fillers, a fake tan. A great deal of her clothing was velour, matching leisure sets, worn with Ugg boots or flip-flops.

"There's no dog with her," Melissa said, shrugging, almost disappointed.

"Violet told her she couldn't have the dog in the bakery," Athena said. "And she—Angelica—was all, 'I'm just getting a coffee, I'm holding her, she's not touching anything.' She was being really rude, and Violet goes, 'I'm very sorry, it's not our rules, the health department, yadda-yadda.'"

"Angelica knows she can't bring that overgrown rat in here," I said. "I've told her a half-dozen times myself."

"She doesn't care," Angelo said. He'd hardly looked up from his laptop. "She doesn't care about anybody but herself."

Angelica had been part of a clique who'd been particularly nasty to Angelo after he came out at age nineteen. I don't know if she ever said anything to his face, but she was there, snickering, when Mike Esposito muttered "faggot" as Angelo walked past them at the Italian-American Federation's annual gala. The slur was unprovoked, the kind of drunken bravado displayed by bullies in movies. Angelo had stood aghast in his tuxedo, an empty plate in hand. We'd been heading toward the lasagna buffet. Melissa, grouchy already in her cocktail attire, had seethed, but Angelo had told us not to react.

"Don't say anything to Nonna or my pops, please," he'd begged. "I don't want it to be, like, a thing." We'd complied, but Melissa never let it go. To this day, she was cold to Mike and Angelica and the rest of their crowd, even people who hadn't been witness to the abuse. A few years ago on Halloween, during the Ragamuffin Parade, she'd called 311 on Mike's mother for parking in the unused driveway of a foreclosed house, and the poor woman's car had been towed. Melissa had only been walking by and seen Mrs. Esposito getting out of the car. They waved to each other, all smiles, Melissa in the angel costume she wore every year. Then she got to the bakery and called the city, reported the car as though it were in front of her own home.

"Well, you know that guy who's always with Angelica—that Russian guy?" Athena was saying.

"Konrad," I said.

"He's Lithuanian," Angelo added. "He's not so bad, except he hangs around those zeroes."

"Ugh," Melissa said, disagreeing. "He's a Yankee fan."

"Right, well," Athena said. "He took the dog outside, but he was really aggressive to Violet."

"What'd he say?" asked Angelo.

"He was all, 'Are you the manager? Do you see the health department anywhere?' and kind of implying he knows you guys and is going to get us in trouble. Then to Angelica, he was like, 'Who is this Chinese girl?'"

Melissa was stone-faced. She asked, "What did Violet say?"

"It didn't seem to really bother her," Athena said. "She just said, 'I'm not Chinese, sir.' He left, though—he wasn't listening."

"Is Violet okay out there?" I asked.

"Violet's good with jerks. She looks fine," Melissa said, spying through the view window. "She's making Angelica's revolting drink." Angelica liked large iced lattes with skim milk, sugar-free hazelnut syrup, and six Splendas, which she referred to as "Splenders."

"Violet was so chill," Athena said. "She just kept smiling and being like, 'I'm so sorry but no dogs, no exceptions.'"

"She deserves a prize," I said.

Melissa had started grinning in a psychotic way. Angelo and I looked at each other. He shook his head. "Mel, don't," he said, and she wriggled her eyebrows in a manner of demented playfulness. "Don't start something right now."

Wild-eyed, Melissa opened the kitchen door. "Hey, Angelica!" she called loudly, with false friendliness.

I couldn't see Angelica, but I could imagine her looking up from the counter. "Oh, hi, Melissa," she said with barely affected politeness. "How are you?"

Melissa didn't answer. Instead she said, "Hey, funny thing, actually. I saw your dad on Tinder. His profile says he's only forty-three years old. What's going on? He's going through something?"

There was a hefty silence. From the kitchen, where Angelo and I were looking at each other with a combination of muffled amusement and abject horror, I tried to picture the expression on Violet's face. Violet, who reacted to nothing on the sales floor, acknowledged no rudeness, powered through difficult customer encounters with the tolerance of a monk. I doubted she'd seen this side of Melissa, this extraordinary ability to harass an enemy without flinching, Melissa's willingness, on the rare occasion when the spirit moved her, to say something so outrageous, and with such a neutral cadence, that it was like an atomic bomb of pure adolescent cruelty dropped into a normal adult interaction. Melissa held the door open with her back and continued to smile at Angelica. Athena, standing behind her, put a hand over her mouth. Angelica's father had a reputation for being a philanderer, and since his divorce, he'd had a few young girlfriends, women his daughter's age, maybe even younger.

"You know what?" Angelica said finally. I pictured her haughtily combing the bottom of her overstraightened extensions with her acrylics. "I don't want this fucking coffee."

Melissa nodded, I think to convey something to Violet, perhaps to throw the coffee down the sink.

"I'll take my business elsewhere," Angelica said. "Where they know how to treat customers."

"I'm really going to hurt for your twenty dollars a month," Melissa said coldly.

"You have no class, Melissa DeMarco," Angelica said. She was shouting, really. "You never had any class."

"That's probably true," Melissa said.

Angelica was still shouting, her voice growing fainter as she left. "No class!" I heard her shriek again out on the sidewalk.

Melissa let the door close. Violet rushed through, leaving the now empty dining room unattended. "Oh my God," Violet said, her eyes glowing with shock and admiration. Athena slow-clapped.

"Don't encourage her," I said. "That was fucked up. That was so mean."

"It really was, wasn't it?" Melissa said calmly. She went back to Maria's workstation, where Maria, who'd gone back to work, was stirring green food dye into cream cheese frosting.

"It's not her fault her dad's an old creep," I said, but my voice was too soft.

"You can't pull stunts like that," Angelo said to Melissa. He was stiff. "She's going to tell twenty-five people she came in here to buy something and you insulted her. She's going to post about it on Facebook."

"Only if she's sure her dad's not on Tinder," Melissa said. "Otherwise, it's too humiliating."

Angelo sighed. "Are we running a business here?" he asked.

"It's going to be so awkward the next time I run into her," I said. "She lives around the corner from me."

Melissa ignored us. A look passed between Violet and Athena, and Athena made eyes toward the dining room, as if to say, *I'll tell you out there.* No doubt Athena had insight on Melissa's feuds with different people in the neighborhood, as well as another key fact: Melissa was beloved. She and Angelo sponsored a handful of local kids' soccer teams and neighborhood organizations, she was on the chamber of commerce, she knew our assemblyman and city councilman personally, she was connected. People said she was just like our grandmother. In a lot of ways, she was.

"No dogs," Melissa said to Violet and Athena. "You don't even have to be polite to people with dogs—just tell them to take the dog out. I hate dogs."

"You hate dogs?" Violet asked incredulously.

"That wasn't about the dog," I said, but no one acknowledged me.

"No one *hates* dogs," Violet said, still stuck on this rather irrelevant piece of the equation. She and Athena trudged back into the dining room.

DAVID WASN'T HOME WHEN I got off work, so I called Matt and told him the whole story of Melissa's outburst. He was enthralled, and laughed hard, and said he couldn't believe it. It was fun to do an impression of Melissa. I could ham it up and feel separate from the incident, an observer, like Violet and Athena.

"You're so funny," he said. "I wish you could come over."

"Me, too," I said, just as I heard the heavy front door snapping shut downstairs. David was home. I told Matt I had to go, locking myself in the bathroom and turning on the faucet to buy another minute while David's footfalls on the stairwell drew closer. I said goodbye to Matt and hung up just as David called my name.

When I came out of the bathroom, my phone in the back pocket of my espresso-stained Levi's, David was already at the fridge.

"Are these salads for tonight?" he asked.

"Yep," I said, remembering the beets now with a twinge of regret. "The one with beets is mine."

"It looks like they both have beets," he said, frowning over the clamshells. "They must have made a mistake."

"Oh, no," I said. I thought of Melissa smiling at Angelica. I was so petty, as bad as my sister. Maybe worse.

"It's okay," David said. "It won't kill me to eat them once."

I could tell, though, as we ate at the kitchen counter, that he struggled. I actually wondered if he would gag.

"I'm sorry I pissed you off this morning," he said. "I really didn't mean to be a dick. I thought it was cute, how you had them wrapped up around a special apparatus, but they were so beaten up. I wasn't trying to say you're a slob or anything."

"It's okay," I said. I didn't admit I'd overreacted, and he didn't seem to expect me to do so. I felt terrible. I shoved a forkful of arugula and beets into my mouth and chewed. The meal was so boring. I knew I'd still be hungry afterward. I didn't tell David about Angelica Corrado when he asked me about my day. I wanted to finish my stupid salad and go to bed.

"Did your mom call you today?" I asked.

"She texted me saying I should listen to whatever you had to tell me," he said, chuckling. "So manipulative!"

"She wants to do the Italy trip," I said. "In September."

I had expected David to balk and say he needed more notice, start talking about some project at work that was going to eat up the fall. But he said, "Finally! Yes, let's do it. Did she say the dates?"

"The third to the tenth," I said. "A few days in Naples, then a train trip to the southeast."

David was thumbing through the calendar on his iPhone. "I can do those!" he said. "Can you?"

"I'm sure it's fine," I said. "You know the bakery—so long as no one travels from Halloween until New Year's Day, Angelo and Melissa will give me the time off. They'll complain, but they'll complain if I'm there, too."

"This is awesome," David said. "I'm going to text my mom and tell her we're in."

My stomach was a ball of wax hardening inside me.

David added, "Oh, Kit. The food. The *wine*." He looked at me expectantly. "All your healthy eating is about to pay off."

"What does that mean?" I asked.

"Nothing. Just, you know. People who are really into clean eating— like you—you'll get to let loose on a trip like this. Guilt-free."

"I'm not guilty," I said. "That's not why I'm doing the Radiant Regimen."

But David wasn't going to entertain any more bickering. He looked at me affectionately and touched his pointer finger to my nose, as if I were a cat. "Boop," he said.

"Boop yourself," I said crankily, and went upstairs to put on my pajamas.

A CHUNK OF MY ire toward David *did* have to do with the Radiant Regimen. I was often in a bad mood because I wanted coffee with half-and-half, because I wanted sugar, because at the end of each day I was not rewarded with alcohol for the intolerable task of living a life and working a job. But I was mad at the program, too. I didn't feel like I was earning a trip overseas, and not just because of Matt. Six weeks in, with another four and a half to endure, I had yet to realize the Radiant Regimen's more divine claims. I wasn't a higher version of myself or whatever. My skin wasn't glowing. In fact, it looked ashier to me lately, uneven and colorless. I never felt awash in endorphins except when I was with Matt. The rest of the time, I was hungry.

CHAPTER FIFTEEN

The next week, on Wednesday morning, Matt texted and said I should come see him before he went away on his bachelor party trip.

—**But that isn't until the weekend, right?** I texted.

—**I am flying to Cincinnati tonight,** he wrote. **To spend a couple days with my folks first.**

—**FOLKS is a funny word,** I texted back, and when he didn't respond for a while, I worried that I'd offended him.

I wanted to see him, but I had my period. It was several days early. I'd gone to the bathroom just after waking up, and there had been a stain on my underwear. They were good panties, and I cursed, seeing the bright spot of new blood. I wasn't delicate about my period, but for some reason I felt weird going to Matt's. I'd never gone over and not slept with him.

After several minutes went by, I texted him again:

—**Melissa wants to hire you for another job.** This was true in the loosest sense. The day before, Angelo had taken out the lowboy against the south-facing wall, which was windowless and wide. Now there were several feet of rare extra space. As he and Guillermo hauled it to the truck Angelo had borrowed, Melissa had said she wished Matt could furnish the rest of the kitchen storage. She'd described a fantasy project.

—**Really? What job?** This time he responded immediately, which was a little mortifying.

—**You know that spot between the walk-in and the dish pit? They got rid of the lowboy. She wants you to make cabinets and a cooling rack.**

—**I'd love to work with you guys again.**

I regretted baiting him. Angelo might want to find someone cheaper to imitate Matt's shelves or buy something practical but unattractive from a restaurant supply.

—**She just brought it up yesterday,** I wrote. I added: **I don't know if there's a timeline or concrete plans or anything** but then deleted it.

—**Well, it'd be great.**

I responded with an idiotic smiley-face emoji.

His next text said:

—**Come over!**

I told him I had my period. I tried to make a joke of it by including a GIF of the scene from *The Shining* when a tidal wave of blood comes rushing from an elevator. I hadn't been apologetic since college about menstruating. I stared at my phone, waiting for him to answer, watching the ellipsis graphic that meant he was typing something. I was annoyed with myself.

—**Come over anyway,** his next message said.

MATT DIDN'T HAVE A real TV. He was watching *Frasier* on his laptop when I got to his apartment, lying with the computer on his stomach. I thought it was a little depressing. The day was sunny, and his windows were cracked open. It wasn't warm enough to have them all the way open, but a light, cool breeze coming in felt good.

He shut the laptop and said, "I was just killing time until you got here. I should have gone to my studio this morning. I feel gross from sitting around too much."

"Do you want to take a walk?" I said.

"I would love to take a walk with you," he said. I could tell he was pleased. Since the museum, we'd rarely been anywhere outside his apartment.

The sky was pale blue, and it was chilly in that pleasant early-April way. I had on only my canvas Carhartt jacket, but I felt good, though my hands were cold. We walked down Kane Street toward the waterfront. We talked about *Frasier*. Matt really liked it, especially Frasier's brother, Niles, whom I vaguely recalled for his feathery hair and confusing accent, edging on a bad impression of a British person. It was dumb.

"Those characters were all so prissy and classist," I said.

"Yeah!" Matt said, laughing, because these were the exact things he liked about the show. "What's your favorite TV show?" he asked me.

"The news," I said.

He chuckled. "What's your favorite show of all time, though? Like if you had to pick one to take to a desert island."

"The *news*," I repeated. "*PBS News Hour*."

"Oh," Matt said. "What's your second favorite?"

"I don't know," I said. "I'm not much of a TV person. I like those BBC miniseries based on old novels. When I was in, like, eighth grade, there was one of *Pride and Prejudice*. I loved that shit. I got it on VHS and watched it about a hundred times."

"So, horror movies and *Masterpiece Theatre*," he said.

"Pretty much."

He was quiet. Then he said, "Aren't you going to ask what my favorite show is?"

I laughed. "Oh, this was a leading question?" I said teasingly. "Say,

Matt, what's your favorite TV show *of all time* since, apparently, it isn't *Frasier?*"

"You really are a dick, you know that?" he said, but in a flirtatious way. "My favorite show is *Twin Peaks.*"

"Ugh!" I said, louder than I meant. "Does that mean your favorite book is *Infinite Jest?*"

"No," he said. "But I do like David Foster Wallace."

"I'm sorry to hear that."

"I find your disdain of my insufferable interests insufferable."

"Fair enough," I said. "What is your favorite book?"

"That's easy," he said. "*Beloved.*"

We'd reached the corner of Columbia and Congress Street and the Pilates studio where I'd told David I attended classes. I'd Googled fitness studios in the area, for plausibility's sake on the off chance that I saw someone we knew, but this was the first time I'd actually been by it. It looked nice. I thought I'd like to take Pilates there someday, when I had more time.

"Well, that answer," I said to Matt, "is perhaps the most redeeming thing you could've said."

"I first read it when I was in high school," he said. "For English class."

"That kicks ass. In high school I had to read *Of Mice and Men* in ninth *and* eleventh grade."

"Well, *Beloved* takes place in Cincinnati, so I think the AP teachers got away with assigning it instead of *The Great Gatsby* or whatever."

"*The Great Gatsby* is *my* favorite book," I said. I tried not to sound too sour, but I was appalled.

"Huh," he said. "I would have guessed it was *Jane Eyre* or something."

"Look," I said. "If you are truly claiming to dislike *The Great Gatsby,* we can still sleep together. But we can't talk. You can actually never speak to me again."

He laughed. "I haven't read it," he said.

I shrieked. We were at the end of Columbia Street, on the desolate sidewalk outside the distribution and shipping centers. There was no one around. Still, I had the prickly sense that I could run into someone at any moment, and I'd have no way of explaining what I was doing taking this not-at-all-scenic walk with this tall man.

"I'll read it," he said. "I like sleeping with you, but I'd be sad if we couldn't talk."

"Me, too," I said.

"Sometimes I wish," he said, but then he hesitated.

"What?" I asked. "You wish what?"

"God, it's stupid," he said. "It's not stupid, but it's stupid to say."

"What?"

"I wish we could date, I guess," he said finally.

I didn't say anything. We approached a bodega and Matt asked if I wanted anything. I shook my head.

"Are you upset with me for saying that?" he asked. "I'm sorry. I shouldn't have. It's not fair—I knew what I was getting into from the beginning."

"Don't be sorry," I said. "I know what you mean. It's odd: I feel guilty for lying to David, for cheating. But I feel guilty with you, too. That I'm not available for anything more." I shrugged. I felt embarrassed and corny. What I'd said hadn't really occurred to me before.

Matt said, "I knew we were going to sleep together when we met. I didn't necessarily think it would go beyond a one-time thing. Maybe I thought we'd hook up for a week while I was working with you. But every time you come over, it's like a bonus. I think, Maybe that's it. But then I text you again, you come over, and I enjoy it. I guess the problem is I didn't think it through."

"I feel the same way," I admitted. "I am always waiting to hear from you."

Matt nodded. "You know, Melissa called me," he said.

"What?" I said. "When?"

"While you were on your way over."

"About the job?"

"Yeah," he said. "Well, she wanted to see about my availability for a month or so from now. She said she's 'working' on Angelo. I wasn't really sure what she meant."

"Oh, just that he's cheap," I said. I was relieved that she'd asked Matt about the job, but it was weird to think of them on the phone. Imagining their conversation, a prickly sweat popped up on the back of my neck. I checked the time. "I have to go soon," I said. "I have work in an hour."

"Can I kiss you?" he asked. We were standing in front of a high chain-link fence topped with barbwire. We both looked around, even though the closest people were in hard hats far beyond the fence, near the dark open mouth of a large warehouse door.

I nodded, and we kissed. He was headed back toward his apartment, so we went in opposite directions. Before I turned to the footbridge over the highway, I looked behind me to see him walking away. He'd gotten far up the street already and looked tiny in the distance. He stopped, as though he felt my eyes on his back, and turned. We waved to each other, and I felt silly and sad that he was going away. I realized I'd forgotten to tell him I hoped he had a good time at the bachelor party, even though I thought bachelor parties were archaic and stupid. I texted him this exact thought.

—**Insufferable!** he wrote back, but then he added, **I'm going to miss you.**

MATT WAS DUE BACK from his trip Monday afternoon. This coincided with long-standing plans David and I had to go to see Annie Lou Samuels at Radio City. She was playing a two-night engagement; I'd bought the tickets back in September. Both shows had sold out in under an hour, and I'd spent the entire morning refreshing my browser over and over, laptop trembling on my thighs. I'd secured seats in the orchestra, twelve rows back from the stage. They cost a great deal of money.

It had been a long and lonely week without Matt. David, on a new deadline with the building in Korea, worked the whole weekend and was on the phone with his boss whenever he was around. I was annoyed by his neglect while at the same time secretly pleased; there was less reason for me to feel guilty as I spent my free time at home, sharing cans of imported tuna in oil with Woogie—the one canned food allowed by the Radiant Regimen, so long as it was wild-caught—while I sent Matt texts and selfies. We used a photo-sharing app that deleted pictures after eight seconds. He sent me brief videos of his dad cooking burgers on his parents' expensive-looking grill, and a trip he took with his mother to a greenhouse. His parents' house was in a neighborhood where everyone had a big lawn with real grass, but there were no businesses, no buildings taller than the two-story homes. The houses were all the same beige brick and far away from one another. Everything looked clean, kind of fake. I thought I could probably kick a hole between his bedroom and the hallway outside; the place looked to be about eighty percent drywall. It was strange to think of Matt growing up there, in that flimsy structure, when he devoted himself now to what was sturdy and finely crafted.

Late at night, he sent me images of his penis, which was something he did on a semiregular basis and always via text. I wondered, dismayed, if he texted instead of using the disappearing app because he thought I'd want to keep those pictures. In truth, the dick pics mortified me, and I always deleted them immediately. Once, he sent one while David was across the counter from me at breakfast, and David had said, "What are you looking at over there? Your face is completely red." I deleted the photo and then the whole text thread, all while fumbling through a preposterous lie about a viral video of two otters violently mating. Even though I didn't really like the photos, I thought about them when I masturbated after David went to work in the mornings, and I always came right away.

On Friday, Matt drove down to Nashville with his friends, and I didn't hear from him again until Sunday night, when he texted to say he was coming home the next day and hoped we could see each other.

I MET MATT'S RETURN flight, nearly an hour delayed, at LaGuardia's Marine terminal baggage claim. I'd left work early, taken two trains and a bus, an hour and a half of travel. Throwing my body against his, letting him lift me into the air and kiss me, I suspended all the concerns I typically had about being out with him in public. Never mind any number of David's colleagues or friends who might be riding the Delta Shuttle. Never mind anything besides the pleasure of my face against his neck. In the cab from the airport to Matt's apartment, I took his hand, put it up my skirt, and guided it between my legs. He made an almost inaudible noise of pleasure, sliding his fingers up the surface of my insides.

"You're so wet," he mouthed, looking at me sideways, his expression one of untamed desire: his mouth slightly ajar, his whole face open and seeking. No man had ever looked at me that way, certainly not David, even when we were kids. I nodded slowly, and we rode the rest of the way to Brooklyn like that, with his hand moving under my clothes and all three of us—me, Matt, and the cabdriver—staring straight ahead into I-278's clogged traffic.

A FEW HOURS LATER, I peeled myself from Matt's sweaty sheets and got dressed in his half-dark room. I was supposed to meet David for dinner before the concert. There were creases in my skirt, and my linen top had turned to a wrinkled handkerchief on the bedroom floor. Matt had fallen asleep on his stomach, naked, his long limbs stretched to the edges of the bed. I didn't wake him. I closed his front door behind me, wincing at its loud click, and tiptoed out of the building. I took the train to the Lower East Side, where there was a farm-to-table restaurant that Diana Spargel had recommended on her blog. It was an indulgence, outrageously over-priced, but I hadn't been to a real sit-down restaurant since January.

The temperature had dropped. It looked like it was about to rain, I realized, and I had no umbrella. I was late, and I had no excuse for being late, and David had texted me unprompted to promise that *he'd* be there on time. When the train finally stopped at Delancey Street, I ran through the turnstile and up the stairs, did the ten-minute walk to the restaurant in half the time. I was panting when I turned onto Rivington, where I could see David climbing out the back of a cab.

"Hey," I called to him, waving.

He squinted through the drizzle that was just starting. I wondered if my lipstick was rubbed off in a conspicuous way, if my hair was mussed. Things I should have worried about earlier. David looked at me without suspicion but also without joy.

"I am so exhausted," he said.

"I'm sorry," I said coolly. A dark feeling ladled into me, scooping up something vital. I had been nervous the whole way into the city, sure I wouldn't make it in time to meet David, but it didn't make a difference. He was late, too, even though he'd made a point of saying he would be on time, and now he was complaining.

THE RESTAURANT DOOR HAD an official RR COMPLIANT sticker with the Radiant Regimen's sunburst logo. Inside, the brick walls were painted white and affixed with brass candleholders. The place had the look of a Mediterranean hotel lobby, with long gold-framed mirrors along the walls and rows of tall, waxy-looking potted plants arranged around the terra-cotta-tiled floor. The hostess led us through the maze of long wooden tables and mix-matched metal bistro chairs to one of the two-tops in the back. We sat down, and I decided to let David take responsibility for the conversation. It had occurred to me recently that he never started talking, while I was always rambling on. I looked at him. He looked back. I don't think I meant it to be some sort of test, but either way, David failed. He smiled stiffly, and I smiled back and rested against my chair, which wasn't very comfortable.

He laughed. "What?" he said, like I was being weird.

"What, what?" I said.

"Why aren't you saying anything?"

"Why aren't you?" I asked. "Why do I have to be the one to start a conversation?"

"I don't know," he said. "That's a good point." He made a serious face, like he was trying to think of something to say.

Before he could come up with anything, the waiter arrived with the booklet-size menu of Italian wine. I began to salivate. David explained we would've loved to have a drink, really, but couldn't.

"I'm afraid we are doing the Radiant Regimen," he said, sounding ashamed.

"Got it," said the waiter. "So, no bread for the table."

"No, thank you," David said.

The waiter, who was wearing suspenders attached to tweed trousers, had an old-timey handlebar mustache, which twitched above a frown. I didn't blame him, really. The restaurant's willingness to cater to strict dietary restrictions was something of a surprise for the Lower East Side, and it would've been unfathomable in central Brooklyn, where all the good restaurants had turned into galleries in recent years, the food a precise art project to be photographed and consumed, never challenged. I understood David's embarrassment. Here we were in this nice restaurant in our dry-clean-only clothing, our expensive haircuts, my complexion rosy and bright from department-store makeup. If I could have known, when I was a teenager, what New York would become, and whom I'd marry, and the life we'd be able to afford, I'd have floated on a cloud through the rest of my awkward adolescence.

But in that too-good-to-be-true future, I was still the same scab-picking self-saboteur, unable to stop glancing at myself, searching and judging, in the paneled mirror running the length of the wall. Forcing myself and my husband to skip the wine, to order an inferior version of the good food.

Nothing's ever enough, and you never get away from yourself.

The busboy brought us a pitcher of cold water with lemon, and then the waiter returned with a plate of roasted radishes dusted with black salt crystals. "Instead of bread," he said, and David and I murmured in appreciation, as though this consolation were even a little appealing. Then we both ordered the Radiant Regimen–compliant version of the flank steak with morels and asparagus—vegetables dressed only in sesame oil, steamed rather than sautéed.

I drank two glasses of water while David told me about a new project in Shanghai. He was making a parametric model, rewriting a few lines of source code to reconfigure a tower's floor plates. I couldn't really grasp the details of the problem or its solution, but I was able to nod along with David's disdain for certain colleagues.

"These *designers*," he said, "think computations are just buttons I press. I spent all day rewriting code for this hideous structure. At six p.m., I get an email asking for 'another tiny change to the shape of the balconies.' The designer is in the Hong Kong studio, so it's morning for him, and he can't comprehend—no matter how many times I explain—that changing even the smallest detail requires me to rewrite code for essentially the whole construction. It's almost like these architects don't care if their cheesy luxury condos actually stand up."

"How frustrating," I said.

"It is frustrating!" he practically shouted. "Oh, and the best part? This guy, this incompetent, glorified *illustrator,* guess what his name is?"

"I give up," I said.

"*Rolf!*"

"Oh," I said. "He's Austrian." David's firm hired a lot of Austrian designers, for some reason. Or it seemed so, based on how much David complained about Austrians.

"Of course he is."

WHEN OUR FOOD CAME to the table, the plates set down delicately in front of us, I nosed right into the meal with my head down, like a starving dog. It was delicious, the meat pink in the center, the vegetables hot and crisp. Even without the sauce or the wine or the bread, the meal had the decadence of professional preparation. I admired the sprig of parsley garnishing my plate, and then I ate it.

David cut his steak into little pieces. Civilized. "Hey, Hoover," David said. "Don't vacuum your food." This was one of Rebecca's lines. "Did you eat anything today?"

I didn't answer and grabbed my water glass, chugged.

He said, "I'm sorry to mother you."

"Mother who? *Me?* The motherless?" I said theatrically. I knew I was being a weenie, but I couldn't stop myself.

"It's just an expression."

"An expression you know I hate."

"I am sorry, Kit," he said. "I just don't want you to choke."

I took a deep breath. He was right. I'd let myself get too hungry again, the whole day going by without anything since breakfast. I should have been nice to him. Instead, I was annoyed he'd noticed.

"I won't," I said. "I promise."

"Are you excited about the concert?" he asked, choosing, in his patient, reasonable way, to ignore my pointless bad mood.

"You know I am," I said. I tried to make it feel true. I wasn't

190

unexcited. But the desire to attend the show now felt like someone else's memory, or something I'd wanted in a dream, and following the vague illogic of a sleeping brain. I loved Annie Lou Samuels's music, and wanted to see her onstage, but I was busy now with preoccupations that hadn't existed when I'd bought the tickets six months earlier. Going to this concert with David felt like a scheduling error, like he—my own husband—had arrived, for dinner and a show, in another man's place.

CHAPTER SIXTEEN

After dinner, the rain turned into a light, disappointing snow as we came out of the subway and headed up Sixth Avenue toward Rockefeller Center.

"March sucks," David said. "I feel like spring gets shorter and less predictable every year. Doesn't it feel like, the last few years, there's only winter and summer?"

"That's not a *feeling*," I said. "That's climate change. It *changes* the climate."

"Well, I hate it," David said in a Valley girl voice. "I think it's a bad look, and somebody ought to do something." Even though I wanted to be an asshole, I laughed. Since we'd been together so long, our inside jokes were just cadences, certain turns of phrase and tones only we recognized as funny. We'd built our own little language out of so many joint experiences, so many nights together on the train after a few drinks, so many movies and books and baseball games and podcasts and parties.

The wet sidewalks bustled with tourists and late commuters, their faces aglow in the city's terrarium light. Outside the theater, David asked if I knew how long the show was supposed to last. His firm had an all-hands meeting at eight the next morning. As he said this, I was taking a photo of the marquee; I held my phone steady against the irritation that had been simmering over dinner and now zipped through my body, a wave of something scalding, something near-crazed, starting at the base of my spine.

"I asked you one hundred times if you wanted to attend this concert with me," I said without looking at him. I knew on instinct, or from our historical record, that his shoulders were up to his ears, his hands stuffed into the pockets of his black jeans.

"I do!" he said. "I'm excited."

"Then don't ask me how late we're going to be out," I said. "Don't say things that make it seem like a chore." This, like his concern over my rapid scarfing at the restaurant, wasn't entirely fair. While trips into the city were a treat for me, David took the hourlong subway ride to midtown every day. He worked there. I should have had more sympathy for him, but it was true that I'd asked if he wanted to come. I'd asked many times.

"I'm sorry," he said, and he did sound sorry, but there was an urgency to his contrition, betraying his fear of my angry reaction to the thing he should not have said rather than actual regret for having said it.

"I forgive you," I said menacingly. I was being so awful, and I knew it, and I couldn't make myself stop.

The doors had opened nearly an hour earlier, but it was an obstacle course getting to our seats: security staff in shiny jackets herded us through metal detectors, then peered into my purse with a small flashlight. We had to spread our arms and legs in a position of yogic surrender so that more security, wielding smaller metal detectors, could scan our bodies one more time. The whole thing struck me as too militarized, even for New York City, even for a venue so famous and well trafficked. I tried to remember what security had been like at concerts I'd attended when I was in the regular habit in high school and college, but it had been a dozen years. More!

Could that really be true?

We had to show our tickets so many times, to one usher after an-other, until we were finally there. The opening act was some synth-pop duo neither David nor I had heard of: Two redheads wearing diapha-nous gauze pants played twin keyboards and sang in a kind of haunting electronic yodel.

I sat and watched them for a few minutes. I very much wanted a drink.

"I very much want a drink," I said.

David's neck was craned, blinking in awe of the theater's ceiling, that wood-paneled firmament over three massive mezzanines.

"Hmmmm," he said. "Well, want to have one?"

"You know we can't," I said.

"It's just one drink," he said, as though he'd never met me. "On a special occasion."

"It's not *just one drink,*" I said in an exaggeratedly aggrieved voice. "One drink is the line between successfully completing all seventy-five days of the Radiant Regimen or failing. We already got through dinner without drinking. Why fail now?"

"Well," he said. "You're the one who brought it up."

"*You* can have a drink," I said. "Since the Radiant Regimen isn't important to you."

He shrugged, smiling. "No, I want to stick it out with you," he said. "This is the longest we've done one of these diets."

"It's *not* a diet," I hissed through clenched teeth.

"Oops," David said, but he didn't care anymore. I took off my coat and touched my torso through my top, comforting myself by running my fingers up the rungs of my rib cage.

"I'm going to go get a ten-dollar bottle of water, I guess," I said. "Would you like one?"

"No, thanks," he said, which meant he would ask for a sip of mine and then drink most of it.

* * *

THE REFRESHMENTS LINE WAS endless, a hundred people long. In front of me, an older guy had struck up a conversation with some young women. By their long hair, chunky jewelry, and oversize sweaters, I guessed they were NYU upperclassmen or recent grads; they had that shabbily expensive, business-class-flight-to-Bonnaroo look about them. I couldn't stop looking. They were so thin.

"I wonder if I'll make it back to my seat before Annie Lou goes on," the man was saying. He tugged at his well-groomed facial hair. It had a few handsome patches of gray.

"Oh, I was here last night," said one of the women, the taller of the two. "And she didn't take the stage until, like, nine-twenty?" She spoke that way women did sometimes, not wanting to sound too sure of facts she knew with one hundred percent certainty, in case he was the type of defensive guy who'd be offended by any kind of female confidence. There was no way to spot those guys beforehand; it was a good tactic.

"So we have plenty of time?" her friend added with similar incertitude, toying with the carved silver bracelets on her skinny wrists.

"Nine-twenty!" the man cried, concerned. "How long does the show last, if she doesn't go on for another hour?"

Both women observed him in disdainful silence, slow-blinking their big eyelashes. Any potential threat of male aggressiveness had been brushed from him like dandruff. The tall one raised her eyebrows and lifted her shoulders an inch, an almost imperceptible shrug. She reached absently for a strand of her long straight hair.

"I don't know," she said after a pause, her questioning tone gone. "I didn't, like, time it or anything."

"Right," the guy said, chuckling in an embarrassed way, realizing how lame he'd sounded.

I was struck by a terrible realization: This man, this *older* guy, in his black Levi's and North Face fleece vest, was David. He had the beard and the expensive sneakers. Worse, he must have been around the same age as David, which meant he and *I* were the same age. If The Vest hadn't been making irritating small talk with these college-y women, they might have reasonably thought he and I were together.

I felt, for the first time in my life, old. I was no longer a member of the young crowd. Other people my age had gotten babysitters to be here. Tonight was, as David had pointed out, *a special occasion.*

The Vest stared into his phone. The young women in front of him had moved on to have a private but loud conversation assessing the cuteness of outfits on people passing by. This was bitchy behavior. It wouldn't have occurred to me to notice and judge a stranger in this way, and I felt bad for agreeing with most of their pronouncements. They had good taste. I wondered if the Girls did this at the bakery when I wasn't around. It seemed nakedly self-conscious. I couldn't imagine Tiana or Athena being so petty. I made a mental note to ask Tiana if she and her friends roasted strangers' outfits for fun when they went out.

"Um, is she on vacation?" one said to the other as somebody walked by wearing a too-summery floral-print sundress and sandals.

Annie Lou Samuels was one of those young pop stars who was actually very talented and therefore appealed to a variety of people. In addition to the requirements typical of enormous fame—she was beautiful and young—her singing voice was incredible, a wholly unique instrument, and she wrote her own songs and played guitar, piano, and, for some reason, upright bass—she'd gone to Juilliard—and therefore had garnered the admiration from the usual crowd of kids and young adults who spent pocket money on live concerts, but also people like me, who almost never went out on a weeknight anymore.

* * *

THE CONCESSIONS LINE INCHED forward. I wondered what Matt was doing. He was probably at the bar down the street from his house—the one with a self-service Laundromat in the back—drinking dark, syrupy beer with his friends. I had a sense that his life was a lot more fun than mine, in central Brooklyn bars full of heavily tattooed arms and useless graduate degrees.

The Vest checked the time on his smartwatch, looked around the lounge. He then turned, quick, and walked away, back through the auditorium doors. The young women watched him go, smirking. "What a dork," said the shorter, meaner of the two.

Their conversation veered, as we drew close to the counter, to concerns about money. The taller one took out her phone, actually signed into her bank app, and looked at her checking account balance. They agreed they could afford to share one bright-magenta frozen margarita—delivered in a clear plastic cup—and a soft pretzel. They were not on the Radiant Regimen. Ha-ha, you perfect-bodied meanies, I thought as I watched them walk away with the refreshments they could barely afford, heading toward the stairs to the third mezzanine, the nosebleeds. It's not so great to be you.

BY THE TIME I got back to my seat, the opening act was done, the stage cleared. David was checking his work email on his phone.

"Put that away," I hissed, and he smiled, sheepish, and said, "In a minute."

I looked around. Where we were seated, almost everyone was older. Except for a few obviously rich kids and one famous actress, the ripped denim and Converse sneakers I'd observed in the Grand Lounge were absent, replaced by loose jumpers and slim leather boots, the sleek but sensible fashion of New York City's working women. Women in their mid-thirties and forties, women with husbands checking email on their phones and asking how long this was going to last.

David put his phone away and began to report the information he'd acquired therein, which had to do with college basketball scores. I pretended to listen until, finally, the house lights flickered.

Once the theater was dark and quiet except for the excitement humming through the crowd, Annie Lou Samuels took to the stage in a slouchy white pantsuit. It shimmered against the spotlights: silk or satin. People screamed. Bass guitar began to play, then the soft beat of a drum, then keyboards, guitar. The stage was bathed in purple light. I stood on my tiptoes and couldn't believe how close we were to Annie Lou. Her arms and legs were long and spindly. She was tan. She sang her melodic astrology hymn and then her disco-inspired nature anthem. Her long hair, reddish brown, moved around her swirling figure like a beaded curtain: perfect, no frizz, no heft. She sang a slow, listing cover of David Bowie's "Ashes to Ashes." She sang the one about the streets of Paris, late nights in the Marais, a man who tasted like cigarettes, the crowds at the *Mona Lisa*. The song lyrics were evocative, wiser than the deepest thoughts I'd had in my twenties, their melodies pure and catchy. I waited for the music to take hold of my entire awareness, all my senses. Despite the bad mood in which I'd arrived at the concert, I'd fully expected to be revived, spirited away.

But now I tapped my foot on the floor and held my arms across my chest and had the sense that I was watching an exceptionally good concert from exactly the seat I'd purchased. I loved Annie Lou Samuels, and I enjoyed the performance—I did—but there was no out-of-body experience, no goose bumps, nothing religious or sexual or otherwise cathartic, the way live music had moved me—a few times to tears—when I was younger. Tears didn't come. Annie Lou looked around in awe, told the crowd she couldn't believe she was here, at *Radio City*, playing to a sold-out theater, but the speech struck me as more of the performance, the least convincing part. It was clear she'd had to say things along these lines for the whole tour, and this was the last stop. I kept my breath. There was another song. I knew all the words. I didn't sing along or even hum. I watched respectfully. Another song. And another.

The concert ended, two encores, the lights went up. I was tired. I was profoundly aware of the time. I'd be groggy tomorrow even without having had any booze. David and I shuffled in tiny steps to the aisle, where we waited in the throngs, the air stuffy and moist from so many breathing mouths, smelling of popcorn and spilled beer. It took so long to finally get into the lobby, then longer to get outside.

Midtown was still lively.

I noticed, as we started toward the subway, that David had a serious look. His face was drawn with the work of thinking.

"Is something wrong?" I asked him.

"No," he said. "Did you like the show?"

"Yeah," I said. "She's good."

"I thought she was incredible," David said with conviction. It felt almost like a scold. "That was one of the best concerts I've ever seen."

I looked at David carefully. "You liked it better than Boyz II Men?" I asked. His first concert, at Nassau Coliseum when he was in fifth grade. Rebecca had taken him as a special eleventh-birthday present.

"Maybe!" he said.

I felt sad then. My heart beat in my lungs as we went down into the subway. I shivered on the platform, and David took a winter hat out of his coat pocket and pulled it over my head. He was going on and on about the concert.

I wondered what it would take to stop loving David. To leave him. I imagined asking him to move out. Boxes with his books and clothes stacked up at the top of the stairs. The cat looking with concern for the carrier, which would remain in the closet. A half-empty closet, my single toothbrush in the bathroom. The idea made me afraid, a lump growing in my throat. I swallowed. It was a bad thought, a worrisome picture, but for the first time, I *could* picture it.

If I left David, I thought, I'd be somewhat broke, back to using cheap shampoo, the roots of my brown hair showing. No drinking top-shelf cocktails or kombucha on tap, no yoga classes, no dinners in restaurants like the one we went to earlier downtown, no dry-cleaned clothes. Certainly no more intensive all-organic diets. The lack of creature comforts would stink, but those weren't the things I feared losing. I had my house; I had my job. I could take care of myself. What I feared was the not knowing. All my annoyance and boredom at David lately, did it mean anything? What was I doing with Matt—what did I want from him?

Looking at David, at his thick lashes, the strong angle of his jaw, I thought I should just tell him. Right away. Say he was wrong to have had a good time tonight. Admit I hadn't noticed him during the concert, hadn't looked over at him once to see his incomparable experience. Say I was a snake and a liar and the life we had together wasn't solid. Say I'd been sleeping with another man.

It was possible. A thing anyone could do, tell the truth.

Maybe, if I said these things, David would turn and walk away, silent. Or he'd shout at me, right on the platform, his voice echoing against the tiled walls. Everyone would look. Maybe he'd weep. He was so infrequently upset with me. It was hard to picture him possessing the knowledge of what I'd been doing with Matt.

We'd find out together, what would happen then. How he would react.

All I had to do was open my mouth and say the words.

I stared at David and opened my mouth.

He looked at me.

"What's up?" he said.

I took a long, deep breath. Swallowed.

"Nothing," I said.

PART THREE // Passover

CHAPTER SEVENTEEN

When I got to work that day in April, Matt was in the kitchen with Melissa and Angelo. He'd built their cabinets at his studio, and now the three of them were surveying the space where they'd go. Matt was supposed to be in the store over the next two or three nights to install the cabinets and then assemble their built-in cooling racks. Angelo had two guys coming in to help later, because the cabinets were solid and heavy, and Matt would need real muscle. ("Real muscle" was Angelo's phrasing, not mine, and he'd spoken in an officious falsetto, squeezing the bicep on my arm with his manicured hand. I'd shaken him off, annoyed.)

It was a nice day, and someone had propped the back door open with a brick, so it wasn't as stifling hot as usual.

"Hey," I said, and Melissa and Angelo acknowledged me silently, a small tic in their twin facial expressions as they continued to talk to Matt. He nodded in my direction.

"Hello," I said. "How have you been?"

"I'm doing well," he said with feigned casualness. It was all so stupid.

I took an apron from the bin and put it on. The standard-size ones no longer fit, so I'd ordered some smock aprons in a variety of sizes from the linen service. They were white with back cross-straps and big pockets, very charming, and when Melissa saw Tiana and me wearing them, she said, "Good! *Good look,*" though when Angelo noticed the new line on the invoice, I thought he was going to cry.

Violet walked through the back door a minute behind me. She had her earphones in and was mouthing the lyrics to a song.

"Go relieve the morning crew, please," Angelo said to us, like we were idiots.

"Is it okay if I clock in first?" Violet said.

"I suppose," he said.

"Thanks," she said. "It'd be chill to get paid for this. I mean, even though I'd totally do it on a volunteer basis."

Angelo glared at her, but Melissa laughed. "*I* wouldn't," she said.

The counter was busy. I was grateful to spend the first few hours working with Violet as Matt loaded the new cabinets into the kitchen. About two hours into my shift, it finally slowed down. Violet took a bathroom break and Melissa went home, followed shortly afterward by Angelo. I used white vinegar to clean every glass surface in the shop, putting a look of determination and full attention into my work so as not to feel too overwhelmed. I was more on edge than I'd ever been. Having Matt there again, pretending to hardly know him, had the surreal quality of a lucid dream. These were tasks—boxing treats, pulling espresso shots, steaming milk, describing menu items, and listing ingredients, constant tidying and handwashing in between each thing—I could have performed asleep, and I did them with the detachment of a sleepwalker.

Matt and I hadn't seen each other in ten days. We'd had an argument. I wasn't sure where we stood. I felt alone and nervous.

Angelo's guys—I heard Richie Bolognese's shrimpy laugh a few times but didn't even peek through the door—used an earsplitting power drill and a rubber mallet. Customers kept asking about the ruckus coming from the kitchen.

"Just new cabinets," I told them. "Sorry about the noise!"

AFTER HIS HELPERS WERE gone and business at the counter had died down, Matt came out from the kitchen and stood at the end of the espresso bar. He looked like he was waiting for something.

"Hi," I said, coming over to him. I was keenly aware of Violet, refilling the sugar packets in little wicker baskets on the dining room tables. She was always listening. "You need something?"

"A vacuum?" he said. "Please." The added "please" was enunciated too formally, making him sound demanding.

"Just a dustbuster or something bigger?" I asked.

"It's kind of a mess—well, you can see for yourself," he said.

I went into the kitchen. He followed. The new cabinets were covered with a fine silt of sawdust, and there were wood shavings everywhere, on the appliances and countertops. There was also a strong whiff of wood stain hanging in the air, as well as ripped-up bubble wrap, masking tape, and other garbage all around.

I groaned. "This is a lot of cleanup, huh?" I asked, but I wasn't really asking.

"I had to do some unforeseen sanding," Matt explained. He sounded half sheepish, half defiant. "I didn't gauge that ridge in the floor seam well enough when I measured the wall."

"Okay," I said. "Come on."

He followed me down to the basement, which was unfinished, dark, and filled with the hum of several industrial dehumidifiers. Melissa and Angelo used the space to store backstock: disposable food containers and paper goods. At the base of the stairs, soiled aprons and rags were piled into the linen service's big canvas bags. There was a second safe tucked in a corner and hidden by a broken freezer. Mostly, though, the basement's floor space was taken up by an assortment of garish, oversize seasonal decorations. No matter how trendy, Sweet Cheeks was still in Bay Ridge, and as Melissa liked to sing while she decorated for each and every holiday: "Brooklyn, we go hard."

Pointing to a life-size Halloween Frankenstein statue and an even creepier animatronic Santa Claus—who ho-ho-ho'ed and jerked his head back and forth when a button was pushed on his back—I said to Matt, "I'm assuming you've met Melissa and Angelo's boyfriends."

"Very funny," he said. "Your corniness is unparalleled, as ever." He flicked his tongue over his teeth when he smiled at me. It was a look I knew well by then, the flash of amusement; he was charmed by me, or maybe he was charmed by his own attraction to me, despite my silly jokes and my nerdy vocabulary and my obvious discomfort in my own skin.

"Here's the shop-vac," I said, pushing the industrial vacuum toward him, its wheels making a violent sound across the cement floor. I lifted the hose and turned, ready to go back upstairs. Matt stood over me, though, and didn't move.

"How are you?" he asked.

I felt my shoulders loosen. "I'm okay," I said. "I'm really sorry about last week. I'm sorry about everything."

LAST SATURDAY, I'D HAD the day off, and David had been with his boss at a talent-recruiting symposium in Boston. He'd left on a shuttle flight early that morning and would return around midnight. These day trips weren't uncommon, but it was rare for him to travel on the weekend.

I'd spent the day with Matt. Close to dinnertime, we were lying around his apartment. I'd been eating small handfuls of raw almonds from a big jar I kept in my pocketbook.

"You should eat some real food," Matt had said.

"Almonds are the realest," I answered. I was in my underwear in his bed, under the covers, and felt warm and comfy with my torso against his bare skin. I was used to being hungry by this point. In fact, I was good at it.

"Well, I have to eat," Matt said tersely.

"What's wrong?" I said. "You sound mad."

He sat up, which meant I had to sit up, too. It felt like he'd shoved me off him, even though he'd actually been gentle. I held the covers over me, suddenly feeling exposed, vulnerable. He ran a hand through his hair.

"I want to be able to go out and have dinner," he said. "With you."

I stared at him, not knowing what to say.

He sighed heavily. "This situation is so fucked. I have no idea what I'm doing. Spending all my time with a married lady." The way he said it—"married lady"—made me feel disgusting and predatory and like I was about eighty years old.

"Okay," I said. "This feels like it's coming out of nowhere."

"Does it really?" he asked in a hostile tone.

"Well, I'd love to put my clothes on," I said. "For this particular conversation."

We both rose from the bed, almost mechanically, and got dressed with our backs to each other.

"Would you like to go get coffee?" I said.

"Oh, so you are willing to go out in public with me after all," Matt said.

"You've misunderstood something," I said. "I'm not avoiding going out in public with you. Not really." I was holding my shoe. My heart pounded. "I just don't drink—well, I haven't been drinking since before I met you. And I have a lot of . . ." I trailed off, looking for the words. "Dietary restrictions."

He looked at me with a desperate frown, almost like he wanted to cry. "This isn't sustainable," he said in a quiet voice.

"Oh, Jesus," I said, as though what he'd said was exasperating, even though my stomach dropped as he said the words. I'd known we were pressing against this conversation, both of us. Things had been building, the sex more intense, the fun and camaraderie vacuumed away and replaced by a new pressure, a sense of precarity when we were together.

"Don't be glib," Matt said. There was a catch in his voice, like a wad of tears caught in his throat. "Don't just brush me off."

We fought then, arguing for over an hour. He said he felt used. I said my situation was what it had always been. We didn't get coffee or dinner. Matt opened a beer and took a long swig from the can. Finally, I had to go home. David's flight was going to land, and I had to beat him to the apartment.

When I left, I asked, feeling like a bad actress, "Is this it?"

Matt said he needed some time to think. I nodded and left without another word.

We hadn't spoken since, except I'd texted to tell him we'd cross paths in the bakery; I was scheduled the days he'd be in for the cabinets. He'd written back:

—**Ok, thanks for letting me know.**

Now I looked at him carefully. I wanted to tell him I missed him, thought of him constantly. I wanted to tell him I needed to be with him again.

But before I could say anything, Violet called from the top of the stairs. "Kit, I need you to make some coffees!" she said. "I've got a line to the door!"

"Sorry, sorry!" I shouted. "Here I come!" I handed Matt the shop-vac hose and ran up the stairs. "Violet," I said as I screwed the portafilter into the espresso socket, "the carpenter made a mess in the kitchen. We'll have to power-wash the whole place if Melissa's going to bake in there tomorrow."

"Of course he did," Violet said. She dropped a chocolate cookie into a waxed-paper bag and handed it to a waiting customer. Wishing her a good night, she turned to me. Her customer-service-pretty smile fell away. "Hot guys are always fucking slobs."

I stared ahead at the espresso temperature gauge, counting back the seconds to two hundred degrees, the perfect pull.

IT TOOK US AN hour past closing to get the kitchen cleaned up. Matt swept and vacuumed beforehand, but once Violet and I were done with our own side work, I used the sprayer in the dish pit to hose the room down while Violet and Matt squeegeed the sudsy water into the floor drains.

When we were done, and all the supplies were put away, I went to the bathroom.

When I came out, Matt and Violet were putting on their jackets, ready to leave.

My heart sank. The whole job, Matt's second and final tenure in the bakery, was nearly over. Plus, here was Violet, beautiful weasel, burrowing in. I was sure she was going to try to pick him up. I'd been bracing for it since she'd made her comment about slobs. There'd been a lewdness to how she said it, her tone at a sexual octave, and I'd thought, Oh, shit.

"I'm ready for a drink," she said. "Anybody interested?"

Matt and I both hesitated. His mouth opened halfway, but then he didn't say anything. Was he waiting for me to answer first? I tried not to look at him. I would've loved to get a fucking drink. But even if I quit the Radiant Regimen, I couldn't go drinking with Violet and Matt. It would be too weird.

"I've got my bike," Matt finally said. "And it's supposed to rain again in an hour or so—I shouldn't chance it."

"Okay, Chief Meteorologist Bill Evans," I said.

There was a hitch in my voice. A pause. And then I started laughing, and Violet started laughing, and Matt said, "I don't get the joke."

"It's not actually funny," I said through laughter.

"It's not funny at all," Violet agreed, wiping tears away, and then we burst out laughing again. She leaned in to me and balanced her hand along my forearm. I'd forgotten about those small touches between women, full of meaning and safety. We were holding each other up, laughing.

"Who is Bill Evans?" Matt demanded.

Violet and I worked to catch our breath.

"This guy on *Eyewitness News*," I said. "It's really not funny. It's dumb."

"We just got slaphappy," Violet said. "It's been a long day."

How could we explain to Matt—a man—why it happens, the moment two women become real friends? The relief, the recognition. There was nothing behind our laughter, except some tension had cracked, and we each had to let go of whatever made us insecure around the other. We had to let ourselves like each other. It was too magical, too important, and no matter how emotionally intelligent Matt was, with his attention to conversation and his excellent cunnilingus skills, he couldn't understand this.

"You can put your bike in the basement and take the train home if you want," I said. Because now I couldn't bear to part with Violet.

I figured he'd say no, but Matt replied, "Cool. Where should we go?"

"Valhalla," I told him. "It's this cute little cocktail bar up by Owl's Head Park."

"Are you crazy?" Violet asked. "That's so far. No way. Let's just go to the Kettle."

I dreaded the idea of taking Matt anywhere close by, where I'd run into people I knew, possibly extended family, Melissa's old friends, Uncle Nicky's friends, someone from Girl Scouts when I was eight. I might've run into somebody at Valhalla as well, but the odds were slimmer.

"I hate it there," I said.

"What are you talking about? It's the neighborhood bar. Everyone goes there. It's like *Cheers*!"

"That's right. And I grew up four blocks away from the Kettle Black," I told Violet. "If we go there, I'm stuck talking to my high school gym teacher all night."

"Okay, but Valhalla's such a long walk," Violet said. "How about Delia's?"

Delia's was Melissa's spot, filled with fruity-smelling hookah smoke. "The music is so loud in there," I said. "I want to go to Valhalla."

"Fine," Violet said. "It puts me closer to home, at least."

"Valhalla's the best bar in Bay Ridge," I said, and Violet didn't disagree.

"Okay," Matt said. "So we're going out."

VIOLET AND I WAITED in the doorway while Matt put his bike in the basement and organized the last of his supplies.

"He has a girlfriend?" she asked, gesturing toward the bakery, toward Matt.

"I don't know," I said. I could feel Violet looking at me.

When he returned, I pressed the alarm code into the keypad on the wall. Violet and I pulled down the rolling gate together, she snapped the padlock closed, I checked the grate lock on the cellar door, and the three of us looked around, like nobody was sure what should happen next.

We started our walk to Valhalla, hands in pockets, chins up in the cool air. After a few blocks, I had no choice but to sneak off and call David; I muttered some excuse about buying a seltzer.

"They have seltzer at the bar," Violet said.

"I only like it from a can," I said, one foot on the sidewalk, one on the curved step up to the bodega's glass door. "You guys go ahead, I'll catch up."

Matt rolled his eyes. Violet—eager, I'm sure, to get in some alone time with him—was already continuing down the street, but he stood there for a second, giving me an incredulous once-over.

"You aren't about to bail, are you?" he asked.

"No, I'm still coming," I said. "I just need to call home first."

Violet stopped halfway up the block, arms crossed, looking like a small blackbird under the hood of her jacket.

"It's cold!" she called. "Are we going or not?"

Matt waved to her and answered yes. To me, he lowered his eyes. "Right, of course," he said.

"Don't be like that."

He turned and jogged to catch up with Violet.

THE BODEGA SMELLED LIKE a mix of coffee and bleach. I waved at Aarpan, the clerk, but he didn't look up from the soccer game he was watching on a laptop propped next to the cash register. I passed through the narrow aisles packed with dried soup mixes and candy until I reached the back of the store, where I called David and pulled two cans of Schweppes from the cooler. The phone rang three times, I paced, my headphones in, a cold aluminum can of seltzer in each hand.

"Hey, babe, I'm just leaving," he said when he finally picked up. I heard an elevator door ding in the background.

"Oh, you're still in the city?" I asked. Relieved but also absurdly annoyed. I should have assumed he'd still be at work, since I'd told him I'd be late again.

"Yeah. What a ridiculous day," he said. "We had a meeting with LOOP Studios, and—"

"Were they actually there this time?" I asked, referring to the notorious cofounders of Lorens Olofsson + Olga Petrus Studios, the married couple behind a renowned design team David's firm sometimes hired, or tried to hire, as consultants on important projects. David occasionally had the chance to rub elbows with some very important weirdos.

"No," he said, sounding disappointed. "They sent their protégé du jour, this twenty-five-year-old Bay Area asshole named *Tad*. He ate a burrito out of a grocery bag."

"During the meeting?" I shrieked. "Very San Francisco of him. Did he tell you how bad the burrito was?"

"I'll tell you about it when I get home. I actually need to talk to you about something."

"Oh, well, I was calling to tell you I'm going to be late," I said. Guilt squeezed my insides, a dull pain right between my stomach and my gut. It was a feeling I should've been used to by that point, but it seemed to only get worse over time, each passing day intensifying the weight of my lies. "I'm actually going out," I said. "To Valhalla with Violet."

"Oh, cool," David said. I heard the pleased surprise in his voice. He wanted me to have friends probably more than I myself wanted to have friends. "So, does this mean you're going to break the regimen? How many days are left, anyway?" Typical of David to not even know how much longer his own discomfort was going to last.

"Only three days," I said, putting both cans of seltzer on the counter and pulling two dollars from my wallet. I handed the money to Aarpan, mouthing, *Thank you*. He took the crumpled bills and waved me away without taking his eyes from the soccer game. "I'm not quitting the Radiant Regimen. No booze. I'm just going to hang out."

"Did you tell your friend about the program? I'm sorry—what did you say her name was?"

"Violet," I kind of shouted. "The shift supervisor Melissa hired when I was—you know—not working. It's fine I'm not going to drink. Violet doesn't care. She might not even notice, honestly. Someone else is going with us, too." My heart pounded in my ears. I'd never come this close to the truth before. It made the lie feel worse, so much bigger and crueler. I didn't know why I was saying these things. "Remember the guy who built the new kitchen shelves—the carpenter? You met him back in February."

"Oh yeah," David said. "That guy seems great. I liked him a lot. What's his name again?"

"Matt. He's okay. Violet likes him, I think." I said this slowly, and was terrified of myself as the words came out.

David said, "Well, I hope you make a love connection. Text me when you're on your way home."

"I will," I said. I paused. "Are you sure it's okay?"

"You don't need my permission to have a social life, Kit."

"I just feel bad," I said. "You had a long day and were thinking about hanging out with me when you got home."

"To be honest, a few hours to myself sounds nice," David said. "I do need to talk to you, but not immediately."

"Talk to me about what?" I asked. I stood on the doorstep of the bodega, my seltzers weighing down the oversize pockets of my jacket.

"Don't worry about it—nothing bad. I'll see you when you get home."

"Okay, then," I said. "See you later."

"Have fun," he told me, and I'm pretty sure we hung up at the exact same time.

CHAPTER EIGHTEEN

The blocks above the thoroughfare on Eighty-sixth Street were narrower and busier than the rest of the neighborhood. Delia's was crowded. Young people spilled from the velvet curtains at the entrance, waiting for cabs on the sidewalk, taking a final group selfie, hugging one another goodbye. Delia's was flanked by Vesuvio Café on one side and a bubble-tea place on the other, but they were both closed for the evening, gates pulled down and padlocked. The Palestinian restaurant—my favorite place to go when I wasn't doing a program—was packed, as always, and a few dozen people waited in line along the brick wall leading to its modest entrance. These blocks also contained a sprinkling of hole-in-the-wall bars with Irish names—O'Grady's and Maureen's and Cork Tavern—and tiny all-night Laundromats, their plastic dryer vents blowing fabric-softener-scented steam onto the street.

Violet hadn't been wrong to complain about the distance. It took me nearly twenty minutes to walk to the bar.

Valhalla was curiously uncrowded. When I arrived, two separate couples were cozied up on velvet-cushioned benches along the far wall. Matt and Violet sat at the end of the bar. I observed them a moment, how they looked side by side. Violet's silky black hair hung down her back, blending with her clothing. Matt leaned toward her, saying something with a sweet look on his face; I could tell he felt loose and easy. In the milky light, they were an obvious pair. If I hadn't known them, I would've assumed they were on a date. I was struck by my sense of how some people just looked *right* together, and Matt and Violet did, both of them attractive and cool, Violet with her dark eyes and oval face and slender frame, Matt with his nice square-jawed smile and aquarium-blue eyes. Their stylish, solid clothes. Violet's edgy makeup, her wide eyeglasses. Matt's black forearm tattoos—a bicycle, a hammer, the tiny silhouette of the state of Ohio.

I pulled a leather barstool over. It screeched on the granite floor, and I made my seat between them.

"Hi," I said, and they greeted me with soft, humming hellos. They seemed neither disappointed nor happy to see me.

"I got you this," Violet said, passing me a glass. "A cherry Negroni. That's your drink, right?"

I took the tumbler, stared into it for a bewildered moment. A bright red maraschino cherry bobbed on the surface of the ice: a delicious, toxic buoy. The gin had that mouthwatering, stinging smell I liked so much. I looked at Matt, my eyes wet. He raised his eyebrows at me.

Seeing my surprise, Violet added, "Melissa told me this is what you drink. I didn't guess."

"She did?"

"Well, no." Violet laughed. "But I overheard her say it. When she was talking about cake pairings with cocktails for that fancy wedding we're doing in the city in May." Violet offered a sheepish smile. On the bar behind her: an empty shot glass and a nearly finished cocktail, clear liquid and a couple ice cubes melting down to pebbles.

Oh, I thought. Violet's getting drunk.

"Can I have another?" she called to the bartender, pointing to her empties, and he nodded.

Melissa and Angelo had been talking about the wedding in May a lot. It was the kind of event Angelo lived for and Melissa detested— five hundred custom-decorated cupcakes in a variety of flavors. I hadn't known about the cocktail pairings.

"What a waste of money," I said. "For one stupid day, to drop thousands of dollars on *cupcakes*."

When he set down her drink, the bartender winked at Violet— he *winked*—and it occurred to me she'd wanted to get a drink at the Kettle Black for the same reason I'd wanted to come to Valhalla; she was already a regular at this bar. She'd wanted something else, something different.

"Thanks, Lewis," she said, turning back to Matt and me after a long swallow. "It's not a waste of money if you're rich. Anyway, I remembered the cocktail because for the groom's dessert, Melissa wanted to do a cherry Negroni and Black Forest cupcakes—"

"—with chocolate chips and whipped vanilla buttercream," I finished the sentence with Violet. Together, Melissa and I had invented this version of Black Forest—my favorite—to serve at my own wedding. Maria had molded frosting into a pattern of roses so delicate and ornate, it looked unreal, woven together as if by thread rather than sugar. "That cake isn't on the menu," I said.

"We sold it all through January, though," Violet said. "It was the seasonal flavor, in honor of your birthday month. Melissa called it Kitting Time, because—you know—she really missed you. Athena said she cried on New Year's Day when she realized you really weren't coming back."

"No," I said. The tops of my ears began to burn. "That isn't true." The shock of hearing this, and hearing it from Violet—Violet, who was being almost sweet, her lid loosened by alcohol—must have been plain on my face. I blinked at her.

"It *is* true!" Violet said. "She and Angelo are obsessed with you."

Matt, who had been listening to this conversation with an open-mouthed grin, added, "When I bid on the job building the shelves—I guess you weren't back at work yet—Melissa brought you up. She called you a genius."

"They both say it all the time," Violet said. "Like, 'Kit's the smartest person you'll ever meet.' That's what they told me in my interview."

"They say stuff like that—they're joking," I said. I looked into Violet's eyes. Matt, I could tell, was near laughing. "They don't *mean* it. It's sarcastic. They're being assholes."

"I don't think you understand what 'asshole' means," Matt said.

The cocktail Violet had given me was cold and slippery in my hand. I wondered if anyone noticed I hadn't taken so much as a sip. I imagined the alcohol sliding down my throat, moving into my blood. Oh, what a relief, to just have a small drink. I took a deep breath. I couldn't stray from the Radiant Regimen, not at this point. I was so close. For once, I'd see something through.

"Melissa and Angelo just like to troll me with the 'genius' stuff. Really, they think I'm a loser." I glared at Matt. "I *am* a loser," I said. "I've never even had a real job, and I live in my childhood home, even though I swore I wouldn't end up in Bay Ridge. I hate it here."

"No, you do not," said Matt.

Violet agreed. "I wish *I* was from here and had my grandmother's house. I'm trying to find a place over here—a studio or one-bedroom—when the lease is up on my Sunset Park dump in September. I long for the day I never have to speak to either of my horrible roommates again."

"And why are we talking about your *whole life*?" Matt said. "You're thirty-four. You aren't chained to Bay Ridge."

"If you're a loser, I can't even begin to deal with what I am," Violet said. "I'm thirty-two—I graduated during the worst part of the recession. After NYU, I did two unpaid internships, trying to get a job in marketing, and when the second place finally offered me a position, the salary was less money per hour than I was making as a barista in SoHo. I didn't take the job, and I've been in service ever since. Every summer I say I'm going to go to culinary school, or apply to an MBA program, but I never do, because I already have sixty grand in student loans and can't take on any more debt.

"Whenever I talk to my mom, she asks if I'm 'ready to move home,' since I don't have a *real* job. I'd rather die than go back to Centreville, but the thing is, I'm not sure why. I have some friends there, from high school, who have kids and cars and houses. In New York, I box cupcakes for a living and have two roommates I found on Craigslist. One of them is twenty-seven years old and her dad pays her rent. She's stupid. I hate her."

"So why do you stay?" I asked.

She shrugged. "It would be impossible to explain in a way you could understand."

"Try me."

"In Centreville, I'd have to get in the car every time I wanted a coffee. I'd have to get on an expressway. It would be like a ten-minute drive to Starbucks. Even if I wanted to walk *an hour* to get a coffee—I couldn't. There are no sidewalks."

Matt was nodding, and he grimaced when Violet said "Starbucks," which she enunciated with clear disdain. Then Matt said, "I think about moving back to Ohio all the time."

Violet and I were aghast.

"But you've got your own business!" Violet said. "You're thriving."

"You have a great apartment," I said. "Undermarket."

Whoops. Violet's eyebrows shot up, but Matt responded before she could inquire how I knew about the quality and price of his apartment.

"Undermarket here is still three times what I'd pay for the same place in Cincinnati. This is a lonely city," he said. "I'm surrounded by all these people, all these other artists and makers, but I feel like I never meet anyone who isn't totally stressed out, hustling all the time just to pay rent. And everyone is on edge." He gestured toward me. "Then, when I *do* meet someone who isn't hustling, they're stressed out because they *aren't* struggling. New York is such a high-strung place."

I couldn't hide the hurt of hearing this, or my irritation over the sanctimonious way they both talked.

"So, Brooklyn is terrible," I said, pointing my eyebrows toward Matt. "And everyone here sucks. But you can't move because then you'd have to drive to Starbucks? That's your problem? Pretty lame existential dilemma."

Matt smirked into the last of his beer, took a swig. "I can see how it would be difficult for you to appreciate. You've got your own problems. Despite the fact that you can't drive. Which basically disqualifies you from being able to live anywhere else."

I let my mouth hang open. Violet pulled her head back so she could look at me and Matt at the same time, narrowing her eyes.

"Wait," she said, pointing between us. "Do you two know each other? Like, from outside the bakery?" Her third drink was nearly gone, and her gaze was starting to separate, a buzzy flutter interrupting her ability to focus her eyes. She tried to make the question sound like no big deal, but I saw her intuition picking up on the weirdness of how Matt and I talked to—and about—each other. Sounding, as we certainly did, like two people who'd fucked.

"We spent a lot of time together when Matt built the shelves in February," I told her.

"And you started hanging out?" Violet sounded almost mad— mad and drunk—and I wondered how much more disappointed than shocked she would be to discover the truth. "You went and played Monopoly at Matt's great—what'd you say?—undermarket apartment?"

"Kit was shopping for a new dining table," Matt interjected. "She commissioned me to build one." He told the lie well, with a calm efficiency I couldn't muster, despite the frequency with which I'd been saying untrue things recently. His lie sounded so practical, and spoken without pause or blushing, as though he really believed it himself.

"Oh," Violet said, satisfied. "So, Kit, your husband makes a bunch of money, huh?"

I didn't answer and looked away. Matt flagged down the bartender and ordered another beer.

Violet repeated herself. "Your husband is, like, what? Kind of rich? I know it's rude to ask, but I don't care because I'm a little drunk." She leaned halfway off her stool, her ass in the air.

"He has a good job," I told her, flustered. I could've said more. If it had been just me and Violet, I might have. I could remind her that Melissa and I owned the building I lived in, and so I lacked a very large expense, but that every year David and I struggled to pay property taxes and maintenance bills—a plumbing issue, gutter cleaning. David had a 401(k), and we had his health insurance but almost nothing saved. He didn't earn an incredible sum of money, and we had a mountain of debt from his graduate degree, and half our furniture was from IKEA. So we weren't rich, though in recent years, we had finally stopped worrying about money all the time. Maybe "not worried" and "rich" were the same thing, though. I often did feel wealthy, sometimes, like the night we'd gone to see Annie Lou Samuels. Of course I did. Throughout my childhood, adults were in a constant state of anxiety over money; the talk of bills and needs hung at the corners of the kitchen ceiling with my uncles' stale cigarette smoke, staining the walls over time, getting inside our lungs.

But Violet wasn't asking about my childhood. She was asking about David.

Matt had turned back toward the bar and was looking straight ahead, pretending to examine the inapplicable happy-hour specials. Lewis brought him another beer. Violet gave Matt's arm a light slap. "What's he like?" she asked.

"Who?" Matt said.

"Kit's husband!"

"Only met him once," Matt said. He took a slow sip of his beer.

"Well, I've never met him," Violet said. "Can you believe it? They live up the block from the bakery, and he has never come by while I'm working. I'm starting to think he doesn't really exist."

"Oh, no," Matt said. "He exists."

"Yeah, I *know*. I'm just *joking*," Violet said with a twinge of hostility. I was jealous of her drunkenness, even as I could sense that she might become moody and loud, make a fool of herself. Say things she'd be embarrassed about tomorrow, if she remembered.

"I'm tired," I said.

"That's because you aren't drinking fast enough," Violet said. "Why aren't you drinking?" She made a pouty face, eyeing the cocktail in my hand. "You think I roofied you, Kit?"

"I'm sorry," I said, reaching to put the now watery Negroni on the bar top. "I want to drink—trust me, I *really* want to—but I'm avoiding alcohol for the time being."

"Oh, right." Violet laughed. "I can't believe I forgot. You do those intense diets."

"She hardly eats," Matt said without looking at me.

My mouth went dry. All the words I knew left my brain.

"She only eats, like, grilled salmon and organic chicken," Matt continued, speaking as though I weren't sitting right there, as though he were gossiping about someone else. "I think she's got some, like, pathological eating thing."

"I don't want to talk about this," I snarled. "And you"—I turned to Matt, pure venom in the look I gave him—"can mind your own fucking business." My voice was much too loud.

"Whoa," Violet said.

A group of young people at a table nearby all stopped talking, a hush of timid elation—a scene! bar drama!—thrown like a bedsheet over their conversation.

"Noted," Matt said, and he drank the rest of his beer in one smooth swallow and placed the glass down—hard—next to my untouched cocktail. "You only want to talk about other people's shit." He looked at Violet. "You know what? Fuck this. Let's settle up." He flagged Lewis back over.

Violet slid off her stool. She draped her jacket and pocketbook in the crook of her bent elbow and seemed to be waiting for guidance. She looked like a punished child, all the intimidating cool-girlness shocked out of her.

"Thanks for getting the drinks?" she said to Matt, craning her neck for his attention as he paid the bill. He offered her a hard nod and a tight, perfunctory smile as he signed the receipt and pocketed his credit card.

"You can get the next round," he said to her. "Where do you want to go? Let's have a nightcap."

I touched my throat where the neckline of my shirt met skin. My hand was warm and clammy.

"Oh," Violet said. She glanced at me, nervous as a deer.

"If you're feeling tired," I said to her, "I'll get you a taxi."

Matt chuckled noiselessly, his shoulders moving under his jacket as we all headed outside. The street was quiet. Matt had never treated me badly before, never been mean, and the sideways nature of his meanness now, its casual air, was disturbing.

Violet stood on the sidewalk, unsure what she wanted to do. I held my phone out to her, the Uber app open on the screen.

"What's your address?" I asked her.

"The thing is, I'm off tomorrow," she said. She sounded almost sad. "This is my Friday."

I should've known. I wrote the schedule, after all. The nervousness inside my belly turned, like a wave unfurling, to nausea, the sickening understanding of what was happening.

Matt was bent over his own phone. Requesting his own ride. I closed my eyes for a second, and in the blue-black nothing behind my eyelids, I told myself to give up. I couldn't stop this.

"Yeah, you should get another drink," I said when I opened my eyes.

Violet's lip quivered a little. "Do you want to come with us?" she asked in the conciliatory way of someone who hopes you say no. Did she realize how she was being used? She couldn't have. But surely she understood that something had happened, a thing beyond her. I hated Matt. I saw now a cruel pettiness in him, a side of his personality I could've been introduced to only in the real world.

"I have to get home," I said. "I *do* have to work tomorrow."

"You coming?" Matt called to Violet. A black Honda Civic pulled up, and he went around to the other side, getting in behind the driver.

Violet hesitated. She touched her face, pressing her fingertips against the flush at the top of her cheeks. "I already have the glow, don't I?" she asked me.

"Nah, you're good," I said, even though she was pretty pink. From the corner of my eye, I saw Matt watching from the window.

All right, Matt, reject me, I thought. Steal my friend. Sleep with her, tell her how crazy I am, laugh about it. Why shouldn't you?

That was the hardest part. Out from behind the shroud of our secret, there was no good reason Matt and Violet shouldn't hook up.

I opened the car door, ushering in Violet, and she folded herself inside.

"Have a good time," I told her. My vision blurred and I blinked; tears, I realized with horror, were creeping into the edges of my eyes.

"Are you sure?" she said in a low voice, leaning toward where I stood in the bike lane between the curb and the street.

I nodded, but I couldn't bring myself to say anything. Matt was buckling his seat belt.

"Happy Friday, Violet," I told her. "Be careful."

"Happy Wednesday, Kit," she said. Her voice contained gratitude and sweetness, the parts of her I'd just met and hoped to see again. I wished she and I were going somewhere together. I wished Matt didn't exist, or David, or any man. All the bars and all the cabs and all the bakeries and museums and movie theaters and subway trains would be so nice if men weren't allowed inside.

I shut the door and watched the car shrink down Fourth Avenue until it was gone.

Matt! In the time it took to exhale, my tenderness for Violet stretched like taffy, constricted, hardened into ear-ringing, humiliating panic. Maybe Matt slept with other women all the time. Violet was just one more. He didn't like her. Did he like her? Were they going to fall in love?

It was all so asinine and so terrifying, a monster of my own creation.

My hands shook as I pulled my phone out of my pocket.

—**Grow up,** I wrote to Matt. I sent the message, my phone sighing out its familiar *swoosh*. Unable to stop myself, I added one more:

—**Asshole.** Another *swoosh,* through the air, or the cable lines, or the satellites, or however texts traveled from one phone to another.

I stood there a moment longer, imaging Matt in the car with Violet. The two of them talking as he retrieved his phone from his pocket to read my message, produced a similarly hostile response to my text. I waited. None came. I shivered, even though the back of my neck was sweaty beneath my hair, and my heart was pounding as though I were running a far, long race.

I looked around. There was nothing to do. No one to wait for. Nowhere to go but home.

CHAPTER NINETEEN

David was still up, sitting at the dining room table, clearly waiting for me. He closed his laptop screen, sat back in his chair. There was food on the table, two rotisserie chickens in plastic takeaway containers. Woogie was underfoot, circling David, meowing and sniffing.

"I brought you dinner," he said. "From a farm-to-table place on Lafayette. Drew and I went to check out a brownfield site on Thirteenth and Avenue D, behind ConEd. Are you hungry?"

"I have never been as sick of anything as I am of chicken," I said. I took off my shoes and padded in stocking feet into the dining room.

"I hear you," he said, standing up. "What do you want instead?"

"Pepperoni pizza, a rare cheeseburger, and a whole Black Forest cheesecake. And a bottle of red wine and then some Sambuca."

"Let's do it," he said. He looked at his watch. "Pizza Wagon still delivers for another hour."

"No," I said. "We are so close."

"Yeah, sure," he said lightly. "But I'm ready to quit whenever you are. We've done great."

"Stop trying to get me to quit," I said.

He fidgeted with the zipper on his vest. There was uneasiness coming off him, filling the room.

"What's the matter?" I asked him.

"Nothing. I guess I thought we could spend a little time together. Hang out."

"Why?"

"So, I have some more travel coming up," he said slowly. "I just found out. And I know you've had a pretty hard time this year, so I wanted to, you know." He rubbed his nose. "I wanted to touch base with you about it."

Touch base! Like we were coworkers.

I flopped into one of the dining room chairs. My pocketbook fell from my shoulder to the floor. I reached for a chicken, popping the plastic lid off. Woogie jumped into my lap and I let him stay there. Ripped off a chunk of the meat, fed him with my hands, letting him lick my slimy fingers clean.

"That's gross," David said.

I ignored him. "Where are you going?" I asked. I ate a little bit of the chicken myself, digging below the skin to get to the white breast meat, making sure to be extra-uncivilized about it. Woogie watched me closely, face leaned in, licking his lips.

"Beijing."

He said it with slow apprehension, and I waited a beat before responding, allowing the distance to sink in.

"For how long? You wouldn't be waiting up to *touch base* unless it was a big trip."

"It could be three weeks. Maybe a whole month. I really wish you wouldn't feed the cat from the table."

I shrugged, pushed Woogie off my lap. He whined, shrill and wild, and tried to get back near the chicken. I got up, taking the chicken with me, balancing with both hands so none of the juices at the bottom of the container spilled. Woogie followed close at my feet into the kitchen, and David trailed behind us. At the counter, I took out two plates. First I took a hunk for Woogie, dropping it in his dish on the floor. He scarfed it, making a lot of sloppy mouth noises, barely taking the time to chew. I knew he'd probably puke and then eat the vomit. Good for him, I thought. A two-for-one.

I washed my hands before separating the rest of the chicken, putting the legs and some dark, oily thigh meat on a plate for David, the white breast meat, cut into tiny pieces, on a plate for me. I gathered what was in the fridge for a salad: arugula, mixed olives, and artichoke hearts. All the while, David explained: An eighty-five-story building in Beijing was going wrong. It was an official computational crisis: The principals at his firm's East Asian studios had promised to deliver a design on a tower for which they had neither the staff nor expertise. As was so often the case in the construction business, this oversight became clear to them only when they were too close to the deadline. Millions and millions of dollars were at stake, so David was being pulled from New York, along with some guy named Garrett from San Francisco and two senior designers at the London offices, and the four would converge like a pale, brainy, sedentary team of superheroes at the Beijing office to work fifteen-hour days in order to have a presentable plan for the clients and stakeholders.

On a different day—yesterday, even—all this might have excited me. A month to myself, one more month with Matt. The Radiant Regimen would be over—I'd be fun! I'd get drunk! I'd eat up to a half a cheeseburger! I could stay at Matt's house overnight—a vacation from my actual life. But this fantasy was soured. Matt was at a bar with Violet. What time was it? Were they still getting their nightcap? Had they gone for another drink at all? Or just straight back to his place?

"You've never needed my approval to travel before," I said to David. My whole body felt stiff with loneliness.

David sighed. "I don't want to turn this into something bigger than

231

it is, but truthfully, you feel far away from me lately—I don't know where your mind is. You go to Pilates a lot—like four times a week, it seems. It's like you never want to be around me. And I feel like it has something to do with this diet—I mean, with the Radiant Regimen. But it also feels like it has something to do with me."

I didn't know what to say. We stood there for a minute. I held two full plates. We should have moved to the table to eat, but this didn't feel like a conversation to have over a meal. It wasn't even time for a meal; it was eleven o'clock at night.

"When are you leaving?" I managed to ask.

"Saturday is the first night of Passover. We have seder at my parents' house—"

"I know about Passover," I said, cutting him off. "*I'm* the one your mother calls with these plans; don't tell me things I told you, just answer my question."

"Sunday," he said.

"This Sunday? As in four days?" The day the Radiant Regimen finished. I didn't say this, though. "Bringing up *my* perceived distance—or whatever—in the context of whether or not *you* should go on a mega-long business trip strikes me as counterintuitive," I finally said. I handed him his plate. Woogie had wandered away to give himself a bath in front of the window. David and I stood there, our dinners held in front of our chests, locked in an awkward standoff. "Do you want to go?" I said. "Are you looking for encouragement so you don't have to feel guilty?"

"I want you to say one way or another," David answered. "Tell me if you think it would be a bad idea for me to go away right now."

"I think you should go," I said.

The thing between us was hard and irritating, a marble rolling across the floor, the scraping sound growing bigger and bigger as we pretended not to notice.

"You could come with me?" he said, his voice thin: a fake offer, a bluff. The same way Violet invited me for the nightcap.

"I have a job," I said. I said it like I hated him, like the very sight of him made me sick.

"All right, then," he said. "I'll tell the travel office to book my ticket."

"Let's eat," I managed to say.

Back into the dining room we went, single file, without talking. We each took tidy little bites, slower and more carefully than either of us had ever chewed.

THE NEXT DAY WAS Thursday. I worked second shift.

There was too much to hold in my mind, and too many of my own secrets to think about, and I forgot I had agreed to come in early and run interviews with Angelo. We wanted to hire another part-timer for the counter. The lines, lately, had been too long with only two people on the floor. Angelo called me a few minutes after ten, when I was undressed and running the water in the shower, waiting for it to warm up.

"Our first interview is here, where are you?" he said when I answered. I stood naked in my kitchen, where my phone was charging on the counter. I'd run from the bathroom, leaving the water on, not even taking the time to wrap myself in a towel. I'd realized instantly why he was calling; my ringtone for Angelo was Bonnie Raitt's "I Can't Make You Love Me," because—I swear—it was his favorite song.

"I'm sorry," I told him. "I'm having a slow start."

"You forgot," he said.

"I just need a quick shower."

"You've never taken a quick shower in your life. Brush your teeth, tighten your greasy ponytail, and I'll see you in ten minutes."

"Can't you interview her by yourself?" I asked, my voice a trilling whine.

"Of course I can," Angelo said. "But I won't. Get going."

He hung up.

* * *

I RUSHED TO THE bakery. The first person we were scheduled to interview sat at the farthest table, her back straight.

"Hi," I said, sticking out my hand. "I'm so sorry to keep you waiting." I failed to hide my breathlessness, a long gasping exhale. "You must be Nicole."

She stood and shook my hand, and I noticed she'd dressed up for the interview: a knee-length khaki skirt, simple faux-suede boots, a cardigan, a small silver cross around her neck. She held a manila folder in front of her, a résumé on crisp white paper. I felt terrible.

"Let me put my things away and go get Angelo," I said. "Has anyone offered you anything to drink? A coffee, hot chocolate?"

"Yes, Angelo did," she said. She ran her hand over a patch of acne at her jawline. I noticed her fingernails were unpolished (a health code plus) but bitten (an absolute health code minus). "I'm fine. Thank you."

"Tiana, can you get Nicole a glass of water?" I called to Tiana, who was just finishing up with a customer. She gave me a *You can't do it?* look, and I responded by mouthing, *Help me.* She smiled, shaking her head.

In the kitchen, Angelo was yelling into his cell phone. It was odd to once again conduct business around Matt's tarp-sealed carpentry, the plastic sheeting duct-taped over the edges to keep it separate from the bakery. He'd never responded to my texts the night before. I went to the handwashing sink and recovered the small mirror Maria hid behind it, inspecting what Angelo had described accurately—without having even seen me—as my greasy ponytail. I fixed a red bandana over my head, pulling all my hair up tight beneath it and tying it in a bow at the front, Rosie the Riveter–style. Placing the mirror back, I washed my hands carefully with scalding water, getting under my nails with a little brush hanging from a chain over the faucet.

I dreaded seeing Matt, who was due in to finish his cabinet later.

234

Melissa was stooped over Maria's workstation, writing a message on a fresh almond sponge cake. Sponge was one of the more difficult cakes to decorate because it was iced with meringue, which was stickier and filmier than the buttercream frosting we used on most cakes. Melissa's own table was piled high with storage bins.

"Look, Berno, I like you," Angelo was saying into his phone. "But I need the deliveries done on time or I have to find somebody else. I can't have you showing up to deliver someone's cake in the middle of the party. I'll just sign up for Seamless." He wouldn't. Delivery apps took a huge cut, and Angelo wanted to know who was driving.

Melissa rolled her eyes. Angelo sighed heavily into the phone, covering his eyes with his free hand for extra-dramatic emphasis.

"I'm gonna have to fire Nick Bernardakis," Angelo said after he finally hung up. "I got this guy in Manhattan Beach who wants to murder me over a sheet cake with a big dent in the corner, twenty minutes after the delivery window. It's like talking to a child when I ask Berno to explain what happened. He gets so defensive. I think he was going to cry just now."

"One time in high school, he started shrieking and, like, hyperventilating in language arts class because a yellow jacket flew in the window and was buzzing around his face," Melissa said. "Mr. Femia sent him to the principal's office for being disruptive."

"Is he allergic?" I asked.

"Oh, yeah," she said. "Deathly, I think."

"Who cares," said Angelo. "Let's get this interview over with. She's been waiting a half hour. The next girl is going to be here any second."

"The next *applicant*," I said.

"Sure, Kit," Angelo said. "Applicant. I don't care what you want to call her. It's time for the second interview, and we haven't started the first one because you're a bozo who can't get out of bed in the morning."

"Have fun," Melissa called in an excruciating singsong as Angelo and I filed out of the kitchen.

* * *

WE FINISHED THE INTERVIEWS around noon. Angelo and I had a funny let's-get-to-know-you routine, a role reversal: Angelo took up the persona of gay good cop, adopting a false effeminacy and asking what the interviewee's favorite flavor of cake was, and if they liked coffee or tea better, and even less relevant questions—where'd they get those cute shoes, what was the last movie they saw in the theater, that kind of thing. Meanwhile, I asked the real questions ("How do you think your last supervisor would describe you?" and "Are you able to lift at least thirty-five pounds?") and explained the dress code, the training schedule for new employees, and our commitment to high-quality ingredients. We alluded to Melissa as though she were some kind of mystical genius rather than the sarcastic, antisocial baker who was currently twenty feet away, behind the kitchen doors, too ornery to come out and meet applicants.

"I think we should hire Nicole," Angelo said. He leafed through the résumés we'd collected. The last person we'd interviewed had said she couldn't work weekends and wasn't available after six p.m., and now he took her résumé and folded it in half, tossed it in the garbage.

"I don't know about Nicole." I pointed to the trash can. "You have to keep résumés on file for a year."

"And yet," Angelo said, gesturing at the trash, "there it lies. Why no Nicole? She was good. Look how patient she was when you made her wait so long."

"We aren't hiring someone as an apology for making her wait," I replied. "She bit her nails. And she touched her face. Multiple times in the fifteen minutes we spent with her. She's a face-toucher. The health department will come in here, see her face-touching behind the counter, and fail us before the inspection even starts."

"She worked at Starbucks," Angelo said. "That's great experience."

"You always say people who worked at Starbucks are going to be good, and they never are. Remember Kathryn?"

I'd caught Kathryn pocketing money from the cash register two weeks after we'd hired her. I never let Angelo forget it, because I hadn't wanted to give her the job in the first place, but he insisted. Her only previous experience was at a high-volume Starbucks downtown.

"They don't even know how to pull espresso at Starbucks," I said. "The baristas just press a button, and some motor oil leaks out on an automatic timer."

"Fine. So, I guess Natasha it is," he said.

"Natasha would be okay, but I think Isra is a better choice. She impressed me. She was genuine, and she has been here before as a customer—she knew the menu."

Angelo pressed his mouth into a straight line, gave me a look. "No," he said. "Let's not get into this."

"Get into what?" I said, even though I felt prepared for a fight. Isra had worn a headscarf. Here was a line between me and Angelo that I usually tried to ignore. "The staff has to cover their hair anyway," I said, lowering my voice.

He whispered, "What are guys like Tony Pasco going to say? And the old-timers?" He pointed to the table where a foursome of elderly people drank coffee and played scopa a few times a week. "They'll treat her bad."

"Who fucking cares what they say? Tony Pasco comes in every day, but he doesn't buy anything half the time. And if you want to cater to people like that, we could just have some stale biscotti in a jar and a radio playing Connie Francis. Plenty of our customers are Muslim, I'm sure you've noticed. Like a third of the neighborhood. What about them?"

"Pasco is an example, is all," Angelo said. "Of the way a lot of people in the neighborhood still think. Tony is one of those guys. He goes, 'Angelo, we need a businessman to get elected and run the government like a business.'"

"Yes, I am aware Tony Pasco sucks," I said. "What is your point?"

"This girl—"

"This applicant's name was Isra."

"I just don't want to hire somebody who's going to get harassed. It puts her in a bad spot, too, see? And I don't want to have to fight with people or kick anybody out. Between this and the way Melissa picks fights with anyone who looks at her wrong—I don't want this kind of thing to come between the bakery and any of the people we've known forever, people who knew Nonna."

"Nonna's dead, so you don't need to worry about her," I said. "You're talking about decisions made for reasons having to do with your own feelings—"

"I'm talking about *Bay Ridge*."

"It's illegal," I said. Angelo rolled his eyes almost imperceptibly. I didn't think he meant to do it. "Isra is the best candidate for the job. She's worked in service and already has her food handler's license. If a small group of people want to pretend it isn't 2016, that isn't our problem."

"You aren't listening to what I'm saying," he said.

"I am listening, but I'm not a mental health professional. And what I'm hearing is that you need therapy."

"I'm not racist," Angelo said. His voice was thin, pleading; he knew how bad he sounded. He knew the fact that he felt the need to declare himself as not racist was, in itself, a mark against him.

I wanted to say: *I hate when you say these things. It makes me so sad.* But I was a coward in the end. I said, "I'm going to see what Melissa thinks."

Angelo glared at me, a flash of anger. But he knew that, in failing to convince me, he'd lost.

"Okay," he said. "Fine. You're right. Isra did a better interview than Natasha. I'll email her and see when she can start training."

"No, no, no. Let me ask Melissa." I grinned; threatening to involve Melissa—who had no patience for these debates and would only want to know who had the most relevant experience and the cleanest fingernails—was so effective in disarming Angelo, I couldn't help but be pleased with myself. "You can tell her how racist you aren't." I made as though gearing up to burst into the kitchen, straightening my back and taking a dramatic step toward the swinging door.

"Don't you dare," Angelo said, reaching as though to pull me back.

But before we could fight our way into the kitchen, the bells on the front door jingled and in walked Matt, bringing a balm of April wind. He wore a beat-up hoodie and his eyes were hung with gray circles. He looked like someone who'd been up too late or not gone to bed at all.

From where she was finishing with a customer at the cash register, Tiana raised her eyebrows at him, amused. "Everybody's in a *state* today," she said to no one in particular.

"He looks terrible," Angelo said to me, barely lowering his voice.

I slunk off behind the espresso bar.

"Matthew," Angelo said as Matt approached. "Hello. We did all the baking a few hours early again, so you should be set to get started. Show me what you're doing today." Before they walked off, Angelo turned to me. "Can you get this man a coffee, please?" he asked in a bossy tone. To Matt: "What do you want? Cortado? Macchiato?" He pronounced the words in a garish Italian accent.

"No, I'm fine," Matt said. "Thank you, though." He gave me a meaningful look and went into the kitchen.

"You embarrass yourself," I said to Angelo, who lagged behind. "You sound like a cartoon man in a pizzeria commercial."

"I was doing Steven Seagal in *Out for Justice*," he said.

"I haven't seen that one, and I don't think I will," I said. I used my whole flat-palmed hand to point toward the kitchen. "Your carpenter is waiting for you."

He spun on his heels and stalked away. I watched the doors swing behind him before turning my attention to the espresso machine. I was mad at Matt and acutely embarrassed for the veiled fight we'd had in front of Violet, for his rejection, for ignoring my texts. I wanted—needed—to know what had happened between him and Violet.

But when he'd come in looking so beaten, a pitiful tenderness had flooded me. I didn't know what to do. I moved my hands mechanically, pouring milk, wiping down the steamer, listening for the sound—the almost inaudible gurgle—the wand made when the perfect temperature had been reached. I tapped the pitcher on the counter: once softly, a second time with a bit more force, and pulled two espresso shots at twenty-six seconds. I poured the drink into a paper cup so the care I'd put into it wouldn't be too obvious. I went into the kitchen.

"Hi," I said to Matt. "I made you this."

Matt and Angelo were kneeling, pulling the tape back from the plastic on the cabinets.

Matt stood. He looked at me before taking the cup. In his gaze, I tried to read whether he'd slept with Violet and, if so, whether it was the best sex of his life. There was no information there, though, just fatigue. He took a gulp of coffee. The cup looked like a toy in his large hands.

"Let me help," I said.

We uncovered the supplies. Matt told Melissa he was going to need a spotter to hold the side panels—tall slabs of oak—in place to stack the cabinets and fix them to the wall. She nodded without looking up or speaking, her head down, her body turned from us.

"I can do it," I said.

"You cannot do it," Melissa replied. "Edwin's coming in."

Edwin was Guillermo's friend. Edwin didn't have papers, so we were able to hire him only for odd jobs. He was extremely handy. Also, Edwin's wife cleaned Angelo's house—I mean, Uncle Nicky and Aunt Tina's house, where Angelo still lived—and Edwin sometimes drove Angelo places when he had to go into the city but needed or wanted to be on the phone the whole time. I didn't want to cost Edwin the work, but neither did I want him there with me and Matt.

"But that's pointless," I said. "I'll just be sitting around until they're done."

"No, you'll be home," Melissa answered. "Angelo will come lock up. He lives closest, anyway."

I opened my mouth, then I closed it. How to protest? What could I say? "But?" I asked. "The safety rules?"

"Matt's cool," Melissa said. "He said if he gets hurt, he'll tell the insurance guy you were here."

"That's an overly complicated crime, considering I'm happy to stay."

"I'm telling you no."

"Why?"

Matt was busying himself with his supplies, pretending to be too engrossed in his own preparations to notice or be invested in the outcome of the awkward exchange happening in front of him.

Melissa said nothing. She was finished for the day, more tired than the rest of us. She must have arrived at three a.m. to get all the baking done so early. She tossed her apron into the laundry bin and walked out of the kitchen without responding. I followed, leaving Matt alone with Angelo.

In the big supply closet, Melissa checked her hair in the mirror. "Yikes," she grumbled, and mussed it a little, then gave up and put on a beanie.

"Melissa," I said. "I want to stay."

She didn't look at me. "You've lost too much weight with this diet," she said after an extended pause.

"Wait." I pulled my head back. "What?"

"You looked pretty normal when you first came back to work," she said. "And now your face is all skinny, and you're wound up all the time. You're not strong enough to do manual labor, and frankly, I don't want to pay *your* workers' comp when you get dizzy and one of your little bird bones snaps."

"Don't you start with me, too."

"Oh, David brought it up? Good," she said, though he hadn't. I realized, heat rushing up the back of my neck, that David might have been apprehensive to travel because he, too, was concerned about my weight. It was infuriating. I'd finally followed through, stuck to a dietary program without giving up, and now everyone wanted to ruin it for me. She went on, "Here Angelo and I were thinking he was going to let you starve yourself to death."

"Don't be dramatic," I said. "It's been a couple months. It's done on Monday."

"So how much did you weigh this morning?"

"I don't know, because I didn't get on the scale. It's against the program rules."

"What'd you eat today?"

"I'm not going to dignify that with a response," I said. I'd had half a banana.

"Okay, then." Melissa put on her windbreaker. It was red with a bright white zipper up the middle. "Have a cupcake."

"Excuse me?"

"Have a cupcake, and you can stay tonight."

We stared at each other for a long minute.

"There's nothing cherry-flavored today, but we've got Chocolate Cloud. Have one cupcake, and I'll ask Edwin to clean the basement and you can help Matt. If it's so important to you."

The anger welling in me was hot and new. Or maybe it was so old that I'd forgotten this kind of rage, buried since early adolescence, when puberty crazed us both with indignation and a sense of what a great injustice it was to live inside our own uncomfortable skin. When the divide between us first cracked open, and I became one kind of woman and Melissa another. I thought of the full-contact fights we had as children, when we were so close, and looked so much alike, and shared everything: possessions, secrets. Now I could've pulled Melissa's hair, slapped her, pushed her down. I could've taken her by the throat and squeezed.

"Go fuck yourself," I said, a little spit flying from my words. "You're a bully, and you are always overreaching—"

"This conversation is actually over," Melissa said. She sounded almost bored. Because she didn't know my secrets anymore, this was just business. We were at work, and I was, at the bottom of everything else, her employee. I might have stormed off, as I'd done in December, but what would be the point? She'd already sent me home. I recalled Matt and Violet saying how much she loved me, saying she thought I was a genius. What a bunch of simplistic baloney.

Melissa pulled lip gloss from her pocket and ran the clear goo over her lips. "See you tomorrow." She stepped toward me and patted my cheek, the way gangsters did in the movies, the way my grandmother used to do when Melissa or I had answered back. *Go ahead, be fresh,* Nonna used to tell us, then place her hand on our face with a tender touch. The gesture had an eerie calm to it, a reminder that we could say anything we wanted; it didn't weaken her authority. We had no power, only useless invective. Words were ours to waste, but the decisions were hers, and they'd been made.

Melissa turned to leave, her shoulders loose and easy. I stood there for a few more minutes with my unbearable anger and, underneath it, a sense of emptiness. I wrapped my arms around my waist, closed my eyes. I ran my hand up my prominent rib cage. Then I got my pocketbook and went home.

CHAPTER TWENTY

I planned to put my pajamas back on, eat a grapefruit, and take a nap. But David was there. He stood in the kitchen, his vest unzipped over his work clothes, oven mitts on his hands.

"What are you doing here?" I said. "It's the middle of the day."

"They're sending me to China on a few days' notice. They let me go home early."

"I can't believe you left work," I said. "You love going to work. It's your one true love." I knew I sounded petty and babyish; I didn't care.

"I do love it," he said. "I think what I do is interesting, and I'm lucky. A lot of people who work as much as I do don't love their jobs— they hate them."

"I know," I said. "You've always been this way."

"What about you?" he said. "I wasn't expecting you home until later." I snorted. "I have a headache," I said.

"Well, I am glad to see you," David said. "I don't feel like we had a real conversation last night. Something is going on with you."

"In what way?" I asked, as if I couldn't imagine what he meant.

"Well, you don't tell me what you're thinking about," he said. "And you go out a lot, but you never invite me."

"That's not true. I never go anywhere."

"Well, you've gotten really into Pilates?" His eyes were sharp below his big, narrowed brows. He moved in front of the stairwell, blocking my way up to the bedroom. His hands were still in the oven mitts. The kitchen was warm, and the smell of something hearty came from the oven.

"Are you baking?" I asked.

"Answer my question," he said. He folded his arms, and with the mitts, it should have been comical. We both should have laughed. But I was terrified. He was stern.

"You work almost all the time. Excuse me if I wanted to do something for myself."

"But what *are* you doing? Just going to Pilates? Really? I have to be honest, it doesn't seem true."

He was, I realized, daring me to say it.

"You have a lot of nerve," I said instead. "To judge me for pursuing solitary interests when your job forces me to spend a lot of time alone. *You'd* rather work than be with me, not the other way around." The accusations came to me as though there were nothing else to say, nothing to admit or explain, when I still barely understood what Pilates was. If David looked at our credit card statements, there'd be no charges for Pilates class. My lies were sloppy, relying on my sureness—unchallenged until now—that David didn't care enough to ask questions.

"Okay. Fair point," David said. "I'm sorry. But what about last night? I felt, I don't know, a little left out. You could have asked if I wanted to have a drink with you and your coworkers."

I couldn't have. "It didn't occur to me you'd be interested," I said.

"Okay, well, what about the first two months of the year? Why did you quit your job only to go back to it?" he asked. "You could have started something new for yourself."

"Like what?" I heard myself yelling, but I couldn't really feel it. "What could I possibly have done instead?"

"Anything, Kit. Jesus." He was yelling, too. "I can't tell you what to do—you have to decide what you want."

"But you're the one who just brought it up!"

"You are impossible to fight with," he said, throwing up his oven-mitted hands. "I'm bringing it up because you quit! You quit right before Christmas and said you wanted to find a new job. A *career*. That is what *you* said."

I was still holding my purse. My work shirt—a pink-and-white-checkered flannel—hung on my frame, my skinny body lost inside it. I wondered if my thinness—hard-won, coveted—looked ugly to him now.

I said, "Don't say 'career' in that condescending tone, as though you have one and I don't."

"I didn't! I was quoting you!" David shook his head in resignation. "You are so frustrating." He took a loud breath, steadied himself. Slowly and with false calm, he said, "You told me you wanted a career and implied the bakery wasn't a career. Then you stayed home and looked at your phone for two months, researching diets. Then you went back to work like it never happened."

"I don't know what this fight is even about," I said, which was mostly true. It was about everything. It was about nothing. "I just want to get in the shower and then read a book." By "read a book," I really meant "skim a blog, stare at Instagram."

"Okay," he said. "I made you lunch, though. Will you come eat, please?"

"But I'm not supposed to be home right now."

"I was going to bring it over to the bakery," he said. I imagined him coming in the back door, Matt in the kitchen with Edwin, a whole weird mess getting even weirder and messier. Well, one agony avoided, at least.

"What is it?"

"A baked sweet potato."

That sounded pretty good.

My head was aching, the violent hammering of hunger let go too long, the tight sensation of a vise inside my stomach, cranking and cranking until every organ was flattened, my energy gone, nothing fed but my ability to be confused and irritated and frazzled.

"I'll eat," I told David. "But I'm still mad. I don't forgive you."

"That's fine," David said. "I'll probably survive."

I ATE AT THE counter. The sweet potato tasted like candy, but in a gross way. I wished it were pie. David got on his laptop in the living room. I could hear him on the phone with his boss, with the travel agent his firm used, with a person at the firm in Beijing, though it was the middle of the night in China. I tried to remember the last time David and I'd had a big fight. I recalled, with horror and a further curdling of my appetite, the worst fight we'd ever had. It was on the way to my grandmother's funeral. The year before we got married. The year before Sweet Cheeks opened. Another life entirely.

My grandmother had a stroke. It was midnight. Early December. A doctor called the landline of the East Village apartment. I was still awake, stoned on the sofa, watching *SpongeBob* on the cartoon channel. I'd only just gotten off work from the café.

"Katrina DeMarco?" asked the doctor, who sounded tired. He had an Israeli accent.

David came out from the bedroom where he'd been sleeping, stood in the doorway. "Who's on the phone?" he asked, annoyed.

"I have your grandmother here," the doctor said. "At the intensive care unit. Maimonides Hospital."

"No," I said. "You're mistaken." I'd spoken to my grandmother on my little Nokia cell phone hours earlier, during my break at the café. She'd been fine. She was going to get a good deal on a couple of Christmas trees from the wholesale florist on Eighteenth Avenue. Uncle Nicky was taking her.

"I'm sorry," he said. "I'm afraid she was brought by ambulance around ten o'clock. I have Nicolò DeMarco here, is this your uncle? I'm afraid he is—well, he is distraught. He asked me to call you."

"I'm confused," I said. "What exactly is going on?"

"Miss DeMarco," the doctor said. "Do you know what power of attorney is? Are you aware you and Melissa DeMarco are entrusted with joint power of attorney in the event that your grandmother is incapacitated?"

"What do you mean," I asked, "when you say 'incapacitated'?"

David was standing in the doorway still, in his pajamas. I felt the earth moving around us.

"Are you able to get to Brooklyn?" the doctor asked.

MY GRANDMOTHER NEVER WOKE up from the coma. Melissa and I signed the papers, the technicians turned off the machines. In the hospital, Melissa's face looked like a stained napkin. Uncle Nicky sobbed: a honking, horrible kind of crying, a child's crying, and Angelo held him. Nothing has been the same since. A few days later, on the way to the funeral, David and I had a terrible fight.

I got my period in the car on the way to the church and, under so much stress, became admittedly histrionic, saying I was going to have to greet mourners all day with blood sticking my stockings to my legs. The driver pulled up to a drugstore without our asking him to do so. David, who had been stoic over the last few days, said, "Doesn't this happen every month?"

I started crying, then I was shouting in the Personal Hygiene/Family Planning/Incontinence aisle of Duane Reade, calling David a mean bastard and claiming, near hysterical, "If men got periods, tampons would be free like toilet paper, and you'd *never* know when it was coming. You can't remember to pay your own phone bill! All your library books are overdue."

Everyone stared at us in the long line to the cash register—David, silent and smoldering, while I whimpered next to him, our funeral clothes already rumpled—while some obdurate old woman at the counter held a handful of coins out to the cashier and made him pick through the change—some of it foreign—until he had the amount of money needed for her pack of Virginia Slims. The whole fight really had to do with how upset I was about Nonna, how much it hurt to know I'd never see her again. My guardian was gone. I wondered if David, realizing this, felt chained to me. He never said or even implied anything of the sort. But that's how it goes when somebody dies suddenly like that—you forget how to be around the living people you have to keep loving, how to carry on even though everything feels ruined.

Anyway, that was seven years ago. Since then, I couldn't remember a real fight. I couldn't remember anything like this—being so sick of him, resentful, wondering who I could be without him—until now.

CHAPTER TWENTY-ONE

The next day was the start of Passover. David had already left for work when I got up. He'd left a note on the counter: *Kit, I won't be able to get home before seder tonight. See you there.*

I tossed the note in the garbage. Then I texted Melissa:

—**Wrkng from home today—sched, orders & stuff**

She responded right away with a thumbs-up emoji. I waited for her to add something more; I knew she wasn't going to apologize, but she could've admitted how rude—how *unprofessional*—her accusations had been yesterday. Or make a snide comment about me skipping work because I was mad. She didn't, though, and I didn't hear from Angelo, either. I wasn't sure Melissa had told him what happened yesterday, how I lost my temper, but I knew they'd been talking about me behind my back for months. *Fine.* I was happy to be alone in my apartment, telling my cat to make me a smoothie.

"You don't do anything," I said to Woogie as he wolfed down a whole can of his gruel. "Wet food," people called canned cat food, not seeming to notice how absolutely disgusting that made it sound. When he finished eating, Woogie sat on his hind legs on the top rung of the stepstool in the kitchen, bathing himself methodically by licking his paw and then rubbing it across his face and whiskers. "Make me breakfast," I said. "Or get a job." Like everyone else in my life, he ignored me.

I SPENT MOST OF the day reading Radiant Regimen testimonials from blogs. A lot of people made claims that seemed grandiose, given that I'd experienced no such effects by this late stage in my own journey: an ability to remain hyperfocused, antlike strength, sagelike calm. Maybe I'd done too much philandering and not enough Pilates, but I was skeptical. Why would stretching with a special set of ropes give me a mental boost when sex wouldn't? The before-and-after photos, however, were more validating. I looked with relish at each influencer in a designer sports bra, arms and stomach dwindled from day one to day seventy-five. I should have taken some photos of myself.

After a few hours online, I felt sticky and gross. Too much sitting. I moved from the kitchen counter to the living room, where I called in some orders for the bakery's paper goods and disposable utensils, then tinkered with the next month's schedule. Mostly, I checked my phone to see who'd texted. No one.

I DECIDED TO GET to seder early. First, though, I made myself look nice. I took a scalding shower. I was attentive while shaving my legs, armpits, and bikini line, stepping out of the shower's stream, moving the razor with care, getting everything, even behind my knees. I shampooed twice and let the conditioner soak in my hair. When I was toweled off forty-five arduous minutes later, I pulled myself into David's favorite of my dresses: a black jersey shift, matched with uncomfortable leather booties and opaque black stockings. In the mirror, after the blow dryer and the makeup and the lint roller, I stood as straight as I could. Because of its A-line cut, the dress didn't look *too* too big. The style was supposed to be worn oversize, so it looked normal, if somewhat loose at the shoulders. It was also a little long, hitting me at the knee now instead of a couple inches above.

I'd never worn the booties before, though I'd had them a long time. They were pointed at the toe and had a chunky heel, about an inch high. It took five minutes to fasten the clasp of the fourteen-karat cherry blossom charm necklace Melissa, Angelo, and David had pooled together to buy me for Christmas a few years ago, even though we had all agreed at Thanksgiving to get one another modest gifts. (I had been livid, opening the necklace right after handing them gift bags with Grumpy Cat coffee mugs and Taylor Swift refrigerator magnets. I'd never worn this necklace, though I took it out of my jewelry box and looked at it sometimes, thought about selling it on eBay and putting the money toward exorbitant gifts for my stupid, inconsiderate loved ones. Oh, I'd get Melissa the fanciest blender money could buy, show her how it felt.)

I took Uber Black to Midwood. The twenty-minute ride from Bay Ridge cost fifty-eight dollars, and afterward I got on my phone right away and tipped the driver thirty percent. Hobbling on my terrible, beautiful booties up the front porch steps, I saw Hiram through the window, his back bent over the piano, the sound of "My Girl" drifting faintly into the night. There was Rebecca doing a goofy little dance on her way out of the front room, and there was Benji sitting on the purple velvet ottoman, and there, to my great shock, was David sitting in the purple velvet armchair.

He was on time! Early! I couldn't believe it.

I pressed the buzzer harder than necessary, releasing its spine-rattling electric cry. Rebecca appeared in the foyer, baffled. "What on earth are you doing ringing the bell, dear?" she asked me. Her glasses slid down her nose. "Oh, you look marvelous."

"Thank you," I said, my tone chilly. Why was I chilly to Rebecca? I wasn't mad at her. She'd done nothing to deserve it. Control slipped away from me, though. I was just throwing grenades in every direction.

"We were just talking about Italy," she said. "David has a lot of good ideas—he's so experienced."

"It's his job to travel," I said flatly.

She clasped her hands together nervously at her torso. "We are going to have a nice seder," she said, changing the subject. I took off my peacoat and handed it to her to hang in the closet—a task, like walking through the front door, that I typically handled myself. She took it without hesitation.

"I was supposed to be at the bakery tonight," I said, my voice slick with feigned insouciance. "Maybe I quit. I'm not sure."

"Oh!" Again, poor Rebecca had no idea how to respond. We tended to avoid talking about my shortcomings, including my frequent futile attempts to quit working for Melissa. "Well, your sister will be helpless without you. But you'll have more time to come over here and hang out with us old folks while David is away."

"If you cook food I can actually eat, I might," I said.

Rebecca had never been anything but patient and accommodating with how I ate. Whenever I look back on this night, there are many, many things I regret. But nothing torments me more than remembering how I treated my mother-in-law. In the twelve years we'd known each other, I'd never been rude to her, and the wrongness of it hit us both at once. We winced. I had an urge to grab her hand and apologize, tell her I was having an awful time. Start crying. Rebecca would be on my side if I pretended I was only freaked out and disappointed because David was going to China. The comfort, however crookedly obtained, would be enormous. I fought the feeling off and walked to the den.

"There she is!" Hiram said, getting up from the piano bench to hug me. I didn't return the embrace, leaving my arms limp at my sides.

"Hey, Kit," Benji said, and I nodded. "You look really nice."

"Yeah, what's the occasion?" Hiram said. "You're like a movie star."

David didn't move from his chair, just observed me. At first I didn't know what to make of his silence, until I realized he was trying to read me the same way I was trying to read him; we were taking each other's temperature. He'd arrived early to be a nice guy, to warm everyone up in case I was still mad. Well, I was still mad.

"God, I must look like a miserable wreck most of the time," I said.

Everybody except David started talking at once: Ridiculous! Crazy! I was beautiful all the time, I just looked even more beautiful today. I was the second most attractive of the Altmanns, Hiram promised, winking at Rebecca, who shook her head, a sweet laugh, a wagging finger.

Finally, David spoke up. "Just take the compliment," he told me.

I glared at him, hoping the look conveyed my message: *I hate you right now, and I'm going to spend all your money on cabs while you're jet-lagged and asthmatic in Beijing, and I'm going to look this pretty the whole time.*

"Guess what? I found a Passover dinner recipe from the Radiant Regimen!" Rebecca said. David and I broke away from giving each other mean stares. "It was on a website. Kit was just saying she hopes I made something she can eat. I sure did!"

"What is it?" Benji asked.

"Baked cod in tomato sauce," Rebecca said. "It's wonderful."

"Smells great," Hiram said.

"Thank God it isn't chicken," David said, attempting to fuse some normalcy into our rapport. "Kit and I have been eating so much chicken. She's really sick of it."

Everyone waited for me to acknowledge his comment, to add my verse of the lament. I examined my cuticles as though I hadn't heard him.

"I was reading up on your program," Rebecca said. "And I have to say, it looks pretty marvelous. All that fresh food. It doesn't really require you to deprive yourself of anything but the junk." She looked nervously at me from the corner of her eye. "And the information on the website about pesticides and toxins was eye-opening. I was convinced."

"We should all do the Radiant Regimen," Hiram said, grinning so his silver fillings showed. He would never go a day without eating at least two handfuls of black jelly beans.

"Hiram!" Rebecca cried. "The woman who invented it, her parents are from Haifa!" She clapped her hands together. Hiram's family had moved from Israel to New York when he was a kid, a part of his personal history that seemed to not interest him even the smallest bit. Only Rebecca ever brought it up, and mostly in the context of who else was Israeli.

"Oh, goody!" he said in a teasing way, making jazz hands. His impression of his wife wasn't meant to be cruel, but its accuracy gave it an unintended meanness.

Rebecca was a good sport, as ever, slapping at his hands playfully. "You stop," she said, giggling.

Hiram took her elbow, beamed at her. They were having a good day together, these people who'd been married thirty-seven years. Could David and I end up like them? Wiry and gray-haired old friends, playing cards in our den, flirting in front of our grown children—still in love, or what looked enough like being in love, but maybe was just the peace of true acceptance? If so, we'd have to start right away. We'd have to shove everything else off the table, let it fall, and say, *It's just us now: focus.* And nobody could get distracted. Nobody could go on month-long business trips, and nobody could have affairs with hipster carpenters.

It was probably already too late. I didn't think we'd be like Hiram and Rebecca someday.

It looked nice, though. It really did.

* * *

THE ALTMANNS NEVER USED their dining room. ("It just doesn't feel like we're *together* in there," Hiram said to me once. "It's not where we belong.")

Rebecca had a special ceramic seder serving set with small rounded dishes on a tray. Besides the five traditional items, there were three extra dishes for modern additions to the seder plate. In keeping with Rebecca and Hiram's relentlessly progressive worldview, a potato represented the Holocaust and all those murdered by oppressive governments across history and around the globe; an orange represented Jews who felt isolated in their communities; and a pinecone was in reverence of the small oppressions we walked past on a daily basis while living our privileged lives.

Hiram filled the cups for the Kaddish, and I was surprised when David held the cup, leaned to the left, and didn't drink. We hadn't discussed it, but I'd assumed he would participate in the seder fully, despite some of the small sips and bites not being Radiant Regimen–compliant. Did he think I'd begrudge him a tradition? I didn't drink the wine, either, but I usually participated only halfway, watching. The Jewish holidays at the Altmanns' were always somewhat disorienting; I found myself moving instinctually to make the sign of the cross, opening my mouth for a recitation I didn't know, and finding the Nicene Creed at the front of my mind. Things I'd done only as a chore, transposed, like when you find yourself in a dream, remembering something that really happened in your waking life long ago. No one ever brought it up. It was a given that I'd join for celebrations, but the Altmanns respected my upbringing, my beliefs, even though they didn't really know what they were, because I'd never really had any in the first place.

AFTER THE HAGGADAH, WE ate the cod, which was indeed delicious. I took small bites, using a teaspoon to scoop the flaky fish onto my fork with a little bit of the tomato sauce. It had a nice garlicky kick.

"No, thank you," I said stiffly when the regular dinnertime wine went around, even though no one asked if I wanted any. When the bottle came to David, he set it down in front of him in a conspicuous way, clunking it against the tabletop so everyone looked.

Benji talked about a sweet old woman—a new client of his—who'd come home to her apartment in Williamsburg last month after a nine-hour shift cleaning hotel rooms. Just three days before, she'd received a notice of eviction from the developers who'd bought her building months prior. It wasn't a valid eviction. She had the better part of a year before the development company could legally evict her, and then they'd still have to give her sixty days. But her door had been nailed shut and padlocked while she was at work, all her possessions trapped inside. It was a rent-controlled apartment, and when the sale had gone through, all the residents had been offered private sums to vacate so the units could be renovated. Everyone else had taken the deal. Now, locked out of her home, her building abandoned, the woman had no idea what to do and went to sleep on her niece's sofa. The next day, when she went to the developer's management office in New Jersey, a brutish man with a shaved head offered insufficient explanations and insinuated that she could be deported.

"This client is Puerto Rican!" Benji shouted, banging his fists on the table. "They just kept telling her it was an issue with her bank, which makes no sense, and she couldn't get an answer from anyone. Why would it be her bank? She paid her rent with money orders. She hadn't been in her house in ten days when she came to us."

"That's terrible," Rebecca said. "That's the worst thing I ever heard. What will happen?"

Benji explained how the developers had offered to settle out of court right away, but they'd already gutted the apartment. The woman's belongings were in a storage space on Flushing Avenue, across from the Navy Yard. The developers gave her the key. In the end, whatever incredible settlement they paid, Benji said, would be a smaller loss than not being able to flip the building quickly into condos.

David was, of course, familiar with the development company and conceded it was a bad business, owned and operated by diabolical morons.

"Now she's going to get a lot of money, though," David said. "Right?"

"Well, that's hardly the point," Benji replied.

"I disagree. I would argue it's the whole point," David said. "She can go live on Park Avenue after this is all over. And I say good for her. In the end, she'll be happy it happened."

Benji opened his mouth to answer, but I was the one to speak first.

"Callous," I heard myself say.

"What?" David said. This was the first time I'd ever taken Benji's side over David's, because it was the first time I'd gotten involved in any Altmann dinnertime quarrel. I always stayed out of it, no matter whom I agreed with (often it *was* Benji). Silly fights about social issues were constant, and as such, they were meaningless; what started with someone's illegal eviction in South Williamsburg could descend into a fiery debate over the shape and size of the unknowable universe. The thing was, I was sure David didn't even mean what he'd said—the tale of this woman's misfortune touched him so lightly only because Benji was never without a depressing story like this one. David's reaction was a way to get a rise out of his brother, who did the same thing in the opposite direction when David complained about zoning or city construction codes. Benji liked being the softhearted hero, and David liked being the shrewd businessman. In reality—in how they voted and where they donated money and how they treated people—their belief systems were the same. Pretending otherwise was how they blew off steam. But now that I'd spoken up, the air had a new charge. Everyone stared at me.

"I said: 'You're callous,'" I repeated, looking directly at him, pursing my lips to keep them from trembling.

David nodded vigorously, his eyes getting wider and wider, almost like he was about to start dancing in his chair at the far end of the table. It was scary, like we were in some surrealist independent horror film: the quiet filling the room, David's tense shoulders stiffening. He picked up the bottle of wine—red wine, a nice Beaujolais—and poured himself a big glass. Setting the bottle down with an even more dramatic thud than the first time, he took a big, showy sip.

"What is going on with you guys tonight?" Benji asked.

"Nothing," David and I replied at the same time. David added, "Kit, apparently, isn't on my side, which hurts my feelings. But I just realized"—he paused, took another sip, swirled the wine in his glass—"that I don't want to be on her stupid diet."

It was as if the room itself held its breath. No one moved.

"I'm glad to hear it," I said. "Since pretending we do anything together is pretty phony, huh?"

"You're both being very immature," Hiram said. He had—for some reason—a look of merriment, a wide grin.

"Well, you decided too late, David," Rebecca said. She cleared her throat, as though her discomfort were only a little phlegm. "Because I made a fresh fruit salad for dessert, and your father polished off all the ice cream last night."

I'D NEVER SO BADLY wanted to leave a place, nor had it ever been more awkward to do so. Rebecca served the fruit salad. I took a few bites but otherwise just stirred it around with my fork, glowering while Rebecca, Hiram, and Benji pretended to have a normal conversation. The tension was awful. I knew it was my fault, but somehow, that just made me more sullen.

When it was finally time to go, David thrust my jacket into my arms without helping me put it on.

"It's so chilly!" Rebecca said. "This spring is turning out to be an endless winter." Nobody said anything in reply.

"Let's call a car," David said in the entryway as we gave his stunned parents terse hugs. (Benji, tired of us, annoyed, had taken a phone call in the next room. Through the open pocket doors, he waved his hand in a dismissive goodbye—more a good riddance.)

David typically wanted to take the bus; a cab ride was a sure sign of just how mad he was. I remembered our fight when my grandmother died. Also in the back of a car. I wanted to bring up the coincidence of it. But wasn't that the worst thing about a prolonged fight with someone you loved? Mentioning anything outside of the argument rendered the argument over. If I was going to stay mad, I had to be consistent with my new hatred of David.

I requested another luxury car, since my account was still set on the Uber Black option. Rebecca was right: The temperature had dropped significantly. David and I waited on the sidewalk without speaking. When the black Mercedes SUV showed up and a suited driver got out, greeting us formally and opening the car's rear door, David sighed bitterly but said nothing. I shoved myself into the car, squeaking across the leather seats, vowing to stare out the window the entire ride and say nothing.

The driver read our address and David said, "That's right" as we pulled away from the curb.

"Buckle your seat belt," David said.

"No," I snapped. So much for giving him the silent treatment. Then, because I couldn't help myself, I added: "Who cares if I go right through the windshield?"

"I care," David said, releasing himself from his own already fastened seat belt to lean across and roughly buckle me up with a loud, angry click. The jostling hurt a little bit, his grabbing my shoulder to move me as he yanked the tight strap over my torso and lap. "Because I'm the one who'll be feeding you through a tube for the rest of your vegetative life." He buckled himself back in. His hands shook. I'd never seen him so angry. It was terrifying and exhilarating. "Though maybe a feeding tube would be easier than trying to get you to eat now."

"What is that supposed to mean?" I said. My insides felt pulled, like a canvas being stretched. Soft symphony music played from the stereo speakers.

"It means I've never really done a diet with you, Kit," David said. "Today I had pizza for lunch. And a beer. I follow the rules in front of you, because I worry if I don't, you won't eat anything at all."

"Wait," I said. Wait, wait, wait, wait. "So this whole time, you've been cheating on the Radiant Regimen?"

"The Radiant Regimen. Sugar Busters. Ketogenics. Whole30. That alkaline thing. I mean, come on, of course I wasn't a raw vegan for a month! It's all dumb. And the frustrating thing is: You're not dumb!"

"Doesn't sound like you really think so," I said. I held the tears in my eyes. David's confession wasn't such a betrayal, in light of the things I'd been doing. But I felt like I'd been punched in the stomach.

"You know I think you're brilliant," David said. "And you don't need me to tell you. You were the salutatorian of our graduating class."

"That distinction has taken me so far," I said sarcastically.

"See, that's your problem. You feel sorry for yourself. It's boring." He sighed, and I heard a grumbling in his throat, more anger being choked back. "I am getting so old, waiting for you to realize you're good enough. Your body is a good body—you have your health, you are attractive. Our life is good enough. I'm just waiting—hoping—you'll get a grip and quit going on every new diet. You just do it to punish yourself. For what, I don't know."

My mouth hung open, my gums and tongue drying out in the car's blasting heat.

"So, you've just been, like, eating whatever?" I asked him. "The whole time?"

He nodded.

"All these—these years?"

"Yep," he said.

"You've been living a double life," I said. I know. *I know*. Even in the moment, I couldn't believe my own audacity. Worst of all, I couldn't see around it; I was really in shock.

We were about halfway home. The Mercedes stopped at a red light on Sixty-fifth and Fort Hamilton Parkway, right across from the big all-night open-air market. I undid my seat belt.

"What are you doing?" David shouted as I opened the car door.

"I need a walk," I said. I slid from the seat, my boot heels clicking against the asphalt. "If you get out and follow me, I'll start screaming—I promise I will."

I'd gone full honey badger. I didn't care. My head swam. David looked at me and I saw it, the heartbreaking desperation he felt—the need to reconnect, wanting suddenly to forgive and be forgiven—at the sight of me going away. We could've just gone to bed, hand in hand, and slept the fight away. I felt it, too. But something wouldn't let me stand down. All the disappointment rushed to the edges of my vision. For a split second I could see the people he and I might have become without each other. They were both clear-eyed. They were happier than we were. I shut the car door. The driver asked David something—if he wanted him to keep driving, I assumed—and David threw his hands up. I saw his silhouette, humming with his exasperation, through the windows.

The Mercedes crawled away at first, neither the driver nor David wanting to leave me on the street like this, both of them turning to see if I'd signal a change of mind, to see if I'd call out, *Come back, come back.*

But I forced them onward by turning in the opposite direction, my toes pounded to jelly in my uncomfortable boots. There was a subway a couple blocks up. It really was unseasonably cold. I was shivering. I checked the time on my phone. It was only ten o'clock. I could be to the bakery in fifteen minutes. To Matt's apartment in half an hour.

CHAPTER TWENTY-TWO

A sweet potato, baked cod, stewed tomatoes, three cut strawberries, and a little chunk of honeydew. It was enough daily calories to live. Matt was wrong. David was wrong. Melissa was wrong. Just because I was hungry didn't mean I was starving. I even felt noble, in a sick way, to be getting just enough. Waste not, want not! These were the thoughts I repeated to myself while the subway crawled from Fort Hamilton Parkway to Union Street.

There were a handful of other riders in the train car, and the only people nearby were an elderly couple, both wearing neon fanny packs around their waists. They spoke Mandarin and glanced my way, making somewhat discernible gestures. I realized I freaked them out because I was talking aloud to myself, whispering "Sweet potato, baked cod, stewed tomatoes" like a mantra. Whoops. I'd noticed my own loony behavior too late; they got off at Thirty-sixth Street, hurrying to switch to the adjacent car before the doors closed.

At the Union Street station, I raced up the stairs and cut across Fourth Avenue, going west toward Matt's apartment. I didn't know how long or late he'd be at the bakery. I didn't know if he'd finished the cabinets on schedule or not. Maybe he was on his way home and would ride his bike right past me. There was a distinct possibility he was finished at Sweet Cheeks but wouldn't come home for hours. He could be out with his friends. Or maybe I'd get to his place and Violet would be there! Violet in Matt's living room. Violet using Matt's toilet, peeing afterward so she didn't get a UTI. Violet's bra and underwear, which I imagined were black lace. Maybe her panties were on Matt's bedroom floor right then. Or maybe she left her sexy bra on while they did it. I was losing my mind. I should text him, I thought. I should get invited or turned down, offer myself the chance to experience a lesser humiliation. But I didn't. I wanted to find whatever was waiting for me at Matt's apartment.

Past the coffin warehouse, past the graffiti-muraled ice cream shop, over the Gowanus Canal, its surface oily and thick from about two hundred years of industrial waste. My feet throbbed—I was practically limping—and my bare ears stung from the cold. My lipstick had worn off, my lips felt chapped. My jaw was clenched. I passed the black-light yoga studio and the ripped, faded awning of the long-shuttered vitamin shop. I cut across the empty blacktop playground and hobbled past the beautiful brownstones on Carroll Street, turned onto Clinton, down past the bar where Matt and his friends hung out.

On Henry Street, in front of his stoop, I looked around. Attempted to catch my breath. There were no lights in his windows on the third floor. In fact, the whole brownstone was dark. For a second I worried the building had been purchased, emptied in the eleven days since I'd been there. I thought of Benji's client. Matt had jumped at the chance to work for Melissa again—maybe that had less to do with being near me than I'd thought. He hadn't told me a thing about his work life in a long while. I hadn't asked. But wait. There, a light flicked on in the basement unit, a sheer curtain behind the window's iron bars aglow in the lamplight beside it. I walked up the steps and pressed his buzzer; when the intercom didn't hum to life after a minute or so, I hovered my finger again but couldn't press. He wasn't home.

I turned to leave. I expected, when I pulled my phone out of my pocket, to see a text from David demanding to know where I was, but there was only an automated message from my wireless provider, letting me know I was nearly out of data for the billing cycle and advising me to upgrade to an unlimited plan.

Just then the intercom crackled. I stepped back to the door. Matt's staticky voice jumped out, muffled. "Hello?"

I held down the talk button and realized my fingers were freezing, sore from an April night that felt like January.

"It's Kit," I said into the speaker. There was a pause, no response, but the buzzer whirred, the lock on the door released with a mechanical slap. I pushed inside. I ignored the agony in my feet as I climbed the stairs.

I turned the knob on his door—it was unlocked—and went into his living room. The lights were off. The air was warm, a space heater clicking in the corner. Matt was there, waiting for me. In the dark I saw his silhouette; he was in cotton boxer briefs, his hair mussed.

There was none of the resistance I'd worried I might encounter.

"Come here," he said as I rushed through the doorway and into his arms, pressed my face into his warm, bare chest. "Oh my God, you're freezing. I had to put the space heater on because my landlord turned my heat off a week ago. I can't believe how cold it got."

"You were sleeping?" I asked, tilting my face up at him.

He took my hands and rubbed them between his hot, big palms. It was nice, the thawing out. I softened back against him. He said, "Yeah, I've been sleeping all day. I'm out of sorts after working overnight."

I shucked my feet out of the booties, sliding down the silver zippers and peeling them off. Touching the top of my feet, I discovered my big toes were bleeding from where my toenails had been smashed between flesh and shoe.

The apartment smelled like its usual stale coffee and fresh sawdust, and even in the dark, I sensed its untidiness. I reached for the vintage Tiffany Nautilus lamp on the green-painted pinewood table by the door. When I gave the lamp chain a gentle yank, Matt squinted into the light. His face was pink and his torso grooved with sheet wrinkles.

"Did you work late last night?" I asked him.

"I just powered through. Melissa had to bake at Angelo's house, and I think she was kind of mad, but we both wanted it to be done."

"So, you weren't there today?" I asked.

"I left around eleven this morning. I worked like sixteen hours straight. What happened the other day? You were there and then you were gone."

"I got into a dumb fight with Melissa."

"I could tell something happened between you two," he said. He went into the kitchen alcove and got a glass of water, which he handed to me. I took a few long sips.

"Melissa said the same thing as you—the other night—but meaner," I said. "She tried to force me to eat a cupcake, and when I wouldn't, she sent me home."

He filled his own glass from the tap and gulped it down, refilled, gulped some more. "Well," he said. "That's bizarre. But you *are* definitely weird about food."

"Yeah, I *know* that," I said. "I actually don't need anyone to point it out."

"Okay, well, you brought it up," he said. "So why'd you come over? To talk about your aggressive sister and cousin and that oversize dollhouse you run? Which, by the way, functions very poorly without you."

I was tempted to ask him to elaborate, but I said only, "No. I came to see you."

He nodded. He started to reply, but I cut him off.

"Did you sleep with Violet?" I asked. I just blurted it out. I couldn't help myself.

He laughed. "I did not," he said. "For the record—though I don't really think this is any of your business—I wouldn't sleep with someone who is so drunk she's slurring her words."

I should have let it go there. But I asked, "But you would have slept with her? You wanted to?"

"Kit," Matt said. "Is David out of town again?"

I shook my head. "He's home," I said. This was probably true. David wasn't out looking for me. "I— It doesn't matter where he is."

"So you're here just to ask if I find Violet attractive?"

"No," I said. "I know you find Violet attractive. Violet *is* attractive—it's just a fact. *I* find her attractive, you find her attractive, everyone who has ever looked at her finds her attractive."

He smiled, nodding in genial concession. "What's going on?" he said. "What are you doing here?"

"I'm here to see you," I said again.

Matt put his glass in the sink and came over to me. He unzipped my jacket and pulled me by the waist toward him. We kissed in a manner both gentle and forceful.

"Get this jacket off me," I said. "Get all these clothes off me."

LATER, I SHUT MYSELF in the bathroom, naked under one of Matt's T-shirts, a threadbare Cincinnati Bengals crewneck that fit me like a tablecloth. Before I dug around in my pocketbook for my travel pack of makeup-remover wipes, I checked my phone. I had four missed calls from David and eleven text messages. My chest ached at the sight of his name. I couldn't bring myself to read the texts. I couldn't bring myself to go outside and call him. I certainly couldn't bring myself to go home. Here, I had done just what I wanted to do, and in the wake of that was terror. I'd scratched the itch to be with Matt so hard it would scar, but this time I found myself barely satisfied. The only thing gone was my anger toward David. I could banish it immediately, I realized, by behaving as selfishly and heartlessly and crazily as possible.

I stared at the phone, at the photo of Woogie that served as my wallpaper. Then I held down the power button until it went black and stared for another moment at its extinguished screen. I saw my reflection: my exhausted, cruel face. Then I found my makeup wipes in my bag and rubbed hard.

In bed, undressed, Matt's body was a warm comfort. I crawled beside him, curling up. I thought I could fall asleep there forever, unbothered, just never leave, and never face my husband again, or Melissa, or anyone. But my stomach gurgled.

"Are you hungry?" Matt whispered. "Do you want something to eat? I have leftover pad see ew I ordered earlier."

"No," I said, even though my head hurt and I knew I needed to put something into my body. I had only another two days. "Do you have any bananas or anything like that? Something fresh?"

He laughed and nuzzled the back of my neck. "I don't even have bread," he said, as though I could've eaten bread. "I could run to the bodega if you want and get some chips." Chips!

"No, it's okay," I told him, shutting my eyes tight. "I had dinner. I'll be fine."

"Okay," he said. He fell asleep almost right after that. I lay there, alone with my hunger while Matt slept. At my own house, there were baked salmon filets in Tupperware, and raw walnuts, and two bags of baby spinach. There were organic blueberries and all sorts of stuff made from coconut. Even if there had been nothing, David would've gone to the organic section in Foodland for me, bought me an avocado, an apple, a jar of raw almond butter. I went to bed hungry but never *empty*. Never like this. Next to me, Matt snored a little, his arm growing heavy across my body, deadweight.

THE NIGHT PASSED IN a series of fits. I'd fall into thin patches of sleep but kept waking, and each time it took a minute to realize where I was. When I remembered, my heart lurched as though trying to escape from my chest. I wondered if I'd die from the stress of my own mayhem. I wondered if David, at our house in Bay Ridge, felt as though he were dying—from panic or anger, from a combination of pains created by the particular mix of my abuse. The simultaneous sense of physical comfort—Matt's real and immediate body against mine—and the anguish of what I was putting David through was the oddest sensation. My phone lay dormant in my pocketbook. I wanted to get up, to wriggle from Matt's embrace, to run. Just as badly, I wanted to never move again. Morning would come, and I waited for it, falling into a light, jittery sleep, my head filled with bad dreams I couldn't remember.

I finally pulled myself out of bed a few minutes past five a.m. Matt, a deep sleeper, murmured and rolled over. I shed his big T-shirt, folded it neatly, and placed it on the bottom edge of the bed. I put my dress back on, slid into my unclean stockings. My necklace, which Matt had helped me remove after it kept getting in our way last night, slapping him in the face or falling into his mouth, was on the nightstand. I dropped it into the pouch of my pocketbook and zipped the pouch closed. The delicate chain would be tangled into ornate knots later, but at least it was safe. I leaned over the bed, rested my cheek against Matt's. His face was warm and his skin, as always, smelled like something I needed to be near. But it was only a smell. He reached for me with the languid limbs of someone still mostly asleep. I stepped away before he had the chance to grab me and pull me back into the bed.

By the front door, I looked with contempt at my shoes. It was impossible to imagine putting my feet back into them. Maybe, I told myself, I deserved to limp all the way home, but that self-punishing line of thinking was too melodramatic and pitiful even for me. I slithered back into the right shoe and then the left, leaving the ankle zippers undone. Pain took over both feet, but I walked softly out the door and down the building's mahogany stairwell, treading over the weather-stained, gritty carpet with the tenderest of steps.

Outside, the purple beginnings of sunrise crept into the sky. I turned my phone back on. I was so tired. My eyes burned. I could not yet bear to see the messages David had left; they popped up in the middle of the screen—**David Altmann (17)**—and I swiped the notification away. No one else had called or texted. Not Melissa or Angelo or Rebecca. I worried David's texts were all furious; maybe he hadn't even tried to find me, maybe in the voicemails he wasn't worried. Maybe he was glad. Maybe he'd said not to come home. Maybe all his clothing and books were now packed in boxes in our apartment's vestibule, ready to go. No more choices for me to make. This new fear swirled in my mind. I didn't want him to go. There was my answer, and in it, an ugly, terrible truth about who I was. I'd wanted it all, just for another night.

I walked up the block and sat down on the bench outside a bread bakery, realizing it was a *forno*. Through the windows, I could see the tiny room, the huge iron door of the oven. In the months I'd been coming to Matt's neighborhood, I'd never noticed it. Matt surely had no idea it was even there. It was the kind of place you could just walk past if you didn't know how special it was, bread baked amid the coal and smoke residue of decades of earlier loaves, which was what made it taste so good. The *forno* was nothing like the treat shop Melissa, Angelo, and I ran. Sitting there, I could feel my grandmother's hand around mine, the way it was when I was little and we were getting bread on Saturday morning. Tears stung my eyes. I missed her so much. If she were here now, she would be disappointed in me.

The small corner room of this *forno* was steamed up, and half the windows were blocked by the hot, fresh bread that a plump middle-aged woman was stacking onto a metal cart. This bakery sold drip coffee from a huge carafe, handed over in small paper cups with pop-top lids: rich black acid with half-and-half and sugar.

As I requested an Uber on my phone, a man walked out of the bodega across the street and lit a cigarette. He made eyes at me and said, "Hey, girl—look at you, sexy-beautiful." I ignored him because it has been my policy, since age twelve, never to acknowledge catcalls or other rudeness from strange men, predawn or any other time. He gave me a sourpuss face. "What's the matter, you can't say hello? You got a boyfriend?"

I knew I should've kept ignoring him, but I was agitated, tired, and near tears. I said, "That's right, I have a boyfriend. As a matter of fact, I have a boyfriend *and* a husband."

He laughed in a sincere, delighted way. "All right, all right, you're busy. Have a good day!" And he sauntered down the block, a new lightness in his step.

The Uber driver was four minutes away, the app said. I rose from the bench to pop my head into the sweltering little bakery's propped-open door.

"I know you aren't open yet," I said to the woman inside. "But could I get a loaf?"

"Yeah, come on," she said, using the back of her wrist to push hair off her sweaty forehead. The bread smelled like bacon and steamy flour. It cost five dollars and twenty-five cents, which I paid in rumpled ones and quarters from the bottom of my bag, because a sign on the cash register read NO CHECKS OR CARDS. I took the loaf—so fresh it was too hot to hold in its paper sleeve—and stuffed it into my oversize pocketbook.

"Thank you," I told the woman, who barely looked up.

"All right, honey," she said. "You take care."

Back outside, my Uber was just pulling up. The driver took the Gowanus Expressway most of the way down, and when he pulled off at Exit 17 and rolled down Eighty-sixth Street onto Fourth Avenue, the bridge was aglow in the distance, lit up by the morning.

The streets were empty, the houses still dark, shopfront gates down.

"It's nice here," the driver said. "You live here?"

"All my life," I told him.

He sighed admiringly and said, "That is good, to be always where you were born. To live in one place."

Looking at the back of his head, I considered what the driver meant. He had a newspaper on the passenger seat with Cyrillic writing. On the front page was a large pixelated photo of two stern, suited men I didn't recognize from the news. I wondered: When was the last time this guy had seen the country where he was born? When was the next time he'd go there?

"You're right," I said, "I'm lucky."

CHAPTER TWENTY-THREE

The bakery's back door was locked, but I could feel that Melissa was inside. Her energy blared like the light of a big-screen TV. I couldn't stand to wear my horrible boots another second, so I removed them before I went in, tossing them into the dumpster. In my wet stocking feet, I dug through my bag until I found my keys, unlocked the heavy door, and stepped inside.

Melissa and Guillermo looked up; Guillermo's face made no expression, his attention returned to the muffins he'd just deposited onto the cooling rack, but Melissa was a little curious, though calm, unbothered, to see me so early.

She said something to Guillermo and handed him some money from the back pocket of her jeans. Taking it, he removed his apron and headed toward the door. "You want something from the store?" he asked me as he approached. "Some aspirin? Some shoes?"

"¡Sácate!" Melissa said, waving him off. She wiped her hands on the rag hanging from her apron. "What do you think?" she asked, gesturing to Matt's new handiwork: a set of smooth steel and ironwood cupboards where the lowboy had been, plus detachable wall-mounted

275

cooling racks and another bay of shelves to match the ones he'd done in February. They looked, as I'd known they would, marvelous. "Your boyfriend really is quite the carpenter. If I could ever afford to open a second location, I'd hire him to do the whole place."

Before I had the chance to respond, she added, "David was losing his mind last night. Talking about calling the police; he was sure you got kidnapped. I said, 'David, nobody got kidnapped in Borough Park. Everyone is at home for the holiday. And the Hasids have no interest in Kit, trust me.'" She smiled, but it was a sad look. She was, I realized, extremely exhausted.

"He left me a bunch of messages," I said. "And texted, like, twenty times. But I haven't read them."

"Well, I imagine you were busy," she said. She pointed to the back corner of the room, where the walls met the ceiling. It took me a long, idiotic moment to realize she was pointing at the security camera, a round plastic console that looked like the outside of a fish-eye lens. "You know, I look at those sometimes."

She picked up her phone and opened an app. On the screen she held out to me, there she and I were in miniature, in real time: the camera pointing at Melissa's workstation and the dish pit, with the swinging doors in between. I'd forgotten Angelo and Melissa's ability to view the security footage from their phones. They never mentioned looking at it.

My mouth was dry, and my empty stomach squeezed tighter. "So you saw us," I said.

"I saw you and Matt Larsson having sex on my table a couple months ago, that's right," Melissa said. "The second night he was here."

"The third," I said. "We didn't actually have sex." I cleared my throat. "We *almost* had sex."

"Good to know. I didn't keep watching."

"Well," I said. "Thank you for respecting my privacy, I guess?"

The oven timer went off and, seconds later, the backup timer. The kitchen was full of delicious smells and high-pitched beeps.

Melissa grabbed big industrial oven mitts from her table. *"¡Ayúdame!"* she screamed, and even though I was the only other person there, it took a moment to understand she meant me—I needed to assist her. I snatched Guillermo's much-too-large mitts from the cooling rack. They came up to my elbows, which was a good thing, because the hot tray Melissa removed from the first oven was massive. I struggled with the weight of it but managed to place it steadily onto the cooling rack. We did four more huge trays, the steam hitting my eyes and blinding me. When we finished unloading, I moved to the rolling rack between the walk-in and the freezer and passed Melissa trays of cupcake pans waiting to go in next. It was physically exhausting work, made even more taxing by the pain shooting from my bare feet. Melissa looked displeased when we finished, though I wasn't sure if her grimace had to do with the slower-than-normal pace at which I offered my help, or because she knew I'd been having an affair in our place of business.

"Are you mad?" I asked. "You look mad."

"Not yet. But it's breakfast time," she said. "And I really don't have the patience to fight with you about it."

Melissa's absentminded magnanimity never failed to surprise me ("You think everyone else holds a grudge because *you* can't forgive the littlest things," she said to me once). In any case, the diet was done. I hadn't quite made it to the end. I never did with these things.

I pulled the loaf of bread from my bag. "Here," I said, holding it out to her. "I bought you this."

"Lard bread!" Melissa shrieked, taking it from me. "Oh my God, it's still warm." She got right to work, clearing a space on her workstation, taking out a clean mixing bowl and whisk. "Seven eggs, cream," she demanded, and I headed to the walk-in. "Do we have any cheese in there?"

We had a container of shredded Parmesan left over from the rosemary and sage shortbread cookies Melissa had been experimenting with last month. I brought the ingredients over to where she was setting up the portable gas burner. She turned the heat low beneath a skillet and added a pat of butter, which liquefied as she whisked the eggs together with a couple teaspoons of cream. When the pan was warm and the butter browning, she dropped the eggs in, tilting the silver mixing bowl with an expert wrist. I used to watch Melissa cook all the time. When we were little kids, and she was obsessed with baking, she fought me after school when *Duck Tales* came on the same hour when PBS broadcast *Baking with Julia*. By the time we'd reached adolescence, Melissa was as advanced an amateur baker as a kid with no formal training could be, and she cooked dinner with our grandmother almost every night. Melissa was never as talented a cook as a baker, but—like many bakers—she did a fantastic breakfast. I preferred Melissa's eggs over just about anything else, besides Melissa's cake. Now I watched, mesmerized, while my sister made a kind of stovetop frittata with three ingredients and a pinch of salt. She sprinkled the cheese in and turned the gas down even lower. We watched it brown and form a soft crust over the tops of the eggs. It had been so long since I'd eaten anything comforting.

Melissa sliced the bread—this particular version was the soft kind, slightly doughy inside with a fatty center of semi-firm cheese and salty salami—and served us each two pieces with a generous triangle of frittata. We took it on paper plates into the still-dark dining room, where I pushed the dimmer switch up just a smidge, so the lightbulbs glowed like candles.

First I divided the frittata up into large bites with my fork and broke off a chunk of the bread in order to scoop a bite of both into my mouth at the same time.

It was the best meal I've ever had. I'm sure of it.

I started to cry a little, mouth full of eggs and dough, and Melissa let me.

"So you've been cheating on David since February?" she finally asked.

"Yes," I said.

She whistled. "I'm somewhat impressed you had the balls."

"Ugh, don't say 'balls,'" I said.

"Sorry," she said. "So, what happened?"

I TOLD HER THE whole story, how it started before I had time to wonder if it would actually happen. I told her about saying I was taking Pilates. I told her David seemed to know nothing. Telling, like eating, was an enormous relief.

"Last night I told David you were at my apartment and had fallen asleep," she said. "And he wanted to come over; he wanted to apologize to you. I had to be like, 'Let her sleep.'" She pressed her lips together, a sliver of aggravation twisting across her face, but as quickly as it appeared, it was gone. "It's okay. It's okay for one time. But I can't be lying like that. I don't want to be—what's the word? An accessory?"

"Complicit," I said. "I'm sorry. And thank you. And I'm really, really sorry."

"Well, you didn't know I knew enough to lie," she said. "I mean, that sucks, too." She laughed. "Did you want us all to think you were dead in a ditch somewhere?"

One way telling the truth and lying are the same: Once you start, you have to keep it up.

"I didn't care," I admitted. "I was mad at you and Angelo for not checking on me when I didn't come to work, and I was mad that you were so hard on me about the Radiant Regimen. And David is just impossible to talk to sometimes. He has to go to China for work, and he lied about following the Radiant Regimen with me, and I guess I used all that stuff as an excuse. Because I wanted to go see Matt and I wanted to be selfish. I am a selfish psychopath."

"Something I love about you," Melissa said, swallowing the last of her bread, "is how you'll be a lunatic, and you'll talk like a lunatic, but somehow you make sense to me. Also, you are the most loyal person I know."

"Well," I said, tears catching at the corners of my eyes again, "I used to be."

"Oh, you absolutely still are. Having an affair—sorry if I sound shallow or something—doesn't seem like much to me, all things in the universe considered. Especially if you end it. Which, to be clear, I think you should."

The back door rattled open. We heard Guillermo make some happy exclamation, and then he stuck his head through the kitchen door. He asked if he could have some frittata, she said yes, of course; he was very glad, she asked if we could please have privacy for a little longer, he said yes, of course, and disappeared back into the kitchen.

"Does Angelo know?" I asked once he was gone. "About Matt?"

"Nah. I didn't tell him, and he hasn't mentioned it, so I'm assuming he's as clueless as that poor husband of yours. But maybe. You never know with Angelo. The things you think he's going to care about, sometimes he doesn't. And, you know, he's not exactly a stickler for monogamy."

"Yeah, but he's not a sneaky cheating liar," I pointed out. "Like me."

"Sure," Melissa said. "But whatever. This isn't about Angelo. What are you going to do? Because, like I said, I can't keep lying like last night. I felt so bad for David. It'd be one thing if you'd come to me when it started and, like, *asked* me to lie, and explained you were gonna have an affair—"

"No way," I said. "You'd tell me I was a maniac."

She shot me a dirty look, a *Don't interrupt me, don't doubt me* look. "Are you going to make us some coffee?" she asked, glancing up at the wall clock. "We have twenty minutes to open, Violet's about to be here, and you don't have any shoes—which, by the way, I must point out—a person's life has to be a decent-size mess to show up at work five hours early, barefoot, and my first question isn't, you know: 'Where are your shoes?'"

I went to the espresso machine, tamped out the coffee for Melissa's double macchiato. She leaned against the skinny side counter that enclosed the espresso bar, and we talked about the things I had been trying to hold in my head, alone, all this time. I told her how much better I liked having sex with Matt than David, and she said sympathetically, "That's not nothing!" and I told her how ashamed I was to face Rebecca and Hiram if I left David, how I dreaded losing the Altmanns, of being on the outside of their lives. Of them knowing I was a cheater. I admitted I also had trouble picturing a future without David.

I said that despite my hating him and avoiding him and wanting to leave him, I still wanted to be arm in arm with David when we walked down the street. I wanted to hear him laugh his honking, dorky laugh in bad horror movies, I wanted to sit next to him at a bar, tasting each other's drinks, play-fighting over who got the last oyster. She slid her palm across the marble-top ledge of the espresso bar and responded softly, "Then you have your answer. You aren't ready to go."

"No, I'm not," I agreed. "But maybe it's over anyway. Once I tell him what's been going on."

"Wait, David? Why would you tell David?" Melissa asked. She cocked her head to the side, confused.

"Well, he has a right to know," I said. "And decide if he *wants* to stay with me. He deserves to know I'm, like, a ruthless betrayer."

"You are so much more self-absorbed than I could've imagined if you truly think telling David would benefit anyone except *you*," Melissa said. "You just want to feel better about yourself and clear your own conscience. Tell Matt it's over, block his phone number, get a vibrator, and get on with your life."

"You really think I shouldn't confess?" I asked her. It hadn't occurred to me that this was an option.

"In court, people plead guilty to get a reduced sentence because they're already caught. *You* have to live with what you've done—why should David? And honestly, you think you won't find out anything you don't want to know about *him* once that can of worms gets opened? A guy who works all the time, who travels?"

The floor moved beneath me for a moment. Melissa, so smart, so practical.

"I've treated everyone so badly. I lured Matt into this."

"Oh, please," Melissa said. "He knew what he was doing. And he'll be fine. Come on. A guy like that? Tall? Good with his hands?" She winked, savoring her coffee in little sips as I gulped down a latte. "If you had any experience on the dating scene in this city, you wouldn't think twice about him."

As she said this, Violet came through the front door.

"Hi," she said, unbuttoning her black jean jacket. She looked me and Melissa over, her eyes hovering at my bedhead and bare, sleep-starved face before resting on my shoelessness. She was choosing how to react, not wanting to be insensitive in the unlikely event that I'd befallen something untoward, a shoe mugging or a lockout. But I could tell by the twitching of her eyelids that she was holding back a laugh.

"Violet," Melissa said, "Kit wants to know what it's like to date in your thirties. She's bored with her life."

"I went out with a guy last night who I met on a dating app," Violet said gamely, opening the closet to put her jacket inside. "He told me I was a solid six. He seemed to think it was a compliment. He didn't pay for either of my drinks, and he ordered fries at the bar and didn't offer me any. He kind of had the plate to one side, like he didn't want me to be able to reach. Then, at the subway, he wanted to kiss! He thought it went well."

"That doesn't sound so bad," Melissa said.

"That's the thing," Violet said, tying her hair back with a black rubber band. "It was the best date I've had in a while. I let him kiss me, and it was like kissing a dog, and if he calls again, I'll go to dinner with him." She shrugged. "I was bored, for the most part. He was boring when he wasn't being rude. But he has a good job, he didn't complain about his ex the whole time, he didn't talk too loud, he isn't married with kids at home."

"Jesus," I said. I wondered about Violet and Matt. Did she also know I'd been hoarding an eligible man? Had Matt told her the other night after they'd left the bar? It didn't matter. She wasn't going to bring it up.

"This is what dating is like," Melissa said. She tapped her foot on the floor. "That's why I'm married to this place. You think I wouldn't like to have somebody like David?"

I had not, in fact, ever considered such a thing.

"Yeah, no offense," Violet added. She moved behind the counter to make her coffee. "You look terrible, and I hope you're okay. I know everyone has their own shit in life. But of all the people in the world I could feel sorry for, I don't feel sorry for you."

"Go home," Melissa said. "Come back later, though, please. Come to work today."

"Yeah, you're training the new girl—Isra—this afternoon," Violet added.

Melissa hugged me, big and comfortable. She was a good hugger. We hadn't embraced in a long time. She whispered, "Good luck," into my ear.

In the kitchen, as I got my pocketbook, Guillermo handed me a plastic Duane Reade bag. He had, in fact, purchased me a pair of shoes, kind of. Three-dollar bargain-bin slippers that lasted just long enough to get me to my apartment door.

CHAPTER TWENTY-FOUR

Melissa texted on my way home to let me know David had messaged her while the two of us were talking in the bakery.

—**Sry if I blew up yer spot but I told him yer diet ended.**

The strength of her loyalty, and how little I appreciated it most of the time, was almost comical. I wrote back:

—**No worries seester,** the way we used to jokingly pronounce the word when we were kids.

INSIDE MY HOUSE, THE stairwell smelled like coffee and toast, as did the kitchen once I walked into the apartment. Woogie trotted over to me, his goofy tail held high, regal and self-serious. He sat down in front of me. My little prince. I picked him up, balancing his big hind paws on my arm. He rested there like a baby, purring into my shoulder. Through the threshold between kitchen and dining room, David sat at the big table. He was in front of his laptop. Woogie sniffed my face.

David looked at me for a long time before he stood up. His eyes were marked by exhaustion, but he'd showered and was dressed, ready to face the day in proper, clean clothing no matter what might happen. I knew I looked terrible in my grimy stockings, my hair mussed and greasy, my skin ashen. I didn't appear to have spent the night at Melissa's. Her apartment was immaculate and had a comfortable guest room. I would have taken a shower and borrowed sweatpants, which would've been several sizes too big, and a pair of sneakers, which would have fit perfectly.

"Hi," I said. "I'm home."

"Are you trying to kill me?" he asked. "Do you want me to have a heart attack?"

Woogie decided he was suddenly uncomfortable and let out a high, violent whine. I put him down. On the floor, he changed his mind again and sat on top of my feet, purring louder than before. I looked down at him, then back at David.

"No," I said.

"I just wanted to see you," he said. "All night, I was up, sick to my stomach, wanting you to come home so I could put my arms around you."

His phone vibrated on the table. He ignored it.

"Well," I said. "I'm here now."

"Yes," David said. "Here you are."

I said, "I'm so sorry."

"What is going on?" he asked. His voice was raised only a little louder than usual. He sounded mad, but more tired than mad, and more terrified than anything. "Are you just getting weirder, or is something going on?"

I sucked in a lot of air, held it, let a breath out slow in a long staccato rhythm. "Both," I admitted.

"So what is happening?" he asked. His lip trembled. "Do I even want to know?"

Melissa, the secret psychologist. I should've known she'd have the best advice. I should have told her what I was getting into a long time ago; I might have saved several people, including myself, a lot of trouble and pain. I could spare David now, at least for this conversation. I wasn't sure I'd never confess. I still wanted to tell him, to relieve myself of the secrets, to expose my lies in a way that would make it impossible to keep telling them. I still wanted to be forgiven.

I started crying, crushed under the weight of how many things felt wrong and terrible, too many to name—my job even though I was good at it, my marriage even though I loved David, this apartment even though I couldn't imagine where else I would live, my body no matter what or how well or how little I ate, and on and on and on. It was striking that in the midst of all these unhappinesses, I had Matt Larsson to think about, too. I could divulge my one big sin and none of my malaise would matter. My whole life would be swallowed up by Matt, what he meant in the context of my marriage and what David meant in the context of everything else.

David came over and wrapped his arms around me. Woogie meowed, refusing to move off my feet, so the embrace was awkward, our bodies not quite close enough, torsos separated so that space was left for the cat between our legs. David cradled the back of my head in his hand, kissing my neck through the piecey hair that smelled like Melissa's fresh sweets and lard bread and the cool April morning air and Matt's salty, earthy skin.

Having been hugged by another man just hours earlier, I found it impossible not to compare. Matt's hugs were bigger, not in the mere sense of his being larger and taller than David but also in the immediacy of his embrace, the instinctual way he pressed himself against me. Matt wrapped me up with his whole body, without thinking. He was warm and heavy, and his grasp was consuming, impulsive, sexual. My body was sore after a night in his arms. Hugs from Matt said, *I want you.*

When David embraced me, it was more bones and muscle, our heads closer together, his ear rested near the top of my head. He moved his hands, liked to squeeze my upper arms and my butt, liked to whisper. I could feel him thinking, how his mind was always at work, and I could feel him reacting to me. He was unable to turn himself over completely to the physical act, unable to give up his thoughts for even a minute. He was careful, deliberate. David's hugs reached forward, said, *I choose you.*

"Don't ever take off like that again," he told me when he pulled away. His tone was severe, razor-edged. He moved some of my hair behind my ear. "You can fight with me all you want at home. You can tell me to go sleep in the living room, you can tell me to go stay with my parents because you hate my guts and can't stand the sight of me. But you can't disappear."

"But now you are taking off," I said. "And I can't fight with you at home because you *aren't home.* You're leaving for China in, what? Five hours?"

"I'm not leaving today. I'm postponing my trip."

He told me how he'd spent the night. He'd been so angry in the Uber, but instantly remorseful when I got out of the car. It terrified him to know how badly I wanted to get away from him. The ride home was agony, he said, made worse by the driver's prying questions and attempts to give David some misogynistic advice on how to diffuse similar situations in the future (apparently, if a woman my age had children, these fights wouldn't happen because I wouldn't have the time or energy). David, being David, decided to debate the driver over what he felt were sexist assumptions instead of just ignoring him, so by the time the guy dropped him off, they were disagreeing on a number of issues regarding a woman's place in society. I couldn't help but laugh as David told me his side of the story. Because that's what our relationship was. We'd had the worst argument ever, shrouded in confusion and secrets. Last night, I'd gotten out of the car, sure I'd never laugh with him again. But I was wrong. Of course I was wrong. It took no effort to sink back down into the sweet, safe muck of my marriage, of knowing and loving him for the entirety of my adulthood.

He told me he'd come home and tried to watch television, a FIFA game on cable that I would have complained about. But his mind paced with horrific worries: I'd been picked up in a white van, brutally murdered, my body thrown against the rocks into Dead Horse Bay. I'd been pushed onto the subway tracks by roughhousing teenagers who hadn't seen me standing near. Hit by a car, hit by a bus, bitten by a rabid dog. Any morbid thing that could befall a person out alone at night, all the tragedies we couldn't prevent or foresee and which lurk in our minds, the possibilities that may be waiting, up ahead in our unknowable futures, coming to tell the end of our stories.

"When things start going bad," David said, "I can't help but wonder how much worse they might get."

"Everyone feels that way, I think," I told him.

"I sent the travel booker at work an email a little after midnight. Said I couldn't leave due to a family emergency. You weren't responding to my texts, and so I called Melissa, who said you were at her apartment, but she was acting so weird. She was too nice—like a different person. Like a *nice* person. I thought, Kit is going to leave me. I couldn't get on an airplane today. What if the plane went down over the ocean? I couldn't die with us fighting like this."

"I love you," I said. "I am so, so sorry."

"I love you, Kit," he said. "And I'm sorry."

"Sorry for what?" I asked.

"For knowing things were bad and ignoring it. For letting you get so distant. For being too interested in my own shit to care about how strange you've been lately."

"So *you're* sorry because *I've* been fucking up?"

He thought about it a second, knowing my reaction might go either way.

"Yes," he said. Choosing honesty. Good old David. "Yeah, I am sorry because you've been fucking up. We are a team, and I let you operate like we aren't. You shouldn't go on any more diets. And you've got to stop quitting your job. Melissa will let you come and go forever, but it's bad for you and for your staff. People need routines. People count on you, and you let them down. And you like your job. You pretend you don't, but you do."

"You're right," I said. "I'm good at my job."

"And you're bad at dieting," he said. "You take it too far, and then you quit or you flip out. Can we just eat food we like? Keep it simple?"

But it wasn't simple. For me, I knew, food couldn't just be simple.

"We can try," I said.

"I'd just like to have dinner sometimes. Without having some long pseudo-ethical conversation about it. I miss just hanging out with you."

David told me that in January he'd refused to go to Rio for work because it was around my birthday and I'd been spending all my time in bed, depressed. He'd apparently called Melissa to see if she'd help get me up and moving, and she had told him to give me a break. She said it was his fault I was depressed, he was too uninvolved in my life, being such a workaholic. Feeling ashamed, he'd skipped a business trip. I hadn't known he was supposed to travel, but I remembered the week in question. It wasn't different from any other, except David was home by seven every night, which surprised me at the time. On my birthday, he'd wanted to go to a restaurant, but I refused, so we binge-watched a few horror movies I'd missed in the theaters. Melissa had called and asked what time she could bring over a cake she'd made me, but I refused her, too, saying I didn't want any stupid cake, and in the end David had gone and picked it up from Sweet Cheeks the next morning. I was adamant: The cake had to go. "Get this fucking cake out of my fucking house," I'd said, like it was a suitcase of heroin or a bomb. At my insistence, he'd taken the cake to work to share with his colleagues. They'd all loved it.

"The thing is, I do have to go on this China trip," he said. "Not today. But soon. It's my job." After a long breath, he added, "I hope you can be proud of how hard I work."

I nodded. This, too, I could try to accept. I was proud of him. Of course I was. Why didn't he know that? Had I really not told him? I tried to remember the last time I'd said something nice to David, something worthy of the admiration I had for him, a compliment delivered with complete sincerity. It had been too long.

"I'm so proud of you," I said. "And impressed. You're the smartest person I know."

"Thanks," he said.

A thick silence filled our apartment. We were suspended in it as though in water, behind aquarium glass. David shifted his weight, put a light hand on the middle of my back. I needed a shower. I needed a million showers. I had work later. I decided I'd ask David to come with me, say hello to everyone at the bakery. He would want to see the newest shelves in the kitchen, and I'd feel guilty and awkward and want to crawl in a hole and hide. For a long time, things related to Matt were going to come up, and my stomach would twist into a tight, cowardly knot.

But these concerns could come later, they were a future Kit's problem, and she'd be better equipped to deal with them because she'd be clean and dressed and she'd have taken a nap, eaten some lunch.

Right now David and I didn't know what else to say to each other, or what to do next, or where to go.

It occurred to me, for the first time in a long while, that we didn't have to do anything. We didn't have to know.

EPILOGUE

It was a rainy summer but not too hot—plenty of nights we didn't have to run the air conditioner. On nice days, we pulled all the blinds and David stood on a chair in the bedroom, cranking the skylight. I opened the kitchen window and took in that familiar smell, salt water and city dirt blowing from the Narrows. We kept the stepladder propped by the screen, so Woogie could look outside and enjoy the fresh air, too. He liked to hunker down on the top rung, so the breeze ruffled his soft orange fur. Watching the pigeons on the house's ledge, he'd chatter, intense and focused within some primal fantasy; whatever notion he had of himself as a hunter, I was sorry to tell him, was grandiose.

"Dream on," I said, and he broke his gaze from the pigeons, looked at me with what seemed like disdain.

I was at the stove the day David left for China, making oatmeal and live-streaming public radio. I'd finally figured out how to sync my phone with the Bluetooth speaker Benji gave us at Hanukkah. The speaker was the exact shape and size of a twelve-ounce can of cocktail peanuts; I'd noticed this once when I absentmindedly put the speaker away in the pantry and then couldn't find it for days. *Weekend Edition* was reporting on a plagiarism scandal that had rocked the crossword-puzzle community.

David, who was in the bedroom packing, didn't want oatmeal. When I called him to come and get it, he was slow to the kitchen. He peered into the bowl.

"Just put a lot of butter on it," I said. "And brown sugar."

He shuffled into the dining room with his unwanted breakfast. I dropped a handful of blueberries into my own bowl. Since quitting Radiant Regimen, I'd made a resolution never to do another diet. But the thing was, I was still going to think about food all the time. I couldn't help it. It wasn't something I could just turn off.

David stooped dutifully over his oatmeal. He was leaving but had told his boss he couldn't be gone longer than three weeks. It was okay. I had plenty to do on my own. The East Coast Confectionery Expo was in Atlantic City the next weekend, and I was going with Angelo and Maria to help run a booth. Violet would oversee the store with Melissa. We'd officially promoted her to assistant manager the Friday before. She and I weren't going to get to work together as much, but we'd recently started having brunch together on Sundays after her early shift ended.

Work had been good. I started noticing the fun parts more. I wasn't as tired. I brought broken cookies and day-old cupcakes home to David, something I almost never did before because I didn't want the sweets in the house. For his part, David started coming home earlier, except the two evenings I went to yoga. After yoga, I'd meet him in the city for a drink.

It didn't have to be the same marriage forever. Maybe David would fall in love with someone else someday. Maybe he'd come back from China in three weeks and be a different man, one I loved more, one I loved less, someone I didn't recognize at all. I didn't have to decide to be with David forever. I could just get up each morning and pick him again. Maybe one day I wouldn't. I didn't need to be sure of anything, either way.

But anything seemed possible that summer. We were planning our trip to Italy—there was a big paper map rolled out on the kitchen counter, and Rebecca had been coming over, rather than me always going to Midwood, and we made lists of all the things we wanted to see. Often, when I was alone, I looked into the mirror above the bathroom sink and felt surprised. I'd gained weight, was rounder especially in my face, and couldn't decide if the change was the beginning of the thing I'd feared most or if I actually liked how I looked. David said I looked great, and whenever he caught me feeling my ribs, he took my hand and held it. Melissa kept telling me how smoking hot I was, a compliment I'd never received from her before during a lull between diets. I didn't know what to think. I felt okay. I had a closet full of pants in four different sizes. I wasn't sure how, exactly, to just get older, but it didn't matter. It would happen on its own. Being hungry all the time hadn't stopped it. Being hungry had never made anything easier.

WHEN IT WAS TIME for David to leave for the airport, I insisted on going with him.

"Don't come with me. It's a waste of time and money," he said. "It's not like you can see me off—you'll get out of one cab at Departures and walk downstairs to catch another in Arrivals."

"But I want to," I said. "I don't have anything else to do today—it will get me out of the house."

"Go for a walk," he said.

"You know, this wouldn't be an issue if we had a car. I'd just drop you off."

I was on this kick: I wanted to buy a car. David would have to teach me to drive. It wasn't a new idea, not really, but as with many other things I wanted, the strength of my desire ebbed and flowed along the river of perceived obtainability. I thought this might be the year David caved in.

He'd learned to drive at sleepaway camp, of all places. But he'd never had a car, and for the entirety of our marriage, he'd maintained a responsible if stringent opinion on car ownership: It was too expensive, bad for the environment, selfish in a city with so much accessible public transportation, impossible to find parking, and the leading cause of accidental death in our country. (With this last point, I was apt to argue: "Would you prefer I die on purpose?" but David didn't find that joke funny.)

"You don't think I'll be a good driver," I said.

"Let's talk about it when I get back," he said. "It's a possibility after we get back from Italy."

"Ha!" I cried. "You're caving!"

"That's not a yes," he said sharply. "Get your shoes on if you're coming." I could tell from his flat expression that David, too, was learning to ride the days, find a way to endure life, and, when possible, enjoy it.

When the Uber driver pulled up, I climbed in first and asked, "Did you just get your car cleaned?" The driver laughed, told me he'd come from a carwash over in Bensonhurst, the good one, all done by hand.

"Perfect day for it!" I said. I put my seat belt on, noticed David glancing over to make sure. "What happens when you get to the Beijing airport?" I asked him. "Do you take the subway or a car to your hotel?"

"The first time I went, they had a car service pick me up. But the traffic—it's indescribable. It's sixteen miles from the airport to the Beijing offices, and the drive took over two hours. The train takes an hour."

"What is the subway like there?"

"Massive. Crowded. The first time I took the train, I got into a car half full of teenage girls in school uniforms—blazers, knee socks. But there were also a couple guys with chickens," he said.

"What do you mean?"

"I mean, they were poultry salesmen, I assume. And were riding the train with, like, a dozen cages filled with live chickens. The cages were on wheels. It was noisy and stank, but the schoolkids didn't notice, really. Everyone is just trying to get somewhere."

"That kicks ass," I said.

David nodded. "I hope you can come with me someday. This will be my fifth trip to China, and I've never seen the Great Wall because it would take a whole day, which is just a day longer until I can come home. In Shanghai, I didn't go to the Bund. But East Asia is another world, and I'm always wondering what you'd think, what you'd say. Beijing is twenty-two times the size of New York. The sky is orange, sometimes the air is orange."

"Oh!" I said. "Did you remember your nasal spray?"

"Yes." The previous week I'd ordered a box of disposable pollution masks. I'd put them in his suitcase before he zipped it closed. I hoped he would wear them.

"When I go on business trips, I always wonder what you'd think," David added. "Every new, strange thing, I find myself trying to imagine your reaction."

I knew what he meant. "You miss me when you go," I said.

He guffawed, a sound of both agreement and shock that I would feel the need to state something so obvious.

As the car glided down the Belt Parkway and passed beneath the Verrazzano, it occurred to me that Matt still, as far as I knew, had never come to bike the greenway. He hadn't craned his neck from below the bridge's one-million bolt tower to look up at the mesmerizing grid of its steel underbelly, or watched the flight path of peregrine falcons roosting in the mast, the way they seemed to disappear when they flew from one side to the other, their nests hidden in the perfect nooks. I never got to tell him how Robert Moses called the bridge "a triumph of simplicity and restraint over exuberance." Matt never took my hand, as David did in the car to JFK, and squeezed it as we left the bridge behind. I missed him. In quick little moments, the loss was painful and large. He was like a whole life I might have pursued if I hadn't decided to stick, for the most part, with the one I already had.

I hadn't seen Matt since the morning I'd sneaked out of his apartment in late April, left him sleeping and hadn't said goodbye. I called him the next day, but he didn't answer. I could feel something, some unnamed space, open between us. An understanding we didn't have to discuss: We'd gone as far as we could without a cataclysmic event, a huge break in our realities. Neither of us was ready to endure the consequences or realize the end of the instinctual part of the attraction, the beginning of a relationship, the work.

So I'd followed up with a text message. It said:

—**Let me know if you want to talk.**

He didn't respond for a full day. Then, the next morning, my phone pinged. His reply said only:

—**I will.**

I hadn't heard from him since. It had been two months.

Violet hadn't brought him up. I'd wondered, for a week or so, if the end of our affair might lead to the beginning of some new relationship with Matt, one in which he dated Violet. He and I could've tacitly agreed to let what had passed between us fall away, let it close, and become friends. On one hand, this fantasy was, I realized, creepy and delusional. But on the other, it would've been nice to keep knowing him.

Anyway, it wasn't as though anyone could truly disappear or sink irrevocably into the past anymore. Matt could've called the next day, and I could've hit the ignore button. Or I could've picked up. I could've woken up in the middle of the night sometime and started scrolling through my phone and seen a new post on Matt's Instagram, a photograph of him with his arm around a woman—a stranger to me—both of them smiling, happy, each excited for the other's company. I knew this would happen. Inevitably. But right then we hadn't spoken, and his social media posts were infrequent and related to the furniture he made. A set of oak file cabinets for some lawyer in midtown. A wall of wavy mahogany cubbies—a place to leave shoes—at a sensory-deprivation spa on Long Island. A three-foot brownstone dollhouse, the sight of which saddened and delighted me in equal measure, for reasons that to this day I do not understand.

AS THE CAR SNAKED down the expressway, the radio played that catchy song I'd been hearing everywhere for the past couple weeks—the slow, melancholy one by the Canadian kid with the hair and the pants. This kid had been famous for years, though this was the first song I was personally able to attach to him. He was finally famous enough to reach someone like me. Good for him. Not everyone could be Annie Lou Samuels. Some music is for kids. But I did kind of like this song, even though it wasn't very good. It got in your head, sang itself to you, made you want to sing it back to no one. I watched Jamaica Bay's gray water out the window, the glowing strips of light where the sun hit, blinding, and the clean, straight line of the horizon beyond. The only wide-open view I'd known in my life, so far.

David was right, of course. The airport was chaos. The driver jerked the car to wedge into an unloading spot, where we rushed to the curb with David's small roller bag, checking our pockets for all the things we might have left in the backseat—our phones and keys—and there was no space, physical or otherwise, for a proper goodbye. He gave me a peck on the lips, told me to be good to myself, told me he'd email often and call on Sundays. I waved him into the terminal, he turned one time, the automatic doors whooshed closed, and when someone else opened them again, David was far away, shrunken to a tiny little toy at the far end of the Air China check-in line, a LEGO-size man getting swept into the bin with the rest of the blocks. This was how we always said goodbye. We didn't.

WHEN MELISSA AND I were kids, my family often went to the beach at the Rockaways during summer, or to one of the parks by the water.

Uncle Nicky had a friend from school who lived out there with his wife and children the same age as me, Melissa, and Angelo, and we'd get together for picnics and cookouts at Bayswater Park. My grandmother liked it because there was a new shelter near the sandy spot where some men played bocce, and she always found people to talk to in Italian, and she could stay in the shade. We called the people at Bayswater our summer friends. The park had a clear view of lower Manhattan and a lot of space to run around. There was a nature preserve, which we could hike through and catch glimpses of all sorts of birds, plus lizards and small frogs darting across the footpaths, all manner of what we understood to be pure wildlife, the kind with which city children are often preoccupied.

What I loved most about the preserve—the edge of the place, where rows of men cast fishing lines out along a scummy surf surrounded by tall brown seagrasses—was watching the airplanes come in and out of JFK. On a clear day, the arriving planes burst into the sky from nothing, tiny mechanical specks growing larger as they descended, coming lower and lower as though they might skim the surface of the shallow water, which rippled below the weight of an aircraft's formidable motion. The planes landed, finally, a safe distance away, the wheels a few yards from actually touching the water before hitting dry, hard tarmac far at the other side of the bay. The departing planes, big Boeing jets preparing for a trip across the ocean, left from a runway farther from the park. You could hear them gearing up for the ascent. I didn't ride in an airplane until I was fourteen and we took a trip to Florida. When I was little, I'd ask Nonna where they were taking the people.

"I don't know, Katrina," she'd say. "Probably to vacation."

WHEN I REQUESTED ANOTHER Uber at Passenger Pickup B, I entered Bayswater Point as my destination. The driver got stuck in endless airport traffic, so I had time to change my mind, but I didn't. I wanted to be alone for a while.

The park had changed, like everywhere else. It seemed smaller. Families gathered on the cut grass, children played on the swings behind the shelter, which was no longer new. The bocce sand was gone, as were the bocce players, and in their place were packs of twentysomething hipsters—all sundresses and tattoos and cutoff jeans—sitting on lawn chairs, drinking beer, laughing. There weren't many people near the entrance to the preserve, which was unmarked and designated by a metal railing that opened onto the main path.

As I made my way through the high grass, the sounds of the radios and car traffic and human laughter subsided. A big dirty egret walked up ahead of me on the path, following the cleared trail to the water as a person would. If this bird noticed my presence, it didn't find me interesting. When I got to the wet sand at the water's edge, the bird took off, dinosaurlike, bending its wings at an impossible angle into the wind, flying up, up, until it was gone. It was still a beautiful and sunny afternoon, but down there, so low to the water, it was windier, the air bright and biting. I kept my hands in the pockets of my thin linen pants.

I took a seat on a piece of driftwood and turned off my phone. The sun felt so good on my face. More planes were coming in than going out, but each one brought a new feeling, or the same feeling made new each time. To be so close to such a powerful and marvelous machine, to feel it exhale, coming to the end of a long trip. If I could have waited long enough, I might've been able to see David's plane leave, but I couldn't stay for so many hours, and I couldn't be certain which plane was his, anyway. He could be delayed in the terminal or held on the tarmac, breathing the already stale air.

So I pretended he was on every plane leaving. The water quivered, and I heard each jet engine's awesome gasp before the beaked nose of the airplane appeared, pointing skyward and lifting itself and all the people inside over the water. It was deafening. I looked at a plane's big white belly and imagined it carrying my life away.

"Goodbye, David!" I said aloud to myself each time. Everything else, I held inside. I breathed deeply, exhaled. I thought: Have a safe trip. I thought: Get good work done. I thought: I'll see you when you get home. I thought: I'm here, and waiting, and it's okay. I thought: We're still mostly young for a little while longer. At least for now, we are in love.

ACKNOWLEDGMENTS

For her enthusiasm, insight, expertise, and patience, I am deeply thankful to my editor, Kara Watson, as well as my agent, Claudia Ballard. Thank you also to Jessie Chasan-Taber and Camille Morgan at WME. Thank you to copy editor Beth Thomas, who made every page better. Thank you, Nan Graham, Sabrina Pyun, Rebekah Jett, Dan Cuddy, Wendy Blum, Abigail Novak, Emily Greenwald, Jaya Miceli, Brianna Yamashita, and the rest of the remarkable people at Scribner.

To the brilliant friends who read early drafts: Carol Gilman, Tyler Ford, Zoey Cole, Meg Wade, René Kramer, Kevin Debs, Jami Attenberg, and Kris Rey. Thank you to Ikwo Ntekim for her candor and bigheartedness. Hannah Obermann-Briendel for being a needed reminder of what it means to be from New York.

An extra-special thanks to Mikey Swanberg, who was a generous first reader and cheerleader, as well as a lot of fun.

Peg Buttermore, Jim Nolan, Jessica Weiss, Gretchen Williams, Dan Parker, Sheri Fink, Dr. Yasmin Collazo, and Dr. Eileen Kemether contributed to my ability to keep writing, whether or not they knew it at

ACKNOWLEDGMENTS

the time. Emma Straub and Eddie Joyce offered invaluable publishing industry insight and advice.

Thank you to the wise and generous teachers who helped me become a writer: Michael Griffith, Brock Clarke, Lorrie Moore, Russel Durst, Judith Claire Mitchell, Maria Romagnoli, Laura Micciche, Jesse Lee Kercheval, and Ron Kuka. I am indebted to Lynda Barry, who taught me how to write the unthinkable, and Leah Stewart, whose mentorship changed my life.

Brian Ringley's support—emotional, financial, social, informational, professional, and otherwise—created the conditions in which I could do this work, and without him this book would certainly not exist. Thank you, Brian.

Finally, I am grateful for my mom, Doe Gavin, who never pressured me to get a real job.